"Intrigue. Suspense. High-stakes drama. Godly Presbyterian Scots. *Duncan's War* educates and inspires us to look back at heroes of the faith in awe and forward to the return of the King in joy."

R. C. Sproul Jr., Director,
Highlands Study Center

"Will lift you into the 17th century and onto the moorlands of Scotland. This is the danger-zone inhabited by evil, danger, death, courage, and faith. A story not to be missed."

Sinclair B. Ferguson, Senior Pastor,
St George's–Tron Parish Church, Scotland

"Unleashes the reader's imagination—a rip-roaring good yarn."

George Grant, Director,
King's Meadow Study Center

"Rich history and principled living woven into an adventure that will capture imaginations."

Susan Hunt, Women In the Church
Consultant for the Christian Education
Committee of the Presbyterian Church
in America.

"A splendid tale told with imagination and skill, set against an authentic background. Enjoy it, learn from it, and be grateful."

A. Douglas Lamb, Vice President,
Scottish Covenanters Memorials
Association, Scotland

"Draws from a genuinely heroic time and tells a story rooted in truth. Children will not forget it!

Robert Rayburn, Pastor,
Presbyterian Church,
ıa, Washington

D0950212

CROWN & COVENANT

Duncan's War, Book 1
King's Arrow, Book 2
Rebel's Keep, Book 3

DUNCAN'S WAR

DOUGLAS BOND

ILLUSTRATED BY MATTHEW BIRD

P&R
PUBLISHING
P.O. BOX 817 • PHILLIPSBURG • NEW JERSEY 08865-0817

Page design by Tobias Design
Typesetting by Michelle Feaster

Printed in the United States of America

Library of Congress Cataloging-in-Publication Data

Bond, Douglas, 1958-
    Duncan's war / Douglas Bond ; illustrated by Matthew Bird.
        p.   cm.— (Crown and covenant ; bk. 1)
    Summary: In Scotland in 1666, fourteen-year-old Duncan learns the value of being true to his faith while fighting against supporters of England's King Charles II, who oppress the Covenanters—those who believe that only Jesus can be king of the church.
    ISBN 0-87552-742-6
    [1. Covenanters—Fiction. 2. Christian life—Fiction. 3. Presbyterian Church—History—17th century—Fiction. 4. Rullion Green, Battle of, 1666—Fiction. 5. Scotland—History—1660–1688—Fiction.] I. Bird, Matthew, ill. II. Title.

PZ7.B63665 Du 2002
[Fic]—dc21

                                                              2002068448

For Brittany, Rhodri, Cedric, and Desmond

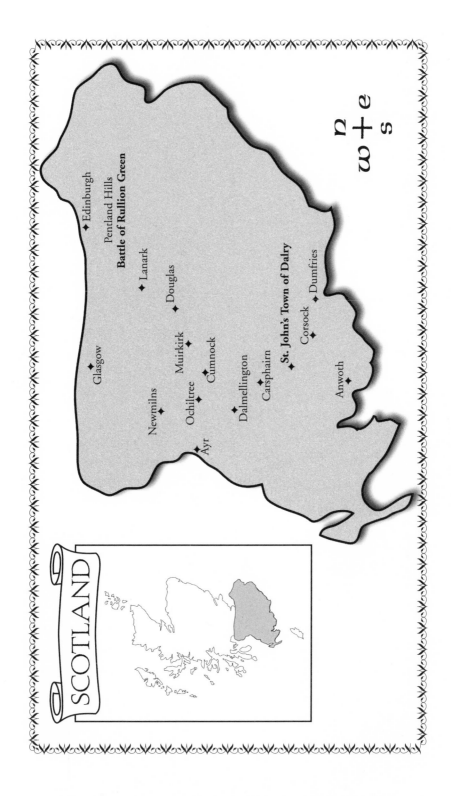

SCOTLAND

CONTENTS

1. Give Way, Ye Coward English! 1
2. Fight or Die! 9
3. Signing with Blood 24
4. Rats! 34
5. The Vicar's on Fire! 44
6. The Devil Kicks up His Heels 54
7. Underground Plans 60
8. Sword Dancing 67
9. London Burns 73
10. Can't Fight Hate with Hate 81
11. Shoot Him 90
12. Sir Brodie 104
13. Ye'll Hang, Sandy 109
14. Through to the Hilt 113
15. Duncan Uses His Head 123
16. This Is No Playacting 131
17. Primed Pistol 139
18. Shoot the Monster! 147
19. Chosen Few 151
20. Duncan's Fall 161
21. Betray and Live 166
22. The Shoemaker 177
23. Battle! 182
24. Kill Him, or Free Him? 192
25. I Smell the Devil! 195
26. Friend or Foe? 201
27. Not Much Time 210
28. The Hanging Show 222
29. Martyr's Bible 230
30. The Smell of Fish 233
31. Farewell, the World 237
32. A Christmas Swim 243
33. Haggis 252
34. Though He Slay Me 257
35. Angus Makes a Deal 262
A Word about the Characters 271
Glossary of Scottish Terms 273
Timeline of Scottish Covenanting History 275
Acknowledgments 277

Life is myself, I keep the life of all;
Without my help all living things they die;
Small, great, poor, rich, obey my call . . .
I hurt, I help, I slay, and cure the same;
Sleep, and advise, and pense well what I am.

King James I (1566–1625)

GIVE WAY, YE COWARD ENGLISH!

Once more unto the breach, dear friends, once more...
Shakespeare

uncan M'Kethe lay prone in the heather, his hand
opening and closing on his weapon. With intense
green eyes he sized up the crumbling battlements of
Dunfarg Castle. Only a narrow ridge separated him from his
objective. With a defiant toss of his head—his red locks flipping onto his shoulder—he scanned his followers. They
moved as one on his signal. He smiled, a grim determined
smile, and slithered silently forward, the heather parting
around his lithe body like the cold North Sea parting for a
haddock.

Cresting the ridge with caution, he halted and peered
around a tuft of moor grass. Where secure gates should have
stood, the entrance to the castle gaped wide and deserted. Just
as he hoped: their attack was wholly unexpected. He stole another glance at his clansman waiting at the ready. For an instant Duncan lay pressed flat on the ground. He hesitated, his
heart beating wildly against his ribs. Could he do it? Then the

words of his father came to mind: "If ye've no cause worth dying for, m'lad, ye've no cause to be breathing God's air."

Leaping to his feet, his stout weapon held aloft in defiance, he roared, "For the Crown and for the Covenant!"

Then, like a berserk of old—save that being fourteen he kept his kilt firmly girt round his middle—Duncan flung himself toward the unguarded castle. His bare feet seemed not to touch the heather as he ran.

"Give way, ye coward English!" he screamed, his weapon circling madly over his head.

Weaving and ducking, he dodged crossbow bolts hastily launched by the startled soldiers on the battlements. Boldly into the breach like a valiant clan chief, Duncan dispatched the first English with a single stroke. And then another, and still another lay stretched at his feet.

But what was this? Sneering English soldiers came at him from every side. Stroke for stroke, he diminished their number by two. More took their place and closed in around him. Then, a blow to the head! Searing pain! The castle spun round and round. He had to fight on. The haze cleared for an instant—an instant of terrifying clarity—he parried a fatal stroke, and with a desperate thrust, his would-be executioner lay at his feet. No time for gloating, and weakened from his wound, Duncan spun on his bare heels. A giant of a man, his sword hissing menacingly, stalked toward him, leering as he advanced.

Suddenly, Duncan caught sight of a black-and-white streak: his clansman bolting to the rescue, teeth barred in rage. Fighting shoulder to shoulder, they stoutly threw themselves on the giant and the remaining defenders. As suddenly as it began, the conflict ended. Not a single enemy soldier breathed. All about them the ground lay strewn with the grim remains of battle.

"The day is ours!" gasped Duncan, gingerly holding the side of his head as he collapsed onto a moss-covered pile of stones.

One eye blackened, his comrade-in-arms sat attentively before him, awaiting his next command.

"Ye rendered good service today," said Duncan, patting the black-and-white head. "And for that I dub ye"—he held aloft his weapon—"with this my herder's staff. I dub ye Sir Brodie. I owe ye my life, Sir Knight. And make no mistake, I pay what I owe."

As he said these words, he solemnly lowered his stick on either side of his comrade's head.

Brodie grinned, a tongue-lolling dog grin, and sat dutifully looking up at his master.

"Come here, boy," said Duncan when he finished the ceremony.

With a happy yelp, Brodie placed his front paws on Duncan's chest and licked the red welt on the side of his young master's head.

"And now ye'll be my doctor, is it, a-tending of my wounds," laughed Duncan, wincing as he touched the tender redness. "A knock I gave myself flailing about with my own stick." He laughed sheepishly. "Aye but, wounds is wounds in a battle."

Eyeing the sun as it peeked reluctantly out from behind a steel-gray barrier of clouds, Duncan opened the goat-hair sporran hanging low from his waist and took out his meal of oatcakes. Breaking one in half, he shared it with his dog.

"Ye've earned yer bannock," he said, scratching Brodie's ears. "And if I'd have fought here alongside Robert the Bruce three hundred fifty years ago when this castle last fell"—he looked around at the crumbled ruin, little evidence of its former glory but the lower part of the central tower—"I'd have wanted none more noble than ye by my side."

With intelligent eyes, Brodie gazed fixedly at his master. As Duncan finished his lunch, the dutiful sheep dog trotted to the broken-down entrance of the castle and peered critically at the small cluster of sheep grazing on the hillside where they had left them only moments ago.

"All's well?" asked Duncan when the dog returned. " 'Course it is," he answered his own question. "Or ye'd be off after 'em like a bullet blown from the musket of a king's dragoon hunting down a son of the Covenant—like me," he added, frowning pensively.

Duncan and his dog had explored these ruins many times, and most of the crofters from the surrounding hills and glens had for generations borrowed stones to repair fences and to patch up chinks in the walls of their cottages. Picked-over as it was, with each visit Duncan felt, with a quickening of his pulse, that this might be the day he'd uncover some long-forgotten treasure. His eyes narrowed as he scanned the mounds of rubble and the jagged remains of ruined walls. It had been a long winter of heavy snow, and spring rains had come in torrents and had lasted for weeks. He poked curiously at a mossy stone with his stick.

Circling the old wall, Brodie at his heels, Duncan picked up a rock and hurled it at the battlements of the remaining tower. On his second try, with a clattering echo, he found his mark: a jagged hole gaping in the tower that must have been made by some heavy missile launched from a catapult during the final days of a siege. It gaped down at him, and he imagined it to be the skeletal grin of an ancient laird who tyrannically ruled the peasants who once eked out a meager living in the surrounding glens.

Brodie waited patiently while Duncan, leaping along the broken-down wall, scrambled to the highest point. Steadying himself, Duncan looked to the south and east. His eyes narrowed and his chin jutted defiantly—England lay that way.

Then for an instant the grayness overhead broke, and the sun shone brilliantly on the green and purple of the hills, some speckled white with sheep, while on the grassy slopes of others grazed the Belted Galloway, black cattle with distinctive white belts around their middles. The spotlight of sunshine shifted, as the clouds rearranged themselves overhead, and reflected off the slate roofs of the hillside village of Dalry—the valley of the king—far below in Glenken, the broad waters of River Ken meandering through the valley. The steeple of the parish church rose above the cluster of cottages, their crow-stepped gables and chimneys outlined in sharp relief. Four years had passed since Duncan had been inside the stone walls of the church, now under the control of popish bishops and the local curate, a drunkard named George Henry. Covenanters and their families were forbidden to worship inside the little sanctuary unless they swore allegiance to King Charles II as the head of the Church and submitted to the blasphemous, slurring homilies of George Henry.

Hunted like beasts by the ruthless James Turner, chief enforcer of the king's will, Covenanter families like Duncan's fled to the hills, worshiping instead at secret field meetings, hearing faithful preaching from the lips of wanted men. Fugitive field preachers, out of loyalty to Christ, the only King in his Kirk, risked their lives for the sake of their scattered flocks. And Turner was determined to see every one of them hang.

The clouds shifted again, leaving the village in shadow. Duncan looked to the south, toward the northern reaches of Loch Ken, just visible at the foot of the glen. He drew in a deep breath. Sunlight sparkled in mottled patches across the blue waters. Duncan watched the brown sails of a fishing boat scudding slowly across the lake in search of salmon.

Several times a year his father traveled to the bustling village of Wigtown on the Solway Firth to sell wool, and Duncan remembered how immense the salty waters of the Solway looked when he first saw them, stretching away westward to the open sea, and to the south—and England. He loved the screeching of gulls, the salty smells, and the sights and sounds of men and boats in the harbor. His father's brother, his Uncle Hamish, worked as a fisherman somewhere near Edinburgh. Though Duncan had never been to faraway Edinburgh, nor had he ever met his uncle, his father told him about fishing on the sea. He told him all about the rising and falling of the fishing sloop on the waves, the fresh salt breeze on your face, and the thrill as the sails filled and the boat surged forward into the frothy seas.

Springtime or not, this was Scotland, and the teasing sun soon disappeared altogether behind the clouds, and Loch Ken faded into the landscape. But Duncan continued gazing approvingly over the muted countryside falling away on every side of his castle—he often referred to Dunfarg as *his* castle. You could see an enemy coming for miles, a perfect place for a fortress, he concluded, leaning on his staff. Duncan often tried to imagine what it would have been like long ago when men fought within these walls for their lives—and for Scotland.

Nosing his way along the rubble, Brodie suddenly halted in his tracks, his ears erect, head cocked to one side. His nostrils flared, and his eyes stared unblinking as he worked this new scent through the mysterious intuitions of his dog brain.

"What is it, Sir Brodie?" asked Duncan. Long ago he had come to respect his dog's instincts. "I wouldn't mind if ye've gone and sniffed out some fresh meat for us. Mother'd be loving ye if ye've gone and done it. What is it?" he urged.

Duncan's mouth watered as he thought about how his mother had roasted the last rabbit Brodie caught—it seemed like months ago. Though filled with oatcakes, his stomach gnawed and growled for meat.

"Rabbit, is it, Brodie?" hissed Duncan, crouching low beside his dog. "A fat one—oh, let it be a fat one."

His face now close to his dog's, he sniffed. A boy's power of scent, though well trained to sniff out mealtime smells, was no match for a dog's keen sense of smell. Though Duncan smelled nothing, he did feel something. A sudden breeze moved his thick red hair, and he felt it on his cheek. He moved to the right and all was still again. Slowly moving left, he felt the narrow breeze again.

"Ye've done it, Brodie," said Duncan. "Though I can't say as I know what it is ye've done."

Following the breeze on his cheek, Duncan leaned closer. Searching the mud, his eyes fell on a dark depression along the inside of the wall.

"Ye've found a bonny hole," said Duncan, a lilting sort of wonder in his voice. "And if air's coming out at such a rate, it must be something more than a rabbit's wee burrow!"

For the next quarter of an hour, boy and dog worked side by side enlarging the hole. Brodie dug away the mud with canine efficiency, and Duncan lifted the stones out of the way.

"We've been over this ground hundreds of times," said Duncan, grunting as he reached farther into the hole, mud smeared on his cheek. "Spring rains must've washed away the soil that covered this passage for—what d'ye think it's been, Brodie?—hoondreds o' years?" When excited, Duncan's r's rolled more than usual, and his vowels tended to rise and fall and stretch themselves in all directions in the process.

Duncan felt his heart beating faster as they dug.

Moments later, his eyes wide with excitement, Duncan said, "Ye really have done it!" He ran a muddy hand through his hair. "Ye've gone and found an old passage!"

FIGHT OR DIE!

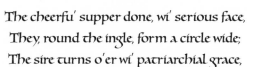

The cheerfu' supper done, wi' serious face,
They, round the ingle, form a circle wide;
The sire turns o'er wi' patriarchial grace,
The big ha' Bible, ance his father's pride.

Robert Burns

With a distracted nod of his head, Duncan signaled Brodie to gather the sheep for home. So occupied was Duncan with the discovery of the passage he barely heard the bleating of his black-faced charges as he followed Brodie and the little mob down the terraced steepness into the glen. Just ahead, a stream chattered its way down the narrow valley and then leveled off for several yards into a quiet pool.

With no apparent signal from Duncan, Brodie shot forward and halted the sheep along the banks of the pool. Duncan smiled. Habit had almost taught his dog how to care for the sheep without him.

He watched the new spring lambs, their clubby legs looking too tall for their fresh white bodies, as they frisked about the older sheep. Most black-faced ewes bore only one lamb each springtime, but this year three ewes had delivered twins.

Duncan never tired of the heel-kicking playfulness of the new pairs of brothers and sisters.

Kneeling at the edge of the stream, he scooped up a handful of water, and scrubbing at his muddy face, he gasped at the numbing coldness of it. With a handful of wet heather, he worked away at his dirt-covered hands and arms. It wouldn't do to show up at home for dinner all muddied up. His mother would only turn him out and send him off for a good scrub.

Wiping his face dry on his plaid, Duncan smiled as two lambs butted and frolicked in the tall grass. As he watched, his mind wandered to the stories filtering up the glens from Dalry that told of Sir James Turner's dragoons prowling about stealing sheep in payment—*they* called it payment—for fines. Worse than that, whole farms had been burned to the ground, and ministers imprisoned for unlicensed preaching. Drunken soldiers burst in on worshipers and demanded anything of value from the poor. One man described the soldiers with arms so loaded with spoil—coats and plaids, even shoes—that it looked as if they'd been stripping the slain after a battle. With his stick he made a savage cut at a clump of gorse. He couldn't help hating the English.

"Now, that's an unkind cut, indeed, Master Duncan," came a voice from the slope opposite the pool.

Duncan looked up at the speaker, an old man, his grinning face topped with a tattered wool bonnet clinging precariously to one side. Long yellow-white hair fell onto his shoulders and joined a full beard of the same hue. Ancient Grier, their nearest neighbor, had lived in these hills forever. Should I tell Grier about my discovery? Duncan wondered.

"But if it were meant fer the enemies of the Laird and the Kirk, I'll be forgiving of ye fer it, that I will."

"A good evening to ye, Ancient Grier," Duncan called up to the old man.

"Aye, 'tis a good evening," mused the old man, stepping nimbly down the hillside.

Duncan smiled as the old farmer joined him at the pool. The old man wore loose-fitting wool trousers, patched and stitched so completely that Duncan had long ago given up trying to tell what the original wool might have looked like. Over a grayish-brown coat, similarly repaired, a plaid draped across his wide shoulders, shoulders once broad and strong but now bent with age. Completing his tattered outfit, the old man wore a pair of knee-high leather boots that widened and folded over at the tops and that looked, battered as they were, like the footgear worn by a pikeman from some twenty-five years earlier during the wars. Ancient Grier had fought in those wars, and Duncan often found in him a ready supply of riveting stories from those heady days.

The old man continued. "Each night after prayers I lay my head on my pillow, and I wonder if I'll wake oop on t'other side. And each morn I wakes on this side—so fer it hae been so, as ye see." Here the old man lifted his white head, and with a broad smile, he continued. "I bless King Jesus and I thanks him fer anoother day 'to glorify and enjoy him,' as it says in the catechism."

"But how, when the times are so bad," blurted Duncan, wondering at the old man's faith, "how can ye possibly enjoy anything with that hell-hound Turner and his dragoons plundering crops and flocks and leaving families to starve to death? Some, they say, not worth rounding up for swinging, he shoots dead on the spot."

"Aye," said the old man. "Go on, give it mouth, lad. Ye'll feel better fer it."

Duncan continued. "My father got word of another fine for not attending the popish services in Dalry, and he said they read yer name out for non-compearance last Sabbath

11

Day, as well. How will ye pay? They'll take everything we have. Like as not, Turner'll kill ye. And how is it ye'll go about glorifying God and enjoying of him when they've done with ye?"

Flushed, Duncan fell silent. He'd said more than he should have.

Grier nodded sagaciously and worked his mouth from side to side in thought, his curly mustache and beard sticking out in a circular pattern as he worked Duncan's question over in his mind.

"Now here's a question that wants answering," said Ancient Grier.

But before he could continue, Brodie nudged his master with his long nose. Duncan glanced up at the flock ambling in all directions. With a slight jerk of his head, he sent Brodie streaking like a bullet in a half circle around the scattering sheep.

"Och, do yer duty, lad," continued the old farmer. "But we'll talk tonight. Yer good mother sent up yer bonnie sisters earlier to invite me to family prayers with ye. I'll bring m'pipes," he added with a wink. "But so's ye hae got an answer to work round in yer young pate till then: In spite of all, I enjoy the Lord, for his mercy, his goodness, his grace, his comfort—my cup fairly overflows with it all. Mind ye, I'd find it overflowing a wee bit more to m'liking if it went and flooded out all the English in the process."

With that, the old man turned and headed back up the hill. Duncan looked after him in wonder. Then he turned and followed Brodie and the flock already moving eagerly toward home. Familiar strains from the Psalter echoed after Duncan as the old farmer sang on his way up the hill to his croft.

> The Lord's my Shepherd, I'll not want;
> He makes me down to lie

In pastures green; he leadeth me
The quiet waters by.

The way widened, and just ahead lay his family's cottage, peat smoke drifting from the stone chimney that rose from one end above the heather-thatched roof. Duncan's stomach growled. His home seemed to nestle securely and inconspicuously into the green and purple of the surrounding hills. Though stories abounded of troubles and cruelties, living high up as they did and several miles from the village of Dalry, the troubles with the English king seemed far away. But Duncan couldn't help fearing—maybe even hoping—that those troubles might someday follow the rumors up the hills—and reach his family.

Pressed together against the dry stane dykes (low walls stacked without mortar) surrounding the M'Kethe croft, the flock of sheep formed a solid mass of winter-thick wool backs broken only by flicking ears and curling horns. Duncan vaulted over the wall and opened the wooden gate from the inside. Brodie took a crouching step toward the flock, and sheep poured through the gate like fighting men through a breach. Clustered against the cottage and encircled by the protective wall, here the sheep would be safe from wolves—and their restlessness when danger threatened served as an early warning for the family within.

Duncan thought again of their discovery. Unless his father asked, he decided not to tell him about it just yet. He and Brodie would explore the passage further before saying anything to anyone.

After securing the gate, he grabbed up an armload of peat from the stack at the south end of the cottage. The M'Kethes always stacked their peat on the south side. Duncan had heard his father say, "Peat stacked at the south end dries better throughout what passes for summer, and dried peat gives ye more warmth throughout the numbing wet times—times when a warm fire is life itself."

Bursting out of the low entrance, braids bouncing and homespun dress flying as she ran, Duncan's seven-year-old sister Jenny flew toward him. Toddling behind came three-year-old Angus gripping his toy long bow and arrows, a grin stretching across his round face.

"Dunckle!" called Jenny, grabbing his leg, then doing her best to scramble up onto his back. Angus wrapped chubby arms and legs around Duncan's leg and held on, squealing with delight as Duncan staggered forward. Eleven-year-old Fiona looked on, her face dimpled with a shy grin.

"Save me, Fiona. I'm done for!" he called in mock anguish, falling to one knee, his arms extended in supplication. Fiona planted a kiss on his cheek and laughed as he struggled under Jenny and Angus's clambering. Jenny finally swung her legs onto his shoulders and sat proudly gripping his hair with her hands, Duncan wincing with each twist of his hair.

Brodie sat on his haunches, his head cocked to one side, and watched the familiar welcome Duncan's little sister and brother inflicted on their big brother.

"I've not seen so wild a gaggle o' bairns in the whole of Scotland," Duncan's mother called good-naturedly from just inside the low doorway. "Fiona, Jenny, ye fetch yerselves back in here and help me lay the table fer supper—be quick aboot it, then!"

Duncan disentangled himself from his sisters and reached for Angus's pudgy fist, intending to hold his hand as they went inside. Prying open the fleshy fist Duncan discovered a moist, warty mound with what appeared to be arms and legs. Angus grinned at his prize.

"Puddock," he informed Duncan proudly.

"Ye have been busy, then," said Duncan, stroking the frog.

"But ye ken what Mother'll do if ye bring a creature like that inside? She'll turn ye into a puddock, she will."

Angus's eyes grew wider.

"We'd best leave it just here," continued Duncan, setting the frog in a niche in the stone next to the doorway.

Taking his little brother's hand, Duncan stretched to his full height as he stepped over the threshold. He felt a thrill of satisfaction as his head brushed lightly against the stone lintel over the low opening. His mother had to duck slightly when she would pass in and out, and his father always bent over with his hand on the lintel, his shoulders turning sideways as he passed through. Though he still had to stretch and roll up onto his toes to do it, Duncan found a good deal of pleasure in that brushing of his head each time he passed in and out of the family croft. It seemed to hold a significance he could not quite explain; nevertheless, his delight in the accomplishment was undiminished. Once inside he planted a kiss on his mother's soft cheek.

"Yer safe returned, Duncan," said his mother, lines of worry softening around her eyes.

Regular reports of fines, arrests, even executions made their way into the hills where Duncan's family kept their few sheep, grew their oats, and eked out their humble living. These were hard times, and though his mother seldom complained, Duncan thought the strain and worry showed more often in her eyes. She was used to loss and disappointments. His mother had delivered six live children into the world. Duncan's older brother had died as a baby and was buried near Inverary, in the highlands where his father had lived as a boy. Between Duncan and his sisters another boy had been born, then swept away by fever before he was old enough to walk. But for all that loss and grief, his mother's blue eyes usually sparkled with cheerfulness, and

Duncan loved the enthusiastic glow that always seemed to animate her features.

"But yer returned dirty," his mother went on, pulling up the corner of her apron and making toward his face. "And all thwacked oop, too!" she added, spotting the bruise on Duncan's cheek. "How ever did ye coome by that?"

"It's just a wee scratch, Mother," said Duncan. "Never mind it." He smiled at her. "Ye are the prettiest mother a lad could ever ask for in all the world." He planted another kiss on her cheek. His sisters giggled from where they put out the wooden trenchers and cups on the table.

"Ye are, Moother," agreed Jenny, who, though the younger of the two girls, was always the first to speak for them both.

"But it won't work," their mother said, looking all the prettier with the last light of day shining through a narrow window and the warm firelight playing on her auburn hair, subdued now from its more youthful flame color by the passage of time. A smile tugged at the corners of her mouth, and a flush of delight shone on her cheeks.

"Ye're still not pulling yerself oop to this table, Duncan," she went on, "wearing half the brae on yer face. Fall to scrubbing, then."

"But I di—" protested Duncan.

"Not enoough to suit me," his mother cut him off, "nor enoough to set mooch fear in the heart of the dirt, I shouldn't think by the look of ye."

While Duncan scrubbed in the basin, his father came in from plowing.

"Blessings aboound!" he said, patting Brodie's head, then planting a kiss on each of his daughters' foreheads, and giving Duncan a manly squeeze and a hearty pat on the back with honest hands made large and coarse from years of hard work. With merriment in his eyes, he then spun their mother around and embraced her. Holding her at arm's length he said, "Tut, tut, poor Solomon. There's none prettier or wiser in all the world."

"That's just what I've been trying to tell her," said Duncan.

"Flatterers all!" she said, a flush of pleasure on her cheeks.

"Not so, m'love," said Duncan's father, planting another kiss on her forehead. "Flatterers mean to hurt ye, and Duncan and I mean to love and protect ye." His face clouded as he added quietly, "Come what may."

When all was ready, they sat around the trestle table, the peat fire hissing in the crude stone fireplace. Duncan's father prayed the Lord's blessing on the food and offered their thanks for it, and the family ate their simple fare: broth and oatcakes spread with soft Crowdie cheese.

"Dunckle gave hi'self a woound," offered little Jenny when she finished her broth.

Duncan scowled at his little sister.

"How'd ye coome by that, lad?" asked his father, his tone rising with concern.

Duncan never lied to his parents, but how could he admit to hitting himself with his own stick while having an imaginary battle?

"Fiona and I ken how he done it," offered Jenny persistently.

Duncan stopped chewing. Ancient Grier said the girls had come up for a visit that day. Could they have been watching him storm the castle? He studied Jenny's wide eyes and features bulging with merriment. Fiona studied the food on her trencher and wouldn't meet his eye. That settled him.

"Playacting, Father," said Duncan, coloring and taking a vicious bite of oat cake.

"Playacting?" said his father. He studied his son silently before continuing. "And the wee lambs while's ye was play-acting? Were they only playacting at nourishing themselves and generally trying to get a decent start on life, answer me that, lad?" Before Duncan could reply, his father continued. "What was it ye were playacting at?"

"It were more rehearsing, Father," said Duncan, and liking the sound of that, he nodded and said it again, "rehearsing it was, Father."

"Did ye keell 'em all?" asked Jenny.

"Now, Jenny, I'll not go and hae ye talking about killing," said their father, his voice firm but his sandy eyebrows raised in firm supplication.

Broth dribbling from his chin, Angus looked with wide eyes from his father to Duncan as they spoke.

"I might be so bold as to call it *training*, Father," said Duncan, hoping to divert his father's attention from Jenny's question. "Training for resisting Covenant breakers and all oppressors of the Kirk." This sounded even better. Duncan continued. "It were no mere playacting. I was *training*, that I was."

"Training, was it?" said his father, his face growing sober.

"We'll soon have to fight them," said Duncan, his eyes pleading with his father, "fight them or die."

"Fight, fight, fight!" sang Angus, slashing his spoon in the air as if it were a claymore. It slipped from his pudgy hand and hit the wall with a thud and then clattered onto the floor.

"Or die fighting 'em," added Duncan's mother, a bitter lilt in her voice. "For shame, Angus," she scolded, retrieving his spoon.

Jenny took another bite of oatcake and smirked at Duncan. Fighting and war were so far removed from anything Jenny had yet experienced in her short life that she decided all this talk must be just part of a game. Fiona grew pale and stared at her trencher, her hands folded on her lap.

"I'll not have ye casting gloom over this fine supper yer mother's gone and prepared for us," said Duncan's father, his voice rising.

"But they're cooming, Sandy," said Duncan's mother, nervously putting a wisp of auburn hair back in place, her eyes casting about as if soldiers might even that moment be lurking in the shadows of the croft.

"Mary, Mary," said Duncan's father soothingly. His eyes fell on each of them in turn as he continued. "The devil wants us a-running about tearing our hair with fear of what might happen to us." He paused and an expression of determination and wonder spread across his face. Duncan had often seen his father look that way. "But our sweet Lord Jesus, he wants us to obey. And, Duncan, I'll not have ye raising the alarm. Ye'll be stirring the pot and scaring the wee ones. Now, there's an end of it."

Duncan had learned long ago that when his father spoke like that the topic was closed. But why didn't his father want to fight? There were wrongs enough. He looked at his father's broad shoulders and muscular arms. And though his father's face was often alive with merriment, when he was angry, his determined forehead and fierce eyes could set fear in the stoutest heart. So why wouldn't he fight? If Duncan hadn't known his father better, he might even have been tempted to think—that he was afraid to fight.

Try as they might, the gloom lingered throughout the rest of the meal. Then Duncan heard it—the faint skirling of Ancient Grier's pipes drifting down the brae and into the cottage.

"There now, Grier approaches fit to wake the dead from here to Dumfries," said Duncan's mother, clearing the table.

"He'll tell us stories," said Jenny hopefully.

Duncan's father's eyes clouded slightly.

"Won't he, Father?" Jenny persisted.

"After prayers," said her father shortly.

Ancient Grier halted outside their croft, the piping now sounding loud and alarming. Duncan's heart beat faster. The

19

wailing of pipes always made him wish he had a two-fisted broadsword in hand and a pack of English or Covenant breakers to throw himself at—he wasn't overly particular which.

He and his sisters, with Angus toddling behind, ran to the door and threw it open. A path of light fell on the old man, his face red and cheeks bulging as he blew air into the goat stomach of his bagpipes. Lit up against the dusk, Ancient Grier marched in place as he played, until with a deflating screech, not unlike the sound of a goose at the chopping block, the tune came to an abrupt end.

"Peace be on this house!" said the old man as they welcomed him into the cottage.

After brief conversation about spring planting, goat kids, and lambs, they all sat down around the table. Duncan's father said solemnly, "Let us worship God." He then led the family in a prayer full of devotion and hope, his voice rising and falling with passion as he prayed. When he finished, he took the family Bible in his great hands and opened it slowly and carefully as if it were some rare and delicate treasure, easily broken if mishandled.

"Hear the Word of our Lord from the Proverbs of Solomon, the sixteenth chapter," he said, reverence and firmness in his voice. " 'Better to be lowly in spirit and among the oppressed than to share plunder with the proud.' " Duncan's father paused, eyeing his son over the sacred pages.

Duncan felt his cheeks burning as his father read the text through a second time before continuing. Why couldn't he have read about slaying enemies and trampling their faces in the streets? There was plenty of that in the Holy Book, too.

His father read on: " 'Better a patient man than a warrior, a man who controls his temper than one who takes a city.' "

Duncan studied his father's face. As he read, the determination in his brow took on a resolve that Duncan thought looked as unshakable as faith itself. But Duncan feared that his father's determination was of a different kind than what was needed to drive out the English or wreak vengeance on Covenant breakers.

His father announced the psalm they were to sing, and when they finished singing, Ancient Grier spoke first.

"Ye no doubt read last evening in the same sixteenth of Proverbs," he said, rising and standing with his back to the peat fire. " 'The lips of a king speak as an oracle.' " He paused, eyeing all in the room fiercely. His voice rose, " *'and his mouth should not betray justice.'* " With each word, Grier's fist came down onto his open palm with a loud smack.

Little Angus squealed and slapped his pudgy fist into his palm like the old man.

"Aye, we read it," said Duncan's father, looking steadily at the old man.

"Which reminds me of our present monarch's grandsire, King James VI—James I, the English called him," Grier continued, folding his hands behind his back, rocking back on his heels and gazing up into the murkiness of the rafters.

Duncan's mother followed Grier's gaze, and she scowled at a rustling in the thatch. She hated the rats that lodged so freely above the family.

"Ye remember the treachery of King James," Grier continued, "betraying justice for saintly Andrew Melville, who was called to London on the pretense of hearing our Presbyterian grievances? 'Course ye don't remember, 'twas more than fifty years ago. But I remember, aye, I remember." Nodding knowingly, he stroked his long white beard, and Duncan and his sisters listened expectantly.

"Now, there was a scoundrel of a king," the old man went on, "who ruled by lies and deceit as he breathed. Breaking his word, he threw worthy Mr. Melville in amongst the rats and fleas of the wretched Tower." He nearly spit out the last words. Then he paused, eyes defiant, as he gazed into the eyes of the children.

"What fer?" asked Jenny.

"I was hoping ye'd be asking," said Grier, nodding in a satisfied manner and resuming his gazing up at the rafters. "All for telling the king the truth about hisself."

"What king would hate the truth so?" asked Duncan.

"An unjust one, that's who," replied Ancient Grier fiercely.

"What did he tell the king?" asked Fiona, softly.

"He told him," said Ancient Grier, clearing his throat importantly, " 'There are two kings and two kingdoms in Scotland: There is King James, the head of the Commonwealth, and there is King Jesus, the Head of the Kirk, whose subject King James is, and of whose kingdom he is not the head, nor a lord, but a member.' Then he called a curse to light upon James's idea of trying to take the place of King Jesus in his Kirk. Sputtering and fuming, James forbade the General Assembly of the Kirk to meet, appointing his favorites to be bishops—bishops in Presbyterian Scotland, mind ye! And then he tried making us a kneeling Kirk and introduced other popish foppery."

"What's popish mean?" asked Jenny.

"Anything not conforming to how the Book tells us God wants to be worshiped, that's popish," said Grier. "James even went and installed a kist o' whistles at St. Giles in Edinburgh. Aye, he did, in the very shadow of John Knox's pulpit."

"What's a kist o' whistles?" asked Duncan.

"English call 'em pipe organs," said Grier, spitting out the name, the flames of the sheep tallow candles quivering precariously with his words. "Roman Catholic churches have pipe organs," he concluded, nodding knowingly.

"Aye, and popish churches have walls and roofs," said Duncan's father, a smile playing at the corners of his mouth. "Would ye have us dispense with walls and roofs in the kirk?"

Grier blinked rapidly and frowned.

"No kist o' whistles in the Psalter," he said defiantly.

"Aye, but we're told to praise the Lord with all kinds of musical instruments," replied Duncan's father. "And I can't see as how an organ doesn't fit that description with all those lovely sounds wrapped up in one instrument." He leaned forward and set another cut of peat on the fire. "It's how ye use a thing that makes it good or bad, Ancient Grier, not the thing itself."

Frowning, Ancient Grier cleared his throat and blinked up at the rafters. "Well, I might just agree with ye," he said, looking levelly at Duncan's father, "if ye said the same, Sandy M'Kethe, about yer sword."

Duncan turned to look at his father. Before he could reply, Fiona, in her quiet voice, asked, "What became of King James?"

"James died," replied Grier, eager to return to his tale. "And thanks be to God for it. But his son Charles—aye, he was even more deluded than his father at thinking he ruled the Kirk and the Parliament—Charles turned loose his Archbishop of Canterbury, William Laud."

"His name'd be Archbishop Praise, then?" interjected Duncan.

"Aye, but there were nothing worth praising about that archfiend Laud," continued Grier. "And before Scotland knew it, he'd forced their popish English prayer book on the Kirk. What followed was riots in the streets of Edinburgh and the Bishops' Wars."

"How'd it all happen?" begged Jenny eagerly.

"Oh, that I'll tell, lassie," said Grier. "And ye'll be liking the telling of it, to be sure."

23

SIGNING WITH BLOOD

If [Archbishop] Laud had been a madman just broke loose,
he could not have done more mischief than he did in Scotland.
Charles Dickens

Sputtering came from a candle melting into a mound of yellow tallow on the table, and light played on the shadows against the walls. From near the peat fire, the spinning wheel hummed rhythmically as Duncan's mother drew out lengths of new wool yarn and laid it in wide loops over two wooden pegs. Angus lined up rows of pebbles at her feet. In and around the rows, he made little forests with tufts of wool snitched from his mother's basket.

"Oh, I wish I hae seen it w' my own eye," continued Grier. "But I rest content to hae heard it on the very best of authority." He lowered his voice confidentially. "It were the Sabbath morning of the twenty-third of July 1637, when into the very pulpit of St. Giles strutted a popish bishop, all swishing in sacerdotal pomp, bedecked with Babylonian glitter and puffing superstitious finery."

Duncan had never been in an Anglican service, but he often wondered just what it would be like. Sometimes he even

24

imagined himself sneaking his way into a service down at the old parish kirk and seeing all.

"It's as bad as all that?" asked Duncan.

"Aye, and worse," said Grier. "That day at St. Giles the usurping bishop, sneering in triumph, read—mind ye, *read*—popish prayers from the accursed pages of Laud's Liturgy right here in Presbyterian Scotland." Grier's eyes goggled defiantly. He continued. "For an instant all was silent in the grand old kirk—save the scurrying of rats scavenging for crumbs under the table."

Duncan's mother frowned. Duncan's and his sisters' eyes grew wide.

"That's when it happened," continued Grier, encouraged by their attention. "A lass named Jenny Geddes—ye bear a noble name, Jenny." He patted Jenny on the head. "I say, Jenny Geddes lept to her feet, and gathering up her stool, she cried, 'Will ye read that book in my lug!' and then with a mighty heave she hurled her stool at the bishop! Determined not to submit to Laud's nonsense, the hot-blooded congregation joined in a frenzy of displeasure. Soon, fiery-tempered Presbyterians clogged the streets of the Royal Mile. Riots followed, and so hated were Laud's men that one of them, Bishop Brechin, kept a brace of loaded pistols in full view on the pulpit when he ventured to conduct the popish rites."

"So *that* Jenny, she'd be a hero, aye, she would," said Jenny, smiling.

Duncan's mother paused at her spinning and looked sternly at Jenny.

"A-leaping up and a-yelling during services?" said her mother, incredulously. "Sounds more like shameful behaving for a lass—under any provocation."

"Aye, yer mother speaks truth, Jenny, lass," added Duncan's father, looking up from where his great hands had been clasped under his chin. He then gazed pensively into the smoldering peat.

Grier stroked his beard and scowled before continuing.

"Then came 'the great marriage day of this nation with God,' the twenty-eighth of February, 1638. A grand day, aye it was. Hundreds of faithful ministers, nobles, and gentry gathered at Greyfriars Kirk, in Edinburgh, mind ye, in peril of their lives. They put down their names on Alexander Henderson's National Covenant—the stoutest of heart put their names down with their own blood."

"Was it a rebellion?" asked Duncan eagerly.

"If ye go and pledge yer support for the king," said Grier, "does that sound like a rebellion, lad?"

"No," said Duncan, a hint of disappointment in his voice.

"Well, mind ye, they pledged loyalty to King Charles in all matters belonging to King Charles, and at the same stroke they pledged loyalty to King Jesus in all matters pertaining to King Jesus. Make no mistake about it, we Scots are no king haters. We just hae more than one of 'em, and King Charles I demanded a loyalty which the faithful give to God alone. Prepared to resist or die, thousands more signed the Covenant over the next weeks—I among them."

"Did ye do it wi' yer bloood?" asked Jenny, grinning hopefully.

"Aye, I did," said Grier, nodding grimly. "That I did."

"Did ye sign, Father?" asked Duncan.

"Yer father was just a wee thing in those days," explained Grier, before Duncan's father could reply.

Fiona looped her arm in her father's, closed her eyes, and leaned against his strong shoulder.

"I hae ever pledged m'highest loyalty to King Jesus in his Kirk," replied Duncan's father, stroking Fiona's head. "And wi' the saints and martyrs who've gone before us, I'd willingly give m'life's blood to defend—mind ye, I say, to *defend*—Kirk and Covenant."

"Yer loyalty none doubts," said Grier, eager to return to his story. "Meanwhile, from all about the realm, faithful Scots rallied to defend—mind ye, Sandy—to defend the cause of religion and the Covenant. Even the earl of Argyll threw in his lot wi' us."

"Did we keel 'em all?" asked Jenny.

"Lass, I'll not have ye gloated over the death of the wicked," said Duncan's father firmly.

"No wicked blood spilt this time anyhow," said Grier with a dismissive wave of his hand. "The king's troops faced off wi' the stouthearted Covenanter army, and King Charles backed down without a fight." Grier chuckled and stroked his beard. "But fearing the growing pressure of Puritans in the English Parliament, Charles visited Scotland and gave out rank, title, and gold to all lairds who'd throw their lot in wi' him."

"Och," said Duncan, holding his head in his hands. "So whose side were we on? And who was on our side?"

"Aye, that's the question, indeed, m'lad," said Duncan's father approvingly. "We are ever on the side of King Jesus—and ever loyal are we to the king or to the parliament that acknowledges the Crown rights of the Redeemer in his Kirk."

"So did the lairds of Scotland throw in with Charles or the Kirk?" asked Duncan.

"The faithful, like Argyll, remained true to the Covenant," said Grier. "They were determined to support either king or Parliament, whichever promised freedom of worship to the Kirk. Worthy Samuel Rutherford and the Scots Commissioners to Westminster negotiated with Parliament, and with the signing of the Solemn League and Covenant in 1643, Parliament agreed to Presbyterian government in the Kirk in exchange for Scottish troops to fight a civil war against Charles."

Grier's eyes narrowed. He spread his arms wide for effect, light from the fire and the candles casting a looming shadow of the old man against the rough walls. "That's where I come into the fight. And with a wee bit of assistance from Cromwell, we Scots brought Charles to his knees at Marston Moor—a bloody fight we had of it that day. Meanwhile, the Scots' betrayer, the popish Montrose, raised Highlander support for Charles and in 1645 routed all Covenanters out of Argyll lands."

Here Duncan's father raised his gaze from the fire and looked at the children. Steady breathing came from a mound on the floor where Angus lay asleep.

"Yer grandfather fled Inverary and Montrose in those times," said their father, "and brought us here, to the lowlands. I was a wee bit younger than ye, Duncan, in those days."

"What was it like, Father?" asked Duncan.

His father gazed silently into the fire before answering.

"Smoke and fire and the reek o' burning," he said, with a far off look in his eyes. "The thunder of cannon and the whistling of bullets and some wailing of bairns." He fell silent before continuing. "I remember hiding in the heather by day and traveling at night, bone weary, asleep on my feet while slogging along wi' yer Uncle Hamish a-drooling on m'back."

Jenny threw her head back and laughed. Fiona looked up pityingly at her father.

"But if Uncle Hamish's as big as ye, Father," said Jenny, "he's too big for ye to be carrying."

"So I thought," replied their father. "But he was just a wee thing then."

"What else?" urged Duncan.

"I remember being hungry—hungry all the time."

"Aye, that's bad," said Duncan soberly.

Grier picked up the story. "With that fellow Cromwell backing us, we Scots routed the Royalists in June of 1645 at Naseby. Charles surrendered to the Scots troops, but he refused to give up his grand notions of ruling the Kirk by what he termed his 'divine right.' So we turned him over to Parliament after they promised not to kill him."

"Why not be rid of him?" asked Duncan.

Duncan's father scowled.

"Aye," replied Grier with a pull on his beard. "There's a question, indeed, lad. Little did we ken that we were seeking to preserve the very royalty that now sets about to destroy us. But things got worse for our side. Cromwell, strutting with borrowed glories, began waning in his promise to keep the Solemn League and Covenant. What's more, he and Parliament and the assembled ministers at Westminster were not getting on so well."

"That's the English for ye," said Duncan. "Can't even get along with their own kind."

"And we can?" said Duncan's father fiercely. "We Scots hae killed more Scots than any of our enemies ever needed to."

"Aye, and Charles played on our disagreements," added Grier. "Watching all, and desperate to get free of prison, Charles entered into a secret agreement with some Covenanters, feigning to allow Presbyterian government in the Kirk."

"Was the king lying, then?" Fiona asked incredulously.

"Aye," said Duncan bitterly. "Lying and using our side to get him free from Cromwell."

"And with the Solemn League and Covenant now seen by many Scots as broken by Parliament and Cromwell," continued Grier, "some of ours set out on a plot to free Charles. Cromwell, now the enemy of Scotland, met them at Preston."

"Them?" said Duncan. "Weren't ye fighting with them, Ancient Grier?"

"No. I was home nursing a wound from the Naseby fighting." He patted his left knee. "I would never stoop to saying so myself, but other of my fighting lads said the whole campaign might hae come out different if I *had* been there. But I weren't, and in 1648 Cromwell routed our Scots army—poor lads. The next year he marched on Edinburgh."

"And what happened to the king?" asked Fiona, her voice coming softly from the shadows.

"Parliaments lie too," Grier spat out. "The English Parliament betrayed its word given to Scotland and executed Charles I. Lifted his head right off, they did."

"And now whose side were we on?" asked Duncan, scowling in confusion.

"That's the question, indeed," said Grier, nodding gravely. "One thing was clear: Parliament had broken the Covenant and could no longer be trusted. So the Marquess of Argyll negotiated with Charles's son and rightful heir, who signed the National Covenant and promised the Kirk her rights. With his own hands, godly Argyll placed the crown on the head of Charles Stuart, later Charles II, our present dissembling monarch. But Cromwell would have none of this rebellion."

"Rebellion?" said Duncan. "How could it be a rebellion? We were now the ones supporting the king?"

"Aye, a question ignored by the likes of Cromwell," replied Grier, taking a more violent yank at his beard. "Now calling himself 'Lord Protector,' Cromwell and his Roundheads marched against us at Dunbar, finally crushing the Scots' army at Worcester in 1651. From the safety of the spire of Worcester Cathedral, Charles watched our lads die on the battlefield below. Aye, the River Severn ran red with Covenanter blood that day. Then he took to his heels, leaving the beleaguered remnant of his army to fend for themselves."

"So that's what we got for being loyal, is it?" said Duncan, a bitter lilt in his voice.

"Ah, but, Duncan," said his father, "there's one King who'll never betray his subjects. Though loyalty to our Redeemer puts us at odds with kings and parliaments and is the cause of all our present woe, King Jesus will never betray ye for yer loyalty to him. And, in his time, a day of reckoning awaits our enemies. So says the Book."

Heavy breathing rose from where Jenny and Angus lay sprawled on a sheepskin at their mother's feet. Duncan's father rose and gathered the now sleeping Fiona up in his great arms and gently laid her on her chaff-filled mattress. He covered her and placed a kiss tenderly on her forehead.

"May he hasten the day of that reckoning," continued Grier, smashing his fist into the palm of his hand savagely.

Angus snorted in his sleep and rolled over.

"I'll be asking ye to keep still, Ancient Grier," said Duncan's mother, "lest ye wake the wee ones."

"My regrets to the bairns," he said. "But there's more than my blusterings like to be disturbing their rest with Charles II ruling the land and the Kirk. Have ye forgotten what our dissembling monarch did when he was restored to his throne? Foul betrayer of the Covenant," he spat out the words, "he declared the loyal Marquess of Argyll a traitor and ordered his execution." His eyes grew wide and goggled at them as he drew his forefinger sharply across his neck with a "Kleek, kleek."

"But why the Marquess of Argyll?" asked Duncan. "He was the very one who had placed the crown on Charles's head."

"Why, indeed," said Grier hotly. "Argyll was only the first of many saints to die." Here Grier looked sternly at Duncan's father. "And thousands more will die—unless Charles be *resisted*."

Duncan's father looked steadily back at the old man, their eyes locked for a moment.

"You know the rest," continued Grier. "Our truest ministers ejected from their pulpits and Charles's favorites, popish drunkards, propped up in their places, to lead the Kirk astray. Roll taken at the episcopal services; fines levied for failure to attend; the faithful hunted down like criminals; field meetings raided by dragoons, threats, beatings and brandings, prison; men even killed before the very eyes of their wives and bairns."

The humming of the spinning wheel stopped short. Duncan's mother raised her head from her wool. "Has it coome to that?" she said, a fierceness in her eyes.

"Aye, and worse," said Grier. "With James Turner—unprincipled mercenary butcher—leading his band of evildoers about the countryside, none are safe, not even we who eke out our living far up in the hills."

Grier paused, eyeing the stock and barrel of the family musket hanging on the wall near the door.

"Peace-loving man that ye be, Sandy M'Kethe," said Grier, "come not on the Sabbath to the field meeting in the glen without yer sword at yer hip and yer gun loaded and at the ready."

Duncan watched as candlelight played on the stout blade of his father's claymore hung over the fireplace.

His father clenched his rough hands together until his knuckles shone white.

"The Lord knows I'll not kill a man—no matter how evil—in cold blood," Duncan's father said, his voice steady and resolved. "Nor will I be standing idle while a wicked man kills another in cold blood. But I'll not go looking for a fight. I'm of the opinion that some of our suffering we bring on ourselves with our own hot blood—perhaps that's another kind of betrayal. In any case, Ancient Grier, true as I am to the Covenant, I'll not go with my heart yearning to worship the Prince of Peace while my hand's a-clutching eager at my blade."

"Aye, and I respect ye fer your reluctance to shed blood, Sandy," said Grier, nodding deferentially. "But if ye'll not fight"—he spread his arms in shadowy supplication—"I hope ye can scatter to the mist and find a good place for hiding your dear ones. Come harvesttime when ye think yer crops are safe in, Turner and his dragoons'll descend on ye like the death angel plaguing King Charles and his London. And then may the Lord hae mercy on yer sweet bairns."

RATS!

Rats!

They fought the dogs and killed the cats,
And bit the babies in the cradles,
And ate the cheeses out of the vats,
And licked the soup from the cook's own ladles,
Split open kegs of salted sprats,
Made nests inside men's Sunday hats ...

Robert Browning

Duncan woke next morning with a start.

"I'll ring yer heart and liver out wi' yer foul slitherin' tails!" resounded from the sod and stone of the walls. Blinking rapidly from under his plaid, Duncan tried calling his sleep-blurred mind to attention and make sense of what he heard. This vicious threat sounded as if it came from his mother's voice—but it sounded so unlike her manner.

Yanking his plaid off his face, Duncan peered out of his bunk.

He rubbed his eyes and looked again. His mother stood atop the plank boards of the trestle table, broom in hand poking viciously at the underside of the heather thatch overhead. Her face was flushed red, and her hair stood out all disarrayed in her frenzy. A shaft of sunlight from one of the narrow windows illuminated particles of dust and stray bits of straw drifting onto the table with each new lunge.

"One too many times 'ave ye made yer procreant cradle in the M'Kethe thatch," she went on with another violent lunge upward with the broom handle. "And I'll not sit idle while ye bring more o' yer flea-infested, disease-ridden kind into the world!" She nearly toppled off the table with the next jab. Suddenly she halted and looked around the interior of the croft. Her gaze rested on the musket, and her eyes narrowed ruthlessly.

Duncan followed his mother's gaze. For an instant the sight of his mother firing the musket into the rafters and thatch splaying every which way with the explosion made him nearly burst out laughing. What would his father, already outside, think when he heard the musket fire and looked back to see the roof of his croft flying in every direction with the impact?

Brodie looked earnestly up at Duncan's mother. He cocked his head and whined as if begging her to come down.

Duncan sprang from his bunk, slinging on his kilt as he lunged toward her.

"Mother, ye'll do yourself a harm," he said, clutching at her skirts in an effort as much to steady her as to persuade her to come down from the table.

"I intend to be doing these infernal rats a harm, not m'-self," she said, one eyebrow raised warily as she made a last jab at the thatch, and then took Duncan's hand as he helped her off the table.

Duncan had learned that his mother, normally so tender and full of compassion, when provoked became a lioness, unmatched for fierceness among women. Though she ordinarily reserved her wrath for the defense of those she loved, Duncan often resolved to never be the cause of igniting the fire or fanning the flames of her ill favor.

"Has mother gang gyte?" asked sleepy-eyed Jenny, her impish face poking out from under the folds of her chaff-filled bolster.

"Mother's not gone mad, Jenny," said Fiona softly. "It's the rats again."

Duncan's mother brushed her skirts and worked at composing herself just as the cottage door opened with a groan and his father stepped into the dusty room. Duncan knew where he'd been.

In all weathers, Duncan's father stole from the croft each morning before anyone stirred. Curious, Duncan had risen early one morning and had followed him. His father fell to his knees under an overhanging rock where he could be sheltered from the fiercest blasts of wind and the cold. Duncan climbed silently onto the rock to listen. His father's voice rose and fell with emotion as he wrestled earnestly with his heavenly Father. Duncan felt the tears come hotter as he listened to his father begging for the souls of his bairns, pleading for the progress of the Kingdom of God in the Kirk, asking for patience to bear up under trials, and adoring the Lord with psalmlike expressions of love, overflowing with the deepest and most profound confidence in both God's goodness and greatness in all he ordains. His father prayed, "The cross of Christ is the sweetest burden that ever I bear. It is such a burden as wings to a bird, or sails to a ship, to carry me forward to my harbor." Due to his blubbering in the heather, Duncan gave himself away that day. He knew that this morning his father had been at prayer and was just now returning.

"I thought I heard the skirling of a daft limmer," said Duncan's father, a smile playing at the corners of his mouth as he searched his wife's eyes.

"It's the rats," she said, turning from her husband, her cheeks flushed crimson. "Rats hovering overhead go and get m'dander up so as they ding me daft," she said, touching her head.

"There, there, m'love," said Duncan's father, folding her to himself with his strong arms. "I spoke to John Kilbride about the rats. He said he'll lend us badger traps. I'll send Duncan after 'em this very day. We'll tease 'em out of the thatch w' a bit of cheese. We'll get yer rats, m'love."

Duncan's pulse quickened. Kilbride's farm lay down the glen near the village. As much as he wanted to get back to his castle and explore the secret passage he and Brodie had discovered, an errand down the glen could lead to the latest news on the troubles, their farm situated so near the village as it was—and he'd see his friend Jamie.

"Now, Duncan," began his father, looking levelly at his son, "make yer way to the Kilbrides' place as fast as yer feet can carry ye. Fetch an armload of traps from John Kilbride and come direct home."

"Ye'll not be going empty-handed," said Duncan's mother. "They've been hard put upon of late. I'll get ye a sack of oats and some cheese." With a flurry of homespun skirts, she filled a sack with food.

"Can I take Brodie along?" asked Duncan, tying the sack of food in his plaid so it would ride securely on his back.

"If yer not taking all day about it," replied his father. "The sheep'll need tending and watering when yer home. I'll be cutting spring grass, and I'll have the wee lasses give the sheep something over the wall—till yer safe home."

As Duncan's father readied himself for his day of work, he paused for an instant and looked at his musket in its place by the door. Duncan followed his gaze. Then his father deliberately turned and gathered up his sickle and seed bag.

"I'll just cut some grass for the sheep and be off to the sowing." After embracing his wife, he left.

She turned and stared levelly at her son. "Ye ken what to do if ye see dragoons?" she asked, worry showing in the furrows of her brow.

"Aye, disappear in the heather," said Duncan, sounding sober. Secretly his heart quickened at the prospect of seeing soldiers—their red uniforms and horses, their guns and swords.

"Haste ye back, lad," she said firmly.

After his mother embraced him, he stepped out of the croft into the warmth of a sunlit morning. From the contorted branches of the sycamore tree on a knoll near the croft, a thrush warbled an exuberant good morning. With the bleating of sheep in his ears, he drew in a breath perfumed with spring grass and the sweet, earthy scent of heather. Duncan felt like singing.

Though a bank of gray clouds lined the northern horizon and seemed to stand at the ready above the hills, for the moment the day looked bright and cheery, and he had freedom all morning and all the excitement of a visit to the village.

The "swoosh, swoosh" of his father swinging his sickle in the tall meadow grass on the slope to the west of their home caught his attention, and he felt a twinge of guilt as he watched the sunlight reflecting on the sheen of perspiration already growing on his father's arms and face. While his father worked hard, Duncan would be doing what he so much loved:

roaming about the glens with Brodie—roaming about under the noses of James Turner and his blood-thirsty dragoons, but they wouldn't catch him. Duncan took another deep breath, and a flush of excitement shone on his cheek.

"Flee all trouble and temptation, lad," his father called without missing a beat in his cutting.

Sometimes Duncan felt certain that his father could read his mind. "Aye, Father," Duncan called back.

"And mind ye don't stumble," his father added, his blade still falling on the grass.

"I'll not stumble, Father," called Duncan.

His lilt must have betrayed offense at the mere suggestion that he might stumble, for his father replied, "Stumbling's of more than one kind, Duncan, m'lad." He stopped cutting and looked earnestly at his son. "Stumblings of the heart, mind ye, break more than bones. Aye, guard yer heart, lad; guard yer heart. Ye can seem to keep the Covenant with yer hands and feet. That's the easy part, but if yer not keeping Covenant with yer heart, ye can't be honoring King Jesus."

As he spoke these last words, his father held his strong arms toward Duncan and seemed to be pleading with him. For an instant Duncan felt the water come into his eyes. One thing he knew: he never wanted to do anything to bring dishonor to his father.

"And no playacting along the way, lad," his father added, looking steadily at Duncan, his sickle now poised over the tall grass.

"Aye, no playacting," called Duncan, with a wave of his hand. Then, turning, he and Brodie ran down the glen toward Dalry.

As he ran, he felt the thrill of his heart beating fearlessly in his chest. Brodie loped easily at his side, tongue lolling and ears fluttering behind. Duncan loved running, and he was fast.

He once ran an errand to Dalry and back up the hills to their croft in less time than it took his father to shear ten sheep. And nobody in Galloway sheared sheep as fast as his father. In moments he passed that first stage of running where his muscles seemed to complain at such demands after lying idle through the night. He knew that what lay ahead was the effortlessness of mind and body, propelled wherever he wanted to go by a pair of very strong legs. The heavy wool folds of his kilt swooshed rhythmically against his bare legs with each stride. Casting a quick glance over his shoulder for one last sight of his family's croft before turning into the wood, and exhilarated with the prospects of his few hours of freedom, he plunged on down the path toward the glen.

The words of the Psalter came to his mind as he ran: "He makes my feet like the feet of a deer . . . You broaden the path beneath me, so that my ankles do not turn." He leaped high over a branch that had fallen onto the path in the last storm.

Leaving the bright sunlight behind and plunging into the murky shadows in the wood, Duncan blinked rapidly to adjust his eyes and slackened his pace. A rich green blanket of bracken and shade clover surrounded the trunks of Scots pine and beech trees. He knew that in the dark of the forest, roots and stray branches cluttering the path could trip him if he didn't watch his steps carefully. It had never happened to him, but his friend Jamie Kilbride would never run as he used to after stumbling in a heap on this very path. He and Jamie had been racing with Duncan well out ahead when he had heard muffled thudding and then a snapping sound. Then came the agonizing scream. He had sickened at the sight of the breaks in Jamie's leg bone. In one break the splintered white bone had pierced right through the skin. Duncan shuddered with the memory and slowed his pace even further.

The wood thinned, and then like lighting a candle in a

dark room, Duncan broke out into sunlight again. The path grew into more of a cart track as Duncan neared the village. Dry stane dykes bordered the widening track and served as fencing to keep in sheep or "Belties," Belted Galloway cattle, the pride of local cattlemen, and to define the boundaries of the farms that surrounded the small village of Dalry. As he ran, Duncan breathed in the smells of civilization: peat reek, cattle, the earthy smells of plowing, and the pinching odors of the village where human beings lived in closer proximity to one another.

"A good day to ye, Thomas MacRoan," called Duncan, waving to a grim-faced farmer at his plow. Duncan thought of new lambs as he watched the farmer's young children prancing along behind the plowing. They occasionally halted in their frolick to pick up stones and heft them to the edge of the little field. Reins looped across his shoulder, the farmer guided the stooped old horse, puffing as its head labored wearily up and down, as it pulled the grinding and squeaking plow through the stubborn sod.

"Aye, and to ye," answered the farmer curtly, while keeping his eyes on the furrow and both hands on the plow.

Just down the cart track, surrounded by the lush green fields of the local farms, lay a cluster of cottages, peat reek drifting above them as the women of the village baked their oatcakes and prepared the noonday meal. Duncan felt a gnawing in his middle.

St. John's town of Dalry was little more than two rows of cottages clinging to the hillside and huddled close together, like sheep just before a storm. At the foot of the narrow street running between the cottages, and just above the steep banks of the River Ken, stood the parish kirk, its spire beacon and crow-stepped gables a reminder of higher things in former times.

It had been four years since Duncan had worshiped with his family inside those walls. In 1662 their faithful minister, Mr. M'Micking, had been ejected from the pulpit and thrown in prison, all for failing to submit to King Charles II as the head of the Kirk. Now the papist George Henry conducted services in the parish kirk. Duncan never thought of him as Mr., a title locals reserved for a minister, a true master of divinity. So incompetent was the drunken cleric that Duncan had even heard he lost track of the days of the week from time to time and conducted Sunday services on the wrong day. Now the kirk and her spire stood only as a defiant reminder of the bitter wrongs of kings and proud tyrants who made it their business to oppress and plunder all within range of their power. Rather than violate conscience, Duncan and his family, along with most families in the district, refused to attend popish services inside those walls.

Since passage of the Parliamentary laws demanding fines of all who failed to attend the episcopal services, faithful Covenanters and their families met secretly for worship in the woods and glens around Galloway. The enforcement of these laws, called the "Bishop's drag net" by the locals, the king entrusted into the greedy hands of the monster Turner and his dragoons garrisoned in the district and quartered in the local homes. Soldiers bribed the weak to inform on their neighbors—and some did. The king's spies watched the trysting places or field meetings in hopes of breaking up the meeting and plundering the offenders for unlicensed worshiping with stiff fines or arrest.

Punishment of a greater kind the English reserved for covenanting field preachers. If confiscating their property failed to stop their preaching, prison and torture awaited them. If those measures failed to break their loyalty to the Covenant—they silenced them at the gallows. Duncan had heard what happened next. To make a public example of them, they cut off their head and hands and spitted them on pikes on the city gates of Edinburgh.

He shook his head violently, trying to clear his mind of the somber thought.

Just ahead on the edge of the village lay the Kilbride farm. He slowed to a walk, catching his breath as he approached the thatched farmhouse. His friend Jamie would be there.

THE VICAR'S ON FIRE!

... how poor Religion's pride,
In all the pomp of method and of art;
When men display to congregations wide
Devotion's ev'ry grace except the heart!
                                        Robert Burns

D uncan!" called Jamie, grinning as he made his way
around the corner of the barn. "Yer not with the
sheep?"

"Aye," replied Duncan, stealing a glance at his friend's leg.
He could still see the scar, and the leg bone had a bend and a
twist in it that made it seem as though the leg was trying to
walk in a different direction from the rest of Jamie. A wave of
guilt swelled in Duncan as he thought of his own legs and how
fast he ran with them—and could still run.

On the other hand, though his friend's leg was crooked,
Jamie possessed an uncommon strength. He could carry heav-
ier loads far greater distances than any other lad Duncan
knew. Sure, Duncan had to slow his pace when walking somewhere with his friend, but at the end of the day, it was always
Jamie who plodded on unwearied. Duncan sometimes won-

dered just how long he could do it. It seemed to be a matter of honor for Jamie, and this uncommon strength had grown steadily into a strength of another and a deeper kind.

"Aye," repeated Duncan. "Father needs the use of yer traps—for the rats. And my mother sent these along." He held out the bundle of food.

"And I'm sure we're grateful to her," said Jamie.

When he returned from delivering the food to his mother in the kitchen, he said, "Word is George Henry's got his days flipped around—again."

"Ye mean he's conducting services today, on the Saturday?" asked Duncan, his eyes flashing with interest.

"Aye, so says Nigel, who heard it from the Widow Ferryman," said Jamie. "And Mrs. Nothing, the ferryman's widow living as she does on the river just at the foot of the hill hard by the kirk, would ken best."

Just then the little valley of Glenken rang with the bell from the kirk.

Duncan stifled a laugh. He saw in his mind the red-faced little man puffing as he yanked on the bell-pulls, unaware in his drunken stupor that it wasn't even Sunday.

Duncan slapped his palm against his forehead. He had an idea.

"Jamie, do ye suppose—" he began.

"Duncan . . ." said Jamie warily. "What is it yer cooking up in that head of yers?"

"What do ye say we make our way down to the kirk"—his eyes shone with excitement—"and hide out? We could watch what he does."

"Och, Duncan, what would ye want to be doing that for?"

"I'm not talking about participating in the service, Jamie," said Duncan, shaking his head. "So we'd not be breaking the Covenant," he went on, "only seeing what he does."

45

Jamie frowned. Though he would never have gone alone, he too was curious about what went on in the parish kirk now that the bishop of Glasgow had appointed the little drunk cleric.

"If we don't go along now, we'll be too late to hide out before he begins," urged Duncan.

Within minutes, puffing hard from running, Duncan and Jamie rounded the corner of the kirk, its stepping gables rising above the graveyard. Duncan pointed to the ground, and Brodie crouched low and lay on his haunches, out of view behind the great sandstone slab of a grave marker. Smiling with satisfaction, Duncan knew that regardless of how much time elapsed before his return, regardless of what the weather might do, or any other provocation short of someone killing his dog, Brodie would never move until Duncan or his father gave the command.

"Hurry, or we'll be late," hissed Jamie.

"Late?" replied Duncan. "We're sure to be the only ones. No one'll come to services on Saturday."

"That's where ye're wrong, Duncan. George Henry'll take roll, and then he'll turn over the list of those who failed to come to services to one of James Turner's commanders. Be sure of it, Saturday or Sunday, they'll load fines on everyone who isn't here—fines or worse."

In a crouching run, they made their way to the narrow Gothic arch of the entrance. They heard the cleric stumbling around in the tiny vestry, but other than that, the church appeared empty. Looking carefully both ways, they scurried across the flagstone floor to the Gordon Aisle. The south transept would provide good cover among the rigid stone effigies where the Gordons of Earlston, patrons of the parish, lay at rest. William Gordon, the present patron, had been cruelly banished from all Scotland forever for refusing to agree to

George Henry's appointment to the kirk. Duncan's father used to sell sheep to the Gordons, and Duncan sometimes envied the great fortified house—the small castle the Gordons used to live in just northeast of the village. Duncan frowned: its stout walls and battlements had not protected even the Gordons from the cruel clutches of tyranny.

Jamie set up a position near the chain-mailed feet of one of the ancient lords of Earlston, while Duncan peered out from over the stone face, the gap between the prominent nose and jutting chin providing a perfect position for Duncan's curious eye.

Within moments, crofters, still wearing their working clothes, their heads down and eyes not looking at one another, began drifting into the tiny nave of the church. Duncan suppressed an urge to stand up and shout at them for breaking the Covenant and stooping to attend a service where Laud's Liturgy, with all the popish trappings, held sway. He hissed as much to Jamie.

"And a fine sight ye'd make, Duncan M'Kethe, being here yerself," said his ever-insightful friend.

Duncan looked up at the solid ribbed vaulting of the nave. He thought of all those Sabbaths out on the moors and braes, the rain beating down on them, maybe snow driven by cruel winds stinging their faces, the very young and elderly growing sick from exposure to the bitter elements. A roof like that over their heads, he decided, would be a fine thing indeed.

The ringing of a small high-pitched bell called him back to attention. The sparse congregation scuffled to their feet. For an instant nothing happened. Then, straining to see over the Gordon nose, Duncan watched the strangest sight. George Henry, a man with a perpetual alehouse stoop to his shoulders, robed in red and white, staggered down the aisle. Now, Dalry was a small village and could ill-afford to support one drunken cleric, let alone a procession of them. But George Henry liked the pomp of the high-church procession, so from his first day he had insisted on the formal procession—though he was the only one in it.

In his left arm, the short, stooped cleric juggled a large brass cross on a tall staff and a tattered Bible—held upside down. Several times he dropped the Bible with a slap-bang onto the flagstone floor. But strangest of all, from his right hand dangled a chain holding a censor filled with burning incense. With a heave, he had begun swinging the chain back and forth. Duncan sniffed the air and screwed up his face in disgust. Each pendulum of the censor seemed to plunge the little man precariously forward, sending him groping for balance with each swing.

Stifling an almost uncontrollable urge to laugh, Duncan pressed his face hard against the stone shoulder of the Gordon effigy. He could hardly tell whether the censor was swinging the man or the man the censor. A low haze of blue smoke hung over the little assembly. Duncan blinked his eyes and gripped his nose. If he sneezed now they were done for.

Finally arriving at the altar, a zigzagging wake of blue smoke lingering in the aisle behind him, George Henry turned toward those who had heeded the tolling of the bell. The cleric's lip curled disdainfully at the sparse congregation as he gave his call to worship: "God or I be hanged over thish pulpit," he paused, steadying himself against the altar screen as he glared, "but I shall force ye all to come in—from the higheSht to the loweSht!"

A service thus begun, it was small wonder that Duncan and Jamie got very little out of what followed. During frequent uncomfortable pauses, George Henry mumbled to himself, noisily shuffling pages, as he hunted for his place in the prayer book. When he failed to find it, he used the opportunity to rail against traitors who rebelled against "the powers that be ordained of God." When he did finally find his place, he seemed blissfully unaware, as he slurred his way through a prayer of confession, that he'd turned more than one page and was nonsensically concluding the prayer by reading a collect for the coronation of a monarch. It didn't seem to matter to the congregation either.

Duncan and Jamie stared in amazement at what happened next. Dark smoke began billowing out of the censor. George Henry paused, screwed up his face, sniffed the air, then narrowed his eyes suspiciously at the congregation. Suddenly flames leapt up his robes. The bumbling cleric had forgotten to set the censor down, and from where it hung at his side it smoldered against his gown. Now in flames, the little curate screeched in panic. Then, flailing at the flames licking at the folds of his gilded vestments, and amidst a barrage of curses, George Henry spun and whirled across the chancel and around the altar. For a fleeting moment as he watched, Duncan even wondered if the fire and the dancing might have all been part of a plan to get more people to come to the church.

With a final roar of blasphemies, the farce of a service ended when George Henry stumbled to the floor and began rolling frantically around the chancel, finally extinguishing the flames. The few shame-faced villagers who had attended left without a word.

Once clear of the kirk, Duncan collected the dutiful Brodie, and he and Jamie collapsed on the banks of the River Ken at the foot of the churchyard. They laughed until their sides ached and the tears streamed down their cheeks.

"I've never seen anything more ridiculous," gasped Duncan when he could finally speak. "Now I ken why we don't compear."

"Aye," agreed Jamie, though his face grew sober. "Aye, but it's all so tragic."

"Now what cause hae ye fer laughing so?" came a voice from the river's edge.

"Greetings to ye, Widow Ferryman," called Duncan and Jamie to the ferryman.

The widow Ferryman's cottage lay at the foot of the churchyard at a bend where the river narrowed. From her doorstep a chain ran across the river, and on that chain, since her husband died years ago, the ferryman's widow pulled strong hand over strong hand carrying local farmers, villagers, and now and then a cow or horse back and forth across the river in her flat-bottomed barge. For her keen ability to see all and know all, the widow Ferryman was known throughout the entire Glenken region as Mrs. Nothing.

"Go on, then," she said, grinning expectantly, "let me in on the joke, lads."

The boys looked at each other before replying.

"Ye weren't at the service today?" asked Duncan.

"Nay, I'll hae none o' his kind o' services," replied the old woman, nodding her head up the hill toward the church.

"But don't they fine ye?" asked Jamie.

"Aye, why don't they put ye in prison?" added Duncan.

"And leave their kind to swim the river?" she said, narrowing her eyes sagaciously.

"So they leave ye be, then?" said Jamie.

"Fer as long as the river keeps flowing, they do," she replied. "And now and again I picks up a bit o' useful information—useful, that is, fer our covenanting side."

"Like what?" asked Duncan.

"Like when Turner—black-hearted swine—and his dragoons are fixing to drag their net through the glen," she replied.

"Ye heard anything of that lately, then?" asked Jamie.

"Aye," she said, looking sober.

"What, then?" asked Jamie.

"Fact is, dragoons are due this very afternoon," she said, "and I'll be forced to ferry them across—they don't pay except in leaving me alone. They'll call at the manse, and when George Henry hands off his list of those who failed to compear at the kirk today—mind ye, it not being the Sabbath makes no nevermind to them—the repeat offenders near to hand will pay."

As the stout woman pulled away on the chain and crossed the river, Jamie's face clouded.

"What's wrong with ye?" asked Duncan.

"My family is near to hand," said Jamie, spinning on his heel and with his steady lumbering gate making toward home. "And my family's repeat offenders."

***

Hard as Duncan ran, Jamie seemed never far behind as they raced to the Kilbride farm with the news.

"Duncan M'Kethe," said John Kilbride, looking up from drenching an ewe. "Ye're back again. And by the look of ye, something's troubling ye. What is it, then, lad?"

Duncan opened his mouth to blurt the news when Jamie called from just behind.

"Word is, Father," he said, "Turner's men are on the rampage again."

"Now, from whom did ye hear it?" asked Jamie's father levelly.

"Mrs. Nothing just told us," said Duncan. "And she—"

"I ken, I ken," said Jamie's father. "She misses nothing. All right, then, we are in the Lord's hands, but we'd best be pru-

51

dent and disappear. I ken the fines have mounted against me for failing to compear at the kirk. And now Turner's men are rampaging up from Dumfries to collect 'em. It had to come, and it has, but just while lambs and spring plantings pressing all about us."

He turned and looked at Duncan.

"Now then, Duncan, if ye're caught here wi' us . . . ye're done for, lad. Ye best scatter to yer brae—and quickly."

John Kilbride turned and began preparing his family for flight. Duncan shifted his weight from one bare foot to the other. He couldn't just leave them.

Jamie had disappeared inside to help his mother and sisters pack. Jamie reappeared with a heavy burlap sack on his shoulder. Duncan knew that somewhere in that sack would be books. If he could save nothing else, it'd be books Jamie would save.

In their characteristically unhurried manner, Jamie and his father steadily hefted the small mound of belongings into a farm cart. Shaking its stocky head, the farm horse stomped its hairy fetlocks and champed at its harness. Jamie helped his mother hoist his three sisters into the cart, where they clambered on top of the hastily packed bundles.

"Where're ye going to hide?" asked Duncan.

"I donnae ken," the farmer said, running his hand through his hair, "but they're sure to take us if we stay here. They'll fire the house. They'll steal my flock." His voice trailed into a moan. Then he said, a firmness returning to his voice, "But God is on our side, and though he fights our battles for us, I'll not just give in to 'em."

Duncan looked down at Brodie. An idea suddenly occurred to him.

"John Kilbride, Brodie and I'll run yer mob up the glen to our place—or Ancient Grier's," he said, the excitement mounting as he spoke. "If ye can disappear for now, we'll tend yer sheep for ye, and ye can join us up the brae when ye can. Ye'll be safe enough there—for now."

It didn't sound as great an idea when he finished. He wanted to tell them about the old passage in the castle.

"The Lord kens I'll not put ye in danger, Duncan," said John Kilbride.

"But my father would want me to help," said Duncan, pleadingly. "I ken he would."

"Turner'd see yer helping us as sedition," said John Kilbride, arguing more with himself than with Duncan. "How could I face yer father if Turner arrested ye for lending aid to me and my family?"

"I'll not get caught," said Duncan. "Jamie knows how fast I run—" Duncan stopped short.

"Aye, Father," chimed in Jamie. "Duncan runs like the wind."

"Nothing else for it," said John Kilbride, his shoulders drooping resignedly. "We'll take what lambs we can in the cart." He took Duncan by the shoulders again and, brows furrowed, stared into his eyes. "Ye scatter to the mist at anything, lad. I'll not be living with myself if ye're lost for helping us."

THE DEVIL KICKS UP HIS HEELS

They chant their artless notes in simple guise,
They tune their hearts, by far the noblest aim;
Perhaps Dundee's wild-warbling measures rise,
Or plaintive Martyrs, worthy of the name;

Robert Burns

Torn between excitement and terror, Duncan drove the small flock of ewes up the glen toward home. He'd never driven nursing ewes so hard.

At first Duncan's heart skipped a beat with every real or imagined sound. Time and again he whirled around, half hoping to see dust rising around galloping red-coated dragoons hieing at his heels. On one such spinning he saw only an old bearded he-goat clopping along the edge of the lane. On another it was only a farmer leading his pony across the road to pasture.

Rounding a bend, he saw a herd of Belties contentedly grazing on a sloping pasture. Nearby a watering pond lay in a hollow where two slopes converged. Suddenly Duncan felt certain he heard hoofbeats and a shout from just over the rise behind him. With a nod of his head he ordered Brodie to drive the sheep out of the road, then he vaulted over the stone wall bordering the lane. Looking frantically around for a place to hide, he dove into the murky waters of the pond, and held his breath. Cheeks bulging and eyes pinched tightly shut, he waited.

Even with strong lungs a boy can only hold his breath so long, and Duncan finally decided that facing dragoons might be better than drowning. Spluttering and gulping air, he rose cautiously from the pond. Not three inches from his freckled nose loomed the wide black face of a Beltie just about to plunge its mouth into the pond and inhale a drink. Duncan gasped in fright and spluttered as he choked on more of the pond. The Beltie's eyes bulged wide in terror. With a snort and a flicking of its tail, and a stomping of hooves in the mud, the bewildered beast turned and lumbered away. After recovering from his own fright, Duncan staggered out of the pond and peered warily through the meadow grass at the road. Not a soul was in sight.

Meanwhile, Brodie nipped the heels of the slowest ewes, hurrying the flock along up the glen. Duncan waited. No soldiers galloped by. His teeth chattered with the cold. Dripping wet he crawled out of the meadow grass and looked cautiously back down the lane toward the village.

What a brave warrior ye are, he scoffed at himself, shaking water out of his hair. He sheepishly looked this way and that. There stood Thomas MacRoan scratching his head. He stared at Duncan. Duncan felt his cheeks go hot and red. Farmer MacRoan had seen the whole thing. Duncan tried to think of some explanation.

"Yer feeling the need of a . . . a wee cooldown, lad?" the farmer said slowly.

"Aye," said Duncan.

"Or, perhaps, ye're needing a bath, lad," the farmer went

on, a smile now playing at
the corners of his mouth.
He leaned on the plow
and broke into a grin.
Then his shoulders
began shaking up
and down, and a
sort of "hee, heeing"
sound came with each
shudder of his shoulders. It grew louder and
louder. Finally unable to contain the accelerating
mirth, the farmer staggered in a fit of laughter, alternately
holding his sides and steadying himself with great effort on
the handles of the plow.

Wringing water out of his plaid, Duncan wondered if his
father would have considered this playacting. Then, breaking
into a run, Duncan hurried after Brodie and John Kilbride's
sheep. He wanted to leave the farmer's laughter behind, and
it wouldn't do for Brodie to show up without him.

As he trotted higher up into the hills and his home came
into view, Duncan felt a wave of disappointment. Nothing
had happened. No soldiers, no furious bounding up the brae,
no scattering the sheep to be collected later by Brodie, while
the dragoons took one or two and, disinclined to the difficulty
of rounding up the flock, rode off to easier pickings somewhere else. All in all, his first encounter with real danger
proved to be rather a disappointment—more of a humiliation.

Late that night the Kilbride family, weary and hungry, arrived in their cart. The report was that Turner's dragoons had
ransacked their house, and, finding little of value, set it
ablaze. Theirs was not the first home destroyed by the king's
soldiers, nor the last, and all that remained was a sod shell,
charred and blackened, unfit for anyone to live in ever again.

But there had been no drag net, no scouring of the countryside, no pillage of the entire village. After all, John Kilbride
was not a minister, and, poor as they were, the Kilbride family was no great catch for the soldiers. What good was another
pile of threadbare wool cloaks and long-since worn-out shoes?
And the books Jamie cherished were only good for burning,
no money to be had selling such sedition writings. So little to
plunder, and no real example to be made of such unimportant
people.

But Duncan couldn't help wondering if that monster
Turner was playing with them as a cat plays with a mouse, bid-
ing time until unrestrained he would unleash the full fury of
the king's wrath against obstinate Covenanters and have done
with them once and for all.

Over the next weeks, Duncan's father, along with Ancient
Grier and several other hill-dwelling farmers, helped John
Kilbride build a small croft out of sod and stone. Duncan and
Jamie cut and dried heather for thatching and helped gather
stones—Jamie carrying more than his share as usual. The Kilbrides were not the only family who sought refuge in the Clat-
teringshaws Hills surrounding Dalry that spring. Homeless
and weary, still more fugitives came during the summer—
some with ghastly tales of horror and brutality, some with a
silent staring numbness born of anguish and loss.

"I'm worried, Sandy," Duncan overheard his mother say to
his father one night after all the family were in their beds. "I'd
not be turning anyone away from the . . . the safety of our wee
glen." Her voice quavered with emotion. "But ye ken the
more of us there are in these braes—" she broke off.

"Be still, m'love," his father said softly.

"Oh, but, Sandy," she continued, her voice rising,
"Moira Henderson and her wee ones just fled to us from the
village. Poor Moira hasnae stopped weeping for these three

days. Turner—all mocking and sneering—shot her man through the head in full view of the wee ones. Then that devil incarnate swine used her very ill—all while her bairns looked on in horror. She nor they will ever get clear of it—nor, I fear, will I."

"Mary, dear Mary, I didnae ken all this," Sandy said, shaking his head.

"Sandy, he will find us," said Duncan's mother, now nearly sobbing. "Turner'll find us and come on with such a terror and woe—I cannae bear to think on it . . ." With a rising lilt, eloquent of her despair, her voice trailed away.

"Mary, Mary, 'tis evil indeed," said Duncan's father tenderly. "But, m'love, we're not alone." And then soothingly, passionately, his voice rose with lines from the Psalter. Duncan imagined his father stroking the auburn waves of his mother's hair with his big hands as he sang:

> God is our refuge and our strength,
> In straits a present aid;
> Therefore, although the earth remove,
> We will not be afraid . . .

> Unto the ends of all the earth
> Wars into peace he turns:
> The bow he breaks, the spear he cuts,
> In fire the chariot burns.

> Be still, and know that I am God . . .

When the Psalm singing ended, his father continued, "Mary, m'love, it's been said that 'Duties are ours; events are God's.' What a broken vessel like Turner might do in the future is none of our present concern. The devil would be kicking up

58

his heels in glee if we chose to worry about the future at the neglect of doing our duty to our neighbors—growing numbers of them that there be—and doing all in the sweet name of our Lord Jesus. Be still, m'love. Be still."

UNDERGROUND
PLANS

—It strikes an awe
And terror on aching sight; the tombs
And monumental caves of death look cold,
And shoot a chillness to the trembling heart.
                                  Sir Walter Scott

With the population of the remote hills swelling week by week, and more mouths to feed, there were also more men than usual to lend a hand with the shearing and planting. This resulted in Duncan not being in as great a demand for some of the work. Jamie, usually with book in hand, often joined Duncan and Brodie when they went farther into the hills to find pasture for the flock.

"Do ye see that old castle, Jamie?" asked Duncan one such day, gesturing with his staff at the ruins of Dunfarg Castle.

"Aye, it's my crook shank that doesn't work so well—not my eyes," said Jamie, grinning at his friend.

Jamie had a strong jaw and a face that seemed to prefer smiling. And though he often grew serious and thoughtful about things, somehow even when his mouth wasn't, he seemed still to be smiling. Duncan could never quite understand how his friend remained so cheerful with all the troubles—and with his crooked leg.

"In my castle, just there," continued Duncan, "I have a secret—haven't told anyone."

Jamie flashed his dark eyes at Duncan, studying his face to decide if he was having him on.

"A real secret? Something worth knowing?"

"Aye, worth knowing," said Duncan, his eyes narrowing as he walked slowly up toward the ancient ruins. "Hounded as we are by that dog Turner and the English," Duncan spat as he'd seen Grier do when he said the word English, "my secret will save yer family and mine, Jamie Kilbride. And excepting myself, ye'll have been the first to ken it."

"Och, Duncan," said Jamie with a dismissive wave of his hand. "As to saving our families, I'll be continuing to pitch my hopes on the Lord, thanks all the same, not on yer heap o' ruins."

"Aye, but God helps those," said Duncan, slapping his friend on the back good-naturedly, "that help their selves."

"Aye, so I've heard," replied Jamie. "Which notion generally leads folk to putting more trust in their selves than in the Lord."

"In these times," said Duncan, "word is, 'Trust in the Lord, but keep yer hand on yer dirk.'" Grier often said something like that.

Duncan ordered Brodie to tend the sheep, and then he took his friend inside the crumbling walls. Clambering over piles of rubble, Duncan finally halted.

"Look around ye," he told Jamie. "What do ye see?"

Jamie did as he was told, and grinning, he turned to Duncan and said, "I see a heap o' ruins. Mind ye, it's a lovely view about the countryside, but I don't see anything that looks like a secret, Duncan, just a heap o' ruins. I ken ye're having me on."

Duncan narrowed his eyes at his friend. "Look closer," he urged.

"I see nothing, Duncan," said Jamie, "nothing but rubble and moss."

"I'm glad of it," said Duncan, nodding seriously. "Now close yer eyes, Jamie Kilbride, and I'll be showing ye my secret."

A grunting and scraping sound strongly tempted Jamie to peek, but he kept his eyes tightly closed until Duncan said triumphantly, "Aye, then, so what do ye make of this?"

Jamie's eyes flew open and he stared in wonder at a gaping hole in the ground, Duncan grinning proudly beside it.

"I've rigged a cover with rocks and moss and some old planking," said Duncan, beaming with pleasure at his friend's astonishment. "Ye didn't see anything, Jamie, and ye were looking for it. Turner's men'll never find this opening, mark me on it." He opened his sporran and pulled out a flint.

"How'd ye come by it?" asked Jamie.

"Brodie found it," said Duncan, striking the flint.

"Does it go deep?" asked Jamie, peering into the blackness.

"Aye," said Duncan in between gentle puffs on a spark from his flint. "And ye are going to explore it with me so we can find out just how deep."

Duncan handed his friend two sheep-tallow candles, lit them, took one for himself, and led the way down the steep, crude stair into the gaping blackness of the old passage. The brightness of the daylight faded as they descended, and the dim candlelight quavered against the rough contours of the tunnel.

"It's big enough for a pony," said Jamie in Duncan's ear.

"Aye, here it is," said Duncan. "But it gets low and narrow in some places."

"Aye," said Jamie, his voice bouncing eerily off the dark, damp walls.

"Do ye think it was an escape route from the castle?" asked Duncan as they walked cautiously farther into the subterranean corridor.

"Almost certainly, it was a mine," said Jamie, "dug by Robert the Bruce when he was taking castles back from the English usurpers in the 1300s."

"How'd ye ken that?" asked Duncan, turning to look at his friend.

"Read about it in a book," said Jamie simply, the sputtering candlelight casting shadows on his face as he replied. "While soldiers fought to keep their enemies from climbing up over the walls, using crossbows, and by hurling stones down on the attackers or dumping boiling oil on them, defense of a different kind was needed to keep attackers from digging underneath the walls. Mining was a kind of warfare, unseen by the eye, but for all that, no less deadly. Defenders frantically dug countermines to try to cut off the attackers before they broke through inside the wall of the castle. Imagine, Duncan, the fierce hand-to-hand fighting that raged underground when counterminers met the miners."

"Aye," said Duncan, shivering as he looked ahead down the dark passage, twisting and turning into the utter blackness. What would it have been like to encounter an enemy down here? he wondered.

He and Jamie were forced to crouch low in a stretch of tunnel where the ceiling pressed low on them and the floor dipped unsettlingly away to their left. Duncan's bare feet slipped on the slimy rock floor. Groping at the clammy walls for support, he nearly skidded onto his hip. He swallowed and tried to quell a rising urge to turn and scramble out of the tunnel as fast as he could go.

Nevertheless, the friends continued down the dark passage, the dungeon-like silence only interrupted by their voices and the slow, ominous dripping of water here and there seeping through the solid rock above. Duncan wondered where they were just then, and what was going on above them. Maybe the sheep grazed peacefully right overhead, ever-vigilant Brodie crouching at the ready. In former days, the whole of the enemy army may have been encamped just above them, waiting for the counterminers to pop out so they could do them in one at a time.

"How'd they ken where they'd come out at the other end of their digging?" asked Duncan, keeping his voice steady only with great effort.

"That's just it," said Jamie. "They wouldn't ken for a certainty. War's like that, Duncan, full of uncertainties—risks you might call 'em."

"I'd want to be first man out of the tunnel," said Duncan, though his voice quavered slightly, and resounding off the walls, it sounded shakier still.

"Not I," said Jamie, "unless the cause were just."

"The cause of the Covenant is just," replied Duncan, steadying himself against the clammy walls as he stepped down into a lower level.

"Aye," said Jamie. "But are we just in owning that cause? Claiming to fight for Christ and Covenant might prove just another sinful way of fighting for pride and freedom. The justice of the cause has lots more to do with my keeping of the Covenant—from my heart." Duncan heard Jamie thump his hand hard against his broad chest as he spoke. "If I go fighting Turner but doing so with hatred and vengeance in my heart for the English and all oppressors of the Kirk . . ." Here Jamie paused. "I'm no less a turncoat to King Jesus than my enemies. And then what good's the fighting and all the dead and dying at the end of the day?"

"Some would say you're afraid to fight," said Duncan,

then adding quickly, "but I ken ye too well to join 'em in saying it."

"An honest man fears what he ought to fear," said Jamie, "so my father says. I, for one, fear God, and if that fearing puts a weapon in my hand and an oppressor of the Kirk and her bairns in my path, I'll do all that fear of God demands of me—but nothing more. And I don't expect knowing what that fear demands will be so easy."

"Did you read that in a book, too?" asked Duncan.

"Aye," said Jamie. "God's Book."

For several minutes the companions made their way deeper into the mine in silence, Duncan frowning as he thought about Jamie's words.

"Look, Duncan," said Jamie, pointing ahead over his friend's shoulder. "There's another passage turning off the main way to the left."

"Ye found it," said Duncan, stepping to the side of the tunnel, "ye go first."

"It's a wee room," said Jamie, gazing about the chamber, "a gallery they call it in the books. It made a place for resting and getting out of the way of the pack animals used to carry out all the rocks and dirt—though I donnae ken how donkeys could find a way in the low bits back there."

"Big enough for a family to hide out, in all events," said Duncan.

"Aye," said Jamie. "No one must ken about this until we need it."

"So ye do think it will be useful?" said Duncan triumphantly.

"Aye, it could be," admitted Jamie.

"While we fight," said Duncan, "our mothers and sisters will be safe from the plundering—and Turner will never ken where they are."

"And the tunnel just keeps going," said Jamie, holding his candle aloft, its flickering light shining in his eyes as he gazed into the blackness. "I do wonder where it ends."

"What with all the folks now hiding out in the brae," said Duncan, "we may need it to stretch on forever."

SWORD  DANCING

O let them unto his great name
Give praise in the dance . . .

Let in their mouth aloft be rais'd
The high praise of the Lord,
And let them have in their right hand
A sharp two-edged sword.

Scottish Psalter (149)

Later that day, after returning to Brodie and the sheep, Duncan and Jamie stopped nearby the castle for a visit with Ancient Grier. His croft was a curious sort of building made of stone and sod like other crofts, but years ago, whoever built it positioned it so close to the steep hill behind that it seemed to be more a part of the cliff than a separate dwelling. Viewed from the side it looked as though it was only half a croft, so close it hugged the steepness against which it was built. And the thatch on the roof blended so well with the grass and thistles growing above that it was difficult to tell where the roof ended and the hill began. On the hillside to the left of the croft lay a meager plot of corn, the fuzzy plume tops of the thin stalks reaching about to Duncan's shoulders.

"I've the English to thank for the end to my loneliness," said Grier, chuckling as the boys seated themselves on the row of large stones set along the side of the croft most likely to catch the infrequent appearance of the sun. "Come to think of it, that'd be the first time I've been indebted to Southerns for anything."

Jamie and Duncan watched as the old man bandaged the leg of a goat kid, now almost three months old.

"The English have given ye nothing but grief, Ancient Grier," said Duncan.

"Aye, on the main that's true," replied the old man with another chuckle. "But they have gone and afrighted everyone in the glens up into m'braes," he continued, setting the kid down and sending it off with a firm nudge from behind. Then he began pensively clawing his fingers through his long beard. "They be bonnie braes," he went on, scanning the landscape, the green now dulled by patches of brown heather and fields of oats turning golden. His smile faded. "But I am wondering just what we'll all be facing when those foul oppressors make their way to us. I'd rather these hills didn't run red with our blood. I look around at the growing population, and I says to m'self, 'Another Covenanter army building strength.' " He gripped the end of his beard in his gnarled fist. "But I am worried for the womenfolk and wee ones. We need a scheme, lads, that's what we need, a scheme for the little folk—and it had best be a good one."

"But I think I've got one," said Duncan excitedly.

"Do ye, now, lad?" said Grier a bit doubtfully.

Duncan looked at Jamie before continuing.

"I found—that is, Brodie actually found—a secret passage," Duncan began, his voice lowered in a confidential tone.

A flash of amusement flickered in Grier's eyes.

"Secret, is it?" he said, nodding encouragingly at Duncan. "Get on with it, lad. Go on, give it mouth, make it less so."

"Up by the castle, it is," said Duncan. "But ye've got to promise not to tell anyone."

"Ye have my word on it, lad," said Grier, eyes wide with mock offense that Duncan should even require his word.

For a moment Duncan wondered if Grier already knew about the secret passage beneath the castle. The old man had lived forever in these hills, or so it seemed to Duncan. One thing was sure. If anyone did know about it, Grier would be the one to know.

The old man listened with growing interest as Duncan told about finding the passage, concealing the entrance, and then exploring its dark twists and mysterious turns.

Nodding slowly, Grier finally spoke. "Generally after a siege, they'd be filling up the mines, but after so fierce o' fighting, Dunfarg lay a complete ruin, never to be used again. 'Why go to all the trouble of filling up the mines?' so they must have thought ages ago." He gripped his beard in his hand and pulled on it in thought. Duncan rubbed the hint of fuzz on his chin. Then taking up what he could between his fingernails, he gave it a pull. He winced and the water came to his eyes. Yanking away on his beard, as Grier seemed always to be doing, must hurt—at least until you had more of one to yank on.

"Jamie, lad, ye've been quiet. What say ye about it?" asked Grier.

"It could be helpful for hiding out the womenfolk and the bairns," replied Jamie levelly, "when it comes to that—and it's sure to come to it."

"I say we gather what food and bedding we can," said Duncan, stroking Brodie between the ears. "And begin storing up supplies so if our families need to flee, it'll be ready for them."

"Aye, as I was a-thinking myself, lad," said Grier, nodding. And then slapping his knee, as if an idea had suddenly occurred to him, the old man looked at the boys and said, "But Duncan M'Kethe and Jamie Kilbride'll not be hiding, I shouldn't think. And if not hiding—ye'll be a-fighting."

The old man rose to his feet and disappeared inside for a moment, returning with his bagpipes, the goat stomach bag under his arm and the drone pipes rising over his shoulder. He gripped a battered claymore in his left hand.

"And there's no better way to prepare yourself for the fighting," said Grier, handing Duncan the sword, "than with the dancing."

Grier had taught Duncan the ancient war dances of the Highlanders since Duncan was old enough to remember. His father had learned them as a boy in Inverary. And though dancing of the baser kind was strictly forbidden among Covenanters, few frowned at such manly dancing put to noble use.

What could be seen of Grier's face, through the mass of yellow-white hair and beard, grew red as he puffed and puffed until his bag filled with air. And then the glen filled with the ominous, defiant rhythm of the Gillie Chalium, Grier stomping his booted foot as he played.

With a set to his jaw, Duncan drew the sword and saluted, its cold steel just touching his nose and forehead as he held it defiantly aloft. He peered around the sword, his eyes narrowed as he gazed at an unseen enemy. Then placing sword and scabbard on the ground, he positioned them carefully into the sign of the cross. At the hilt end of the sword he stood at rapt attention until the piping signaled him to begin. With bare toes pointed, Duncan followed the music of the skirling pipes, advancing and retreating at just the right moment into each of the quarters made by the crossed sword and scabbard. The music came faster, more relentless. The pleats of Duncan's kilt swished as he spun and lunged, his arms aloft and hands

poised like the antlers of a stag. Jamie began stomping with his good leg in time with the piping and dancing. He clapped and hooted as the music became more frenzied and Duncan danced with still more power and determination. Then with a flourish, and a light-footed stepping away from the swords, the dance ended.

Puffing for air, Grier let the pipe fall from his mouth and said, "And with not so much as a feather's touch of the sword, lad. Aye, yer dancing bodes well for yer fighting, Duncan, m'lad. Had ye touched even so much as the scabbard yer enemies would be dancing over yer sword, not ye over theirs. Aye, it were good dancing." The old man's eyes narrowed until they nearly disappeared. "May it be good fighting—aye, and soon."

Duncan mopped his brow with his plaid and collapsed with a grin onto the ground. He fingered the hilt of Grier's claymore. As he regained his breath, he felt a twinge at Grier calling the fighting good. He knew his father would never call fighting good. He might call it necessary, though his reluctance made Duncan sometimes wonder at him admitting it was even necessary, but he'd never call it good.

"Give it a go, Jamie?" asked Grier.

Jamie laughed. "Gimping's my gift, not dancing. Crookshanked as I am, I'd more likely set my comrades to rolling on the sod in fits of laughter than put them in a fighting way with my dancing. No, I'll leave the dancing to Duncan."

"Aye, but ye'll not leave the fighting to Duncan, will ye, lad?" asked Grier.

Duncan grew sober and looked at his friend. How would he answer?

"If the fighting's just and leads to peace," said Jamie soberly, "aye, I'll fight."

LONDON 9 BURNS

For Zion's King, and Zion's cause,
And Scotland's covenanted laws,
Most constantly he did contend,
Until his time was at an end.
Epitaph to Samuel Rutherford

The heather on the hillsides had grown a musty sort of brown, and the once green clusters of leaves on the beech trees now made a crackling rustle as the wind blew their yellowing foliage. Harvesttime had come, and with it came long days of cutting oats and binding sheaves, of hauling peat and repairing thatch. Duncan and Jamie worked side by side through the harvest, Duncan always faster but Jamie the last one to put down his load each night.

"A good crop, it is," said Duncan's father. With a grunt, he hoisted the last sack of oats off his shoulder and onto the growing pile of grain that now nearly filled the barn.

"Aye," agreed Duncan. "And more than we can eat."

"The Lord has dealt bountifully with us, lads," his father continued, mopping his brow with the back of his work-hardened hand. "Ye remember that tomorrow on the Sabbath we'll be

73

a-gathering up the brae at the trysting place to worship our great Provider. Mind ye render thanksgiving to him for blessing us all with a crop such as we have here. Is not that like our merciful God? When we have more mouths to feed, he grants us an abundant harvest enough to fill us all. Praise be to God for it."

Staggering under a sack of oats, the rough sacking scratching his sweaty neck and shoulder, Duncan managed a smile. It was so like his father to find only the good in the midst of calamity. Calamity they had aplenty. New reports of plundering came in daily, and still more, peasants and nobleman alike, stripped of all their earthly goods staggered into the hills confirming the disturbing reports. He knew his father was right to be thankful, but then if Grier was right, too—with a grunt, he heaved the sack off his shoulder and onto the pile—when they finished all this back-breaking work of harvesting and storing these crops, Sir James Turner's dragoons would sweep down on them like locusts and steal it all away. He looked bitterly at the sacks of grain filling the barn. What would his father do when the king's men came plundering? Would shooting thieving dragoons be just? If they didn't stop them, the soldiers would seize the lot and leave his mother and sisters—all of them—to starve through the harsh winter. Is it defending the Covenant to stop soldiers from the unjust plundering of innocent people?

When Duncan awoke next morning and peered out over his plaid, the sharp cold of autumn stung his face, and his breath came in little clouds. He hunkered down into a ball and tried to curl up on the depression in his chaff-filled mattress made warm by his body. With a scraping against the hard-packed floor, the door of the croft opened, and Duncan's father came inside, his arms loaded with peat. In a moment, the comforting smell of burning peat filled the room, and soon after, the chill lessened. Duncan dressed quickly and joined his father where he sat reading at the hearth.

"What are ye reading?" he asked.

" 'Tis a wee book full of letters," said his father, smiling as he looked up from where he sat reading. "Written by one of the best of God's ministers."

"Would that be like reading someone else's post, then?" asked Duncan with a grin.

His father laughed.

Duncan pulled a sheepskin near the fire and curled up on it for warmth. He'd seen Jamie reading the same book: *The Letters of Samuel Rutherford.* His father often told him how as a young man he'd once heard Rutherford preach when he was on a trip to the Solway Firth to sell wool. Mr. Rutherford must have been a great preacher, Duncan had decided, judging by the impression that one sermon had made on his father. He often spoke of it.

"I heard him preach once," said his father. Duncan smiled.

"Is he still living?" asked Duncan.

"No, died in 1661," replied his father. "The young probationer, Mr. Alexander Robertson, now preaches in Mr. Rutherford's pulpit—when out of range of James Turner—in the wee parish kirk in the glen of Anwoth. When hounded, he preaches on the braes and wilds surrounding the kirk. He's a bold and loyal Covenanter, but like to come to an early end for his hot blood—combined as it is with the injustice of the times."

"I'd like to meet Mr. Robertson," said Duncan, his eyes eager.

Sandy M'Kethe looked at his son for a moment. "Perhaps ye shall, soon enough, lad."

"How did Mr. Rutherford die, then?" asked Duncan. "Was he hanged?"

"No," replied Duncan's father. "When called before the Court of High Commission, where he would surely have been condemned to death, and having suffered so much for his love of King Jesus that he was soon to die of illness, he sent back a bold refusal, 'I go where few kings and great men come.' "

"He meant heaven?" said Duncan.

"Aye," replied his father. "Kings hated Mr. Rutherford and all like him. King Charles I banned him from preaching in Anwoth and exiled him away up to Aberdeen, thinking none of the Catholic Royalists in Aberdeen would care to listen to such preaching. So Mr. Rutherford wrote letters to encourage the faithful during those times of suffering. He wrote hundreds of them, and they're each one like individual sermons penned lovingly and full to overflowing with the loveliness of Christ." He turned the little book over, the dim firelight shining on the pale calf-skin leather of its binding. "So loved were his words that most everyone kept his letters, and just two years ago someone collected the lot into this fine little book."

"Will ye read one to me, Father?" asked Duncan.

"Aye, that I will," said his father, eyeing Duncan for a moment, then turning up a page that he seemed to think suited his son.

"Here we are, lad. Ye heed well what he says. '. . . a young man is often a dressed lodging for the devil to dwell in. I recommend to ye prayer and watching over the sins of yer youth; for I know that missive letters go between the devil and young blood. Satan hath a friend at court in the heart of youth; and then pride, luxury, lust, revenge—' " Here Duncan's father paused and looked steadily into Duncan's eyes before continuing. " '—revenge, forgetfulness of God, are hired as his agents. Happy is yer soul if Christ man the house, and take the keys himself, and command all (as it suiteth him full well to rule all wherever he is). Keep and entertain

76

Christ well; cherish his grace; blow upon yer own coal, and let him tutor ye.' "

Here his father stopped and looked again at his son.

"Defying hell's iron gates, m'lad, means oh so much more than merely taking yer sword in hand against the enemies of the Kirk. Ye might fight that battle"—he paused, a pleading firmness in his eyes—"I say ye might fight that battle, as many have before ye, my son, but in the end lose the only battle that matters."

"What battle, Father?" asked Duncan, knowing the answer.

"The battle for yer soul. Aye, this may all come to blows, but see to it that yer heart is right before God. Approach with like passion the battle for yer soul, and all will be well when it comes time for the grim duty of waging war with yer hands."

"Enough now," called his mother from the little scullery. "I be needing Duncan to fetch washing water. I'll not have my family going to field meeting looking and smelling like so many sheep, that I'll not."

Duncan scowled in thought as he waited his turn at the well, Brodie dutifully at his heel. That bit about revenge that his father had read to him—he stroked Brodie's ears absently—it bothered him. He stepped aside as Dame McBirnie shuffled toward the well, her heavy cane, more like a small cudgel, thump-thumping on the hard-packed earth as she made her way.

"I'll draw for ye, Dame McBirnie," he said, reaching for her bucket.

"And a kindness it is in ye, lad," she said, pausing in her stooping shuffle and squinting up at Duncan. She had a way of holding the knobbed end of her cane and eyeing around it, looking at you with only one eye as she talked with you.

Duncan wondered what an old woman like Dame McBirnie could possibly have done to be now a fugitive in the

hills with the rest of them. The reports of plunder and oppression of the peasantry had increased. Reports had it that
when someone was unable to pay a fine levied by Turner, another old woman had been publicly whipped through the village. Still another account told of more men scourged and
sent to prison, and of boys whipped and shipped to Barbados
as slaves. He shuddered at the thought. They were cowards—
all of them, and he hated the English king and all who sup-
ported him. Revenge was exactly what he wanted.

"Now, laddie, whatever is it that makes ye troubled on a
day like today?" she asked, pulling his face toward her for a
better look.

Duncan tried smiling, though with the old woman's hand
pinching his face, his smile looked more like a grotesque
bulging of lips and cheeks. All the while, her one wide eye
goggled at him, and she held the cane menacingly close to
his face.

"Twoubled?" said Duncan through distorted lips. "Dwo I
whook twoubled?"

"Aye, ye be troubled about something," she said, releasing
his face and then giving him a slap on the cheek with her
bony hand. "But ye have no cause fer it, lad. Have ye not
heard the news?"

"What news?" replied Duncan, rubbing his face.

"Why, the news about London town," she said, looking at
him in amazement.

"I donnae ken much about London," said Duncan, "nor
care to."

"Aye, but ye'll be caring to ken this," the old woman went
on, nodding knowingly. "They've gone and fired the whole
place."

"What?" said Duncan, nearly dropping her bucket of water. "Fired? Ye mean it's burned?"

"Aye, burned, near to the ground. The English burned down London."

"But how do ye ken this?" asked Duncan, looking doubtfully at her.

"I have my sources, laddie, aye, I do," she said, winking at him. "I'm told it started more than a week ago, September the second, and raged on for four days, leveling nearly the whole cursed place. Eight and eighty of their popish kirks lie now in ruins. What more does a country deserve, led by the likes of that fornicating, Covenant-breaking Charles Stuart. Last year it were the plague, killing off nearly a hundred thousand of the English." She spat out the word English just like Ancient Grier. "And now this . . ." She shook her cane roughly in the direction of England.

"Did many of the English . . . did they die in the flames?" asked Duncan. He knew his father would not want him to hope that many did die, but he found it hard not to.

"That's a question, indeed." She spat again. "Few enough—two and ten, I'm told." With a disappointed shrug, she rammed her cane down in the dirt.

When Duncan returned home he told his father and mother about the great fire in London.

"What does it mean?" he asked, unable to conceal his excitement.

"I don't pretend to ken what it means," said his father. "But I do ken that our duty remains the same. All this lies securely in the mystery of God's all-wise providence. And we must be content not to ken what God is doing, only to obey."

"Maybe they'll stop oppressing the Kirk," said Duncan, though not really believing it. "They'll be busy enough rebuilding the place."

Duncan's father looked sober.

"Aye, but they'll be a-wanting money to do their rebuilding with," said Duncan's mother bitterly. "Be sure of it, lad, they'll be a-hiring some dandy, wigged fellow to rebuild the whole place—all for a price. So the thieving's like to go on, for in all their plundering they gain silver. Fifty thousand pounds Scots' money it's rumored they've gone and stolen from our poor people of the west country already. Be sure of it, they'll carry on with their thieving in the name of the king, but I shouldn't wonder if things won't now be worse than ever."

"I shouldn't be wondering if yer right, woman," said Duncan's father reprovingly. "But where sin abounds, grace abounds still more. Though poor in wordly goods, we have riches none can take from us, m'love. But ye've heard of how the bishops stripped John Gordon and his brother Robert of all their riches and lands, and of John Neilson of Corsock. All his estate was laid waste and forfeited to the Crown. Along with his wife and bairns, he plunged from a life of riches and honor to that of a vagrant wanderer. Why?"

"I ken, I ken," his wife said, close to tears. "And Laird Neilson's godly wife Mary Maclellan, high born of the house of Barscob, so ill-used. They've stripped them of everything. And all for owning of the Covenant, for refusing to betray King Jesus."

"Peasant or noble born, we're all servants of King Jesus," Duncan's father continued gently. "And the servant's not above his Lord, dear Mary. They stripped our precious Lord Jesus of everything and divided up his robes—then his very life he gave up. He predestined us for glory—but that comes later; for now we suffer, like wee lambs for the slaughter, we suffer."

CAN'T FIGHT HATE
WITH HATE

The sound of so many voices, combining with the murmuring brook, and the wind which sung among the firs, affected me with a sense of sublimity. All nature, as invoked by the Psalmist whose verses they chanted, seemed united in offering that solemn praise in which trembling is mixed with joy as she addresses her Maker. The devotion, in which every one took a share, gave the Scottish worship all the advantage of reality over acting.

Sir Walter Scott

Do ye think Turner and his minions'll find us?" hissed Duncan in Jamie's ear as they made their hushed way through the glen. The M'Kethe and Kilbride families were joined by others as they, determined not even under oppression to break the Sabbath day, gathered for corporate worship. Though his father was loathe to leave the sheep without Brodie, he gave in to Duncan's pleading to bring the dog. Brodie would be the first to know if any dragoons approached.

Jamie shrugged in reply.

Duncan's eyes studied the rim of the hillside that lay between them and the garrison at Dumfries. He imagined what it would be like to see first the horses' heads, ears laid back and manes flowing as they galloped over the hill, followed by the glint of sunlight on steel helmets and breastplates as the dragoons swept down on them, their muskets loaded, and swords flashing in defiance. Tightening his grip on Fiona's and Jenny's hands, he looked around at the farmers and their wives and children that made up the humble procession. All carried Bibles and some had Psalters in hand. Several men carried muskets—Duncan's father held on his shoulders the sleeping form of little Angus—and he caught sight of a sword here and there. But what could they do against trained and well-armed soldiers?

"I'm not afraid," whispered little Jenny.

Duncan looked at the wide eyes that betrayed her boast. In the last months, she had heard brutal stories of Turner and his cruel dragoons sweeping down on other field meetings in Galloway, Dumfries, and Ayrshire. She had heard what they did to children. He was about to tell her she most certainly was afraid, and now a liar, too, but he checked himself, giving her hand a reassuring squeeze instead.

He glanced at Fiona on his right. He never knew quite what to expect with Fiona. She clutched her Bible firmly to her chest and seemed to be gazing at something ahead of them. Duncan took a quick look forward and then back at his sister. Smiling at him for a moment, she then resumed her gazing. There was longing in her eyes, Duncan decided, and there was peace.

Now in the forest, Duncan's eyes darted from tree to tree. At every turn he wondered if a trap awaited them. Bracken fern and shamrock made a lush ground cover at the base of Scots pine and rowen trees rising to the left of the narrow path. The broad, twisting trunks of beech trees clung to the steepness rising to the right of the path, what remained of their browning foliage rustling against the dim sky. As he looked at the groping roots of a beech tree clinging to the rock cliff on his right, Duncan wondered how trees survived in such harsh conditions.

Autumn leaves crackled under the tread of the little band. Duncan was grateful for the babbling burn occasionally visible through the bracken and Scots pine. It might help conceal noises that otherwise might alert a vigilant dragoon scout lying in wait on that ridge just above them. The more people that gathered in any one of the field meetings, the greater the danger of detection—or as had happened in several places, betrayal by their own people. The English were smart—smart at tyranny. They knew that all too many people, when offered enough money, would sell even their neighbors. James Turner himself once fought on the side of the Covenant, but now found it paid too well working for the king. He was not alone in his treason.

They climbed higher into the hills. Still no one spoke. Duncan's eyes went from the forest behind them to the edge of the hills, left and right, then a quick glance at Brodie. Though Brodie almost never growled or barked, if soldiers approached, Duncan was certain Brodie's ears would first stand straight up, and then he would halt in a stalking position, all senses at the ready. Brodie padded along, alert but giving no sign of alarm.

They left cultivated farmland and forest behind, and now crags rose from the high moorland that stretched above and seemed to join the sky. Duncan listened to Fiona's labored breathing as the way grew steeper. He squeezed her hand encouragingly, and as they left the forest and tramped up the thin grass of the hillside, terraced by the sheep, he gave her an extra pull now and then to help her over the steeper parts. And then a narrow valley, like a gaping wound in the moor, appeared on their right, its narrow entrance partly concealed by a thorny gorse bush. This narrow corridor led into a widening hollow, a natural sanctuary scooped out of the hills, Duncan's father often said, as if by the tender hand of a loving heavenly Father as a refuge for his children. Here, those who had no man-made kirk, could worship the Lord in peace and safety—so it had been. Boulders lined the tiny valley where the elderly worshipers might sit when weariness overcame them in the service.

Perhaps the most striking feature of the valley, one that led many to confidently declare that God made this hollow specifically for the faithful to use as their kirk, was a curious projection of rock at the end of the hollow opposite the narrow entrance. A wall of stone rose behind the pulpit and acted as a sounding board, projecting the preacher's voice, so that from anywhere in the hollow his words rang loudly and clearly. It had taken little assistance with hammer and chisel to make full use of this rock as a pulpit where Mr. Crookshanks, Alexander Peden, Mr. Welsh, or another of the fugitive ministers might preach the Word of God to the faithful.

Huddled in the gathering place, several worshipers had already arrived. Among them were refugees of noble birth: John Neilson, lord of Corsock, and his friend and brother-in-law, John Maclellan. The English had seized Maclellan of Barscob's fortified house nearby in Balmaclellan, depriving Barscob of all his rights and leaving him a destitute wanderer, all for his refusal to betray the Redeemer and the Covenant.

Worthy Mr. Crookshanks ascended into the pulpit and gazed at the congregation. Two men with muskets positioned themselves like sentinels below him on either side of the pulpit.

Duncan knew that Mr. Crookshanks as a minister had more to lose for being here than did the rest. If the troopers caught him leading a conventicle and preaching without the sanction of the bishop—a sanction never to be given one so firm and faithful as he—then he would be arrested, tortured, and executed. This was not his first offense.

"Our trust is in the strong arm of Jehovah," he began, calling the flock to worship, "an arm, I say, that is far better than the weapons of war, or the strength of the hills." Gripping his Bible in his left hand, he spread his other arm wide as he spoke, the black folds of his Geneva gown fluttering in the light breeze. "Under the frowning gray of this Sabbath sky, we gather with grateful hearts to bow before our Sovereign, our Lord and Master, King Jesus, whose smile alone we seek, and in whose service we long to live and are prepared to die." His Gaelic cadence rising and falling lent passion to his words. "Today is, indeed, one of the days of the Son of Man, let us rejoice and be glad in it."

Duncan scanned the rim of the valley as he fidgeted from one foot to the other. If he could only see over that rise. Looking around the congregation, he caught sight of Jamie. Suddenly he remembered the service where he and Jamie had witnessed George Henry catching himself on fire with the smoking censor. The unwanted convulsing of a giggle began rising in his throat as he pictured the ridiculous scene. He clamped his hand over his mouth. With an effort he brought his attention back to Mr. Crookshanks.

"We desire not the countenance of earthly kings," said the minister, "for the spiritual and divine Majesty, the Lord of Hosts is shining on this work we are gathered to do in his holy name. The great Master of assemblies is in our midst, and he has prepared for us a table in the wilderness. Praise and glory be to his worthy name."

There could be no greater difference between George Henry's service, Duncan decided, and this one. He soon forgot all else, even the unseen enemies outside the glen. He felt a thrill at Mr. Crookshanks's words, and a longing to see the King of kings filled his young soul.

"Join your voices with the saints throughout the ages," continued the minister, "with the singing of Psalm 72." The little glen filled with that solemn praise mingled with holy joy known only by those who humbly worship in spirit and in truth.

Duncan particularly liked the verse that went:

> They in the wilderness that dwell
> Bow down before him must;
> And they that are his enemies
> *Shall lick the very dust.*

As the psalm neared its doxological conclusion, Duncan felt himself carried along with the wonder and glory of God, and somehow he felt that they were not alone. Somehow, time and place, the English oppressors and the betrayers of the Covenant, it all seemed less clear, less important, less troubling.

> Now blessed be the Lord our God,
> The God of Israel.
> For He alone doth wondrous works,
> In glory that excel.
> And blessed be his glorious name
> To all eternity.
> The whole earth let his glory fill.
> Amen, so let it be.

Duncan tried to sing as his father sang: loud and full of passion, expressed in swelling phrases and eyes lifted heaven-ward. More than any time throughout the week, it was here that Duncan longed for the Lord to come down so he might see him, to speak so that Duncan might hear his voice. When Duncan told his father this one Sabbath on the way home from the field meeting, his father had said, "Turn that longing to faith, m'lad. We're always wanting things our way—the way of sight—but God has called us to a pilgrimage of faith, and that means not seeing with these eyes. But how to turn yer longing to faith, ye might ask? Hear his voice in his Word and in the preaching of his Word. In it he does speak to ye, lad. Hear him, heed him, and do what he says."

Duncan's thoughts were interrupted as the minister led the little congregation in prayer, a prayer filled with the most earnest supplication, but somehow reverent familiarity rang in every phrase, as if he were talking with someone he really knew—and whom he dearly loved. For a moment Duncan thought of his relationship with his earthly father. He loved and respected him more than any man on earth—though at times he did not understand him, and sometimes he was even a little afraid of him.

"My text today, dear people," continued the minister, "is from the prophecy of Isaiah chapter twenty-six and verse five. 'He humbles those who dwell on high, he lays the lofty city low; he levels it to the ground and casts it down to the dust.' "

A rustle rippled through the worshipers.

"As many of ye have heard, a great fire has swept through London town."

Dame McBirnie, from where she sat near the pulpit rock, looked triumphantly around the faces of the congregation. She caught Duncan's eyes and lifted her cane. Mr. Crookshanks seemed not to notice and continued.

"London, the dwelling of our earthly king, surely is a lofty city, filled with grand palaces, theaters and churches . . . churches filled with pomp and artifice, method and pageantry, churches very unlike the one in which we here gather in this wee glen. A lofty city, indeed. And one filled with heavenly defiance and earthly wickedness, one where the words of kings and great men are honored, but where the words of God are, by most, held in disdain . . ."

Duncan listened eagerly. It sounded as though Mr. Crookshanks was going to rail against London—maybe even against the king. Field preaching was already treasonous, but how much the more so if he railed against the king. An idea occurred to Duncan that flooded his young heart with excitement. Maybe Mr. Crookshanks was going to call for a full-scale rebellion against the king. Maybe at last it was time to fight.

"But God humbles all the lofty," said Mr. Crookshanks, "and brings low all who lift themselves up against the high King of heaven. Sometimes he humbles sinners in terminal judgment for their unrepentant wickedness, but still at other times God, who delights in mercy, humbles us in his mercy. He levels to the ground and covers us in the dust as his gracious means of lifting us up and clothing us with the pure righteousness of the Lord Jesus." He paused and looked almost severely at the congregation. They huddled in their wool wraps against the growing cold of the autumn air, all eyes riveted expectantly on the minister.

"But knowing yerselves to be sinners, unworthy of the free grace of our great Savior, how is it that some of ye are gloating over this great conflagration of London? Filled to the brim with wickedness, to be sure; and deserving of the fires of God, to be sure; vice and evil in her playhouses as well as in her Kirk, to be sure; in short a place not at all unlike yer own sinful heart . . . and mine. If London is in need of the humbling, perhaps we are, too."

If that wasn't just like Mr. Crookshanks, thought Duncan, scowling. No call to rebellion against the king in this.

"Quiet, Brodie," he hissed severely, thumping the dog on the head with his knuckle. Brodie lay crouched and rigid, a deep grumbling in his throat, his eyes fixed on the southeastern rim of the little valley.

"Mr. Crookshanks's right, ye ken, Duncan," whispered Fiona, slipping her pale hand into his.

Duncan clenched his teeth and thumped Brodie again.

"Ye can't fight hate," Fiona whispered in his ear, "with more of it. We're called to love our enemies, Duncan."

Duncan thumped Brodie again.

"After all, we were Jesus' enemies," she continued, her voice soft and matter-of-fact. "And he loved us while we were yet his enemies."

She just doesn't get it, thought Duncan as he turned, an angry retort ready for his little sister.

But as he turned, what caught his eye on the ridge above them nearly froze the blood in his veins.

SHOOT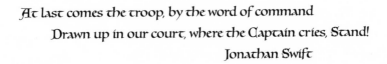HIM

At last comes the troop, by the word of command
Drawn up in our court, where the Captain cries, Stand!
Jonathan Swift

Rising just visible over the southeast ridge of their meeting glen, Duncan saw the head of a fully harnessed horse—and immediately behind, the armored helmet of a dragoon lieutenant rising and falling with the motion of the horse. Within an instant, most of the horrified congregation heard that distinctive medley of noises made by a soldier mounted on a horse: creaking leather from the harness and saddle; snorting, and the stomping of hooves; the metallic clanking of equipment—and of weapons.

Every eye was fixed on the lone dragoon. All expected him to be hastily joined by an entire company of the king's soldiers. And what would follow, none dared to imagine.

The young lieutenant reined his horse in with a startled yank. The horse reared. Duncan thought for sure that he saw a flash of fear flicker in the young man's eyes, but it may have only been surprise. The king's soldier blinked rapidly and seemed about to say something. His horse pranced in a circle, the soldier's head snapping around to keep his eyes on the band of worshipers. The muscles of his jaw worked as he clenched his teeth in indecision. Moans of dread came from several of the women. Lurching sobs rose from one woman who collapsed in a crumpled heap on the grass. Fiona's face grew paler, but she kept a firm grip on Duncan's hand and made no sound.

What happened next was a story to be told many times, with elaboration, though none was needed. When after a minute no other troops joined the young man, Duncan's father rightly concluded that he was sent out from the main army as a scout, an advance guard whose job it was to gather information, return, and bring up the main body of the troops and lead them to their unsuspecting prey. Just as the young man looked about to turn and ride away, Duncan's father stepped forward and boomed after him, "Sir, we invite ye to remain for the sermon—no, we insist ye remain with us for the worship of God." The soldier made no reply. "Ye must know that just like yer horse there, yer soul is thirsty. Come join us as we partake of the Living Water, as we partake of the Bread of Heaven—eat with us and be filled."

The young soldier stared at Duncan's father; then, almost reluctantly, he again began to turn his horse.

"Now, hear me, laddie," barked the voice of Ian Troon, one of the men stationed next to Mr. Crookshanks. "Ye'll lay the reins of yer beast down and stand wi' us fer what remains o' the sermon." Ian raised his musket and held it steadily on the young man, "or, sure as I eat oats, I'll shoot ye dead on the spot." To give substance to the threat, he pulled back the hammer of his musket with an ominous click.

The dragoon's eyes narrowed, and he started to reach for his musket.

"I wouldnae if ye value yer life," said Ian, his voice steady as his gun. "Carry on, Mr. Crookshanks. We hae been joined by a new member of the congregation." Mr. Crookshanks resumed his sermon.

"Now hear me, lad," Duncan's father whispered in Duncan's ear. "Take Brodie and sneak yer way up onto the ridge where ye can watch. The troops are not like to be far behind him. This is no playacting, Duncan. Haste ye back with word the instant ye see them. Now be off with ye."

"Ye'll be careful, Duncan?" said Fiona, softly, her eyes pleading with him.

"Aye, that I will," he replied, giving her hand a quick squeeze.

Duncan felt a surge of excitement as he scrambled through the brown heather on the slopes above the meeting place. His heart beat wildly. It had begun, and he was finally doing something against the English king. He paused and looked back on the circle of worshipers and the lone dragoon, his hands raised reluctantly in the air. The valley stretched far below, but from where Duncan lay on the ridge, he saw no troop of dragoons sweeping toward them. Looking around, Duncan spied a crag jutting high above them on the crest of the brae.

"From there, we'll see all, Brodie."

Duncan scrambled to his feet and began running up the slope, sometimes clawing with his hands on the steeper ledges.

If only I had a gun, he thought in frustration as he glanced over his shoulder at the panorama of the glen. From here he could pick off dragoons one by one. He stopped and sighted down an imaginary musket. "Blam!" In his sights he imagined a red-coated dragoon in full gallop, legs flying upward as he flipped backward off his horse. "Blam!" Another tumbles off and rolls down the brae, never to hunt down innocent people again. "Blam!" Sir James Turner himself, right between the eyes. Disheartened, the remaining soldiers rein in their horses, hastily gather their dead and wounded, and flee down the glen, galloping nonstop all the way to Dumfries. Duncan grinned and nodded as he reloaded, ramming wadding down his imaginary musket, complete with sound effects.

"We set the fear in them, Brodie, aye we did," he boasted, patting his dog affectionately on the head.

Brodie made no reply but crouched low, his ears at full alert.

Duncan raised his "musket" to his eye once again, intending to give them one last volley for good measure. Suddenly, as he eyed down his thumb and the crook in his left hand where the wished-for musket would have rested, charging around a bend came first one red-coated dragoon, and then another until far below he saw galloping toward the field meeting below an entire company of mounted soldiers, swords flashing and muskets at the ready. Duncan's arms fell to his sides, and he blinked several times to make sure he wasn't imagining the charging troop thundering ever closer to the unsuspecting worshipers.

"They've come," he said, his voice hoarse. "They've come."

Sheltered as they imagined, in the sanctuary of the meeting place, none of the worshipers could see what Duncan saw. But the lone dragoon held at bay by Ian Troon's musket knew it was only a matter of time. Sitting high atop his horse on the ridge above them, though it was unlikely that at first he could see them, some clank of weaponry or vibration of hooves beating the ground caught his attention. Duncan watched the lieutenant turn his head, slowly, hoping not to arouse suspicion. Then he glanced back at Ian Troon, who stood absorbed in the sermon. With a flip of his reins and driving his spurs into the sides of his horse, the young lieutenant turned and galloped toward the sounds of his approaching regiment.

"We've got to sound a warning," said Duncan, despair in his voice, "or Turner'll descend like death itself."

With a wrenching knot growing tighter in the pit of his stomach, Duncan feared what the soldiers would do to his family—to Fiona. And he knew what they would do to Mr. Crookshanks. Suddenly his despair turned to rage.

"Come on, Brodie," he yelled and plunged down the slope.

Brodie watched his young master fly, break-neck, down the hill toward the congregation. Instantly Brodie sprang to his feet. But he did not follow Duncan. Like a low-flying bullet he streaked directly toward the retreating lieutenant and the pursuing dragoons.

Thinking Brodie was at his side all the while, Duncan screamed as he plunged toward his family, waving his hands wildly as he ran.

Duncan's mother heard him first.

"The lad's gang gyte hisself," she whispered in her husband's ear.

Duncan's father looked up and saw the frantic gestures of the descending figure.

"He'd not go interrupting services for nothing," he whispered back. "He's sounding the alarm, warning us.

"A thousand pardons, Mr. Crookshanks," said Duncan's

father, his loud voice interrupting the minister. "Duncan's descending, yowling a warning, a warning we'd best heed, or be ruined. And ye, our minister, are most in peril, preaching without consent of the bishop and in defiance of the king, as ye are."

"All ye with arms," cried Ian Troon, "check yer powder. We'll give them a call to worship like none other."

"Hold!" boomed Duncan's father as muskets and flint lock pistols appeared from under plaids and, with a ramming and clicking, men began loading. "Hold! I say. The king's dragoons are like to be armed to the teeth, and in moments they'll surround us on that wee ridge." His hand swept around the grassy rim of the little sanctuary. "If any weapon's visible, the man touting it will be first to fall—and many innocents will follow. Show yer weapons and we have a massacre. Put up yer guns, and we may live to see the day when we can worship peacefully."

"Aye, Sandy's right," said one.

"Ye all ken me for a man of action," Ancient Grier's voice rose above the rest. "I've fought the English." He turned and spat before continuing. "I fought with them. I fought against them." He paused, looking around the little band. Women and children with anxious faces looked back at the old man. He went on. "If it were just the men, and all of us armed"—pulling on his beard, he fixed his eye on Duncan's father for an instant—"I'd say we make a stand, defend our rights, and do what harm we're able. But with women and all the wee bairns . . . We defy these dragoons here in this place, we'll take one or two with us, but mark my words, defy them and, sure as I hate them, we'll all be shot."

"Hear the aged," came an old woman's voice.

"Grier speaks the truth," said old John Sorwick from

where he sat dejected on a large stone. "Though, mark ye, it's all one. We're like to be shot anyhow. I wouldnae be surprised if within the hour this glen is littered with our b—"

"They'll be most keen to seize the minister," Duncan's father broke in firmly. "We'll best defend him by disrobing him—begging yer pardon, Mr. Crookshanks—and making him look like all the rest. In this Ancient Grier speaks true. If we look at all like armed resisters of the king . . . we're all dead men . . . wives and bairns included, but our minister will die only after torture and ignominy of the worst kind."

"What Sandy M'Kethe says is true," chimed in John Short, a butcher from Dalry. "Though I'd like nothing better than to see one of them dragoons down the barrel of m'gun."

"If ye please, Mr. Crookshanks," pleaded Jamie's father. "We'll just fold up yer gown and store it away in the rocks. And ye can then mingle with the rest of us without fear of seizure." Anticipating the minister's objections, he urged, "It's no betraying of the Covenant to be prudent."

"M'conscience won't let me slink away at the first sign of God's enemies," said Mr. Crookshanks. "Mind ye, I've no armor for m'back."

"This here's hardly the first sign of God's enemies for ye, Mr. Crookshanks," said John Short.

"Worthy Mr. Crookshanks, ye donnae ken what they'll be doing to ye," said John Kilbride. "We'll not aid them by sitting idle while they do it."

By this time Duncan arrived on the rim of the meeting place. He gasped for breath as he related what he saw and what was about to come upon them.

"Twenty or thirty of the king's dragoons," he panted. "Coming on—and fully armed. The lieutenant rode to meet them." He paused, scowling as he looked around for Brodie. From here he could not yet see the dragoons, but he knew from which direction they came. "They'll be here any minute!" Again he glanced around for Brodie.

"Like as not, it's Alexander Thomson's company of the guard," offered John Short. "Let loose from the new fine-raising garrison at Dalry."

"Thomson plunders for Turner," said John Maclellan of Barscob. "And like as not, this band is led by Corporal George Deanes, who plunders for Thomson. All unprincipled rabble and haters of the Kirk. I do hope yer plan works, Sandy M'Kethe. If ye go and miscalculate with this sort . . . we're like to all be doomed where we stand."

"Let us sing our confidence in God alone," said the minister. With that he began singing, and by ones and twos the congregation joined in:

> Unto the ends of all the earth
> Wars into peace he turns:
> The bow he breaks, the spear he cuts,
> In fire the chariot burns.
> Be still, and know that I am God . . .

Duncan tried to sing, but with his eyes glued on the rise below, fearing every moment that the troops would soon descend, he couldn't join in with much heart. *What's keeping them? They should have been here long ago. And where is Brodie? Maybe I imagined the whole thing. After all I was playacting,* he thought sheepishly. *What if he raised the alarm, disrupting the service, and all for no reason?* He grew pale with the thought. His father's voice speaking to the minister interrupted his anxious musing.

"We'll not argue with yer conscience, Mr. Crookshanks." Duncan's father stepped toward the minister. "Nor ask ye to violate the dictates of it." He nodded at Jamie's father, who along with several other men fell in with him as he came to the stone pulpit. "But for the sake of yer continued ministry to yer flock . . ." Here Duncan's father placed his arm firmly around the minister's shoulders. The other men gathered around and hoisted him down from the pulpit, removed his gown, and set him among the clustered congregation.

"They'll no doubt ask which one of us is God's minister," said Jamie's father.

"And m'conscience compels me to answer," said Mr. Crookshanks, resolutely, "gown or no gown."

Duncan ran partway back up the brae. What kept them? Were they just playing cat and mouse? Or were they not really there at all? He turned, and the sight that met his eyes both thrilled and terrified him at the same time. The dragoons had halted, but not in any form or rank. At least two men lay sprawled on the sod, their horses galloping back down the glen. Other horses reared, and men cursed. And then he spotted Brodie. He watched in wonder as Brodie stalked and nipped at the horses' heels. Retreating, he then circled around like a fury and struck on their flank. Another horse flipped its rider onto the sod. He rolled, his red coat swirling about him, until with a sploosh he came to rest in the ooze of a low bog.

"Ye're doing it all alone," said Duncan in amazement. But how long could Brodie keep it up? The officer in charge clutched at his pistol. Duncan's blood ran cold. He ground his teeth as he watched. The officer pointed . . . withdrew; aimed again . . . then withdrew, yanking the reins of his terrified horse in frustration. Between the rearing of the horse and Brodie darting and skulking, seemingly in all directions at once, the officer seemed unable to get off a shot. But he looked a man to keep trying, Duncan thought, his face pale and drawn as he watched.

"What see ye, lad," he heard someone faintly shouting from below. It sounded like Ancient Grier's voice.

Duncan hated to take his eyes off Brodie, but just as he was about to yell a reply, for the first time he felt a twinge of real fear. What if a sharp-eyed dragoon, angered from Brodie's diversion, what if he heard Duncan yell a reply and then spotted him up on the brae? Could a carefully aimed shot hit him from down there? And just what would a lead bullet feel like when it crashed into his arm or leg . . . or chest? He shuddered, turned, and fled down the hill to deliver his reply at closer range.

"Brodie's holding them off," he panted, his voice breaking with emotion and the strain of it all. "He's doing it all alone."

"We scatter to the mist, then," said Ian Troon. "And pick off one or two English from up the brae."

"I'll none of yer talk, Ian," said Duncan's father severely. "We scatter now to the barren brae, lonely and open as it is, and they'll be doing the picking off, shooting yer bairns and mine and asking questions later . . . perhaps when none can answer. No, we stay together and hide the minister, trusting God for our protection. Don't ye be looking to the hills, man. Look rather to the Lord."

And then, a pistol shot cracked. It shattered off the fells and through the glen. To Duncan the retort of that pistol seemed to echo and reecho on and on. Its crack and whistle settled into a wailing that Duncan never forgot.

With a scream of rage, Duncan felt his feet pounding on the rim of the meeting glen. He heard his own screams as if they came from someone else. As he rounded the ridge intending to plunge down the brae toward Brodie and the dragoons, and the sound of the pistol, he stumbled. Apparently sensing what her brother in his rage was about to do—and knowing the peril if he did—Fiona gathered up her skirts and raced after him, hoping to cut him off on the low side of the ridge before he plunged farther down and into the jaws of the dragoons.

She clutched at him as he rose, his knee bleeding from the sharp stones on which he fell.

"Duncan, ye cannae go," she said firmly but with tears in her eyes. "They'll only kill ye."

"But they've killed Brodie," he sobbed, "they've killed him."

"If they've killed the lad's dog," John Short's voice rose from among the worshipers, "they're like to be on us any moment."

"Duncan," called his father sharply, "take Fiona and scatter to the mist. There's no time for ye to join us. Stay hidden with her on the brae."

Duncan, his face streaked with sweat and tears, hesitated.

"Do it now!" boomed his father's voice.

Duncan looked at Fiona's pale face and seemed to awaken. He knew if he tried to run up the brae with Fiona, she would not be able to go as fast, and they'd be spotted sooner by the dragoons. He grabbed her hand and traversed along the brae to a large stone surrounded by a tangle of brown heather.

Meanwhile, protesting that he must answer if asked, Mr. Crookshanks was positioned so as to be completely surrounded by his congregation, and several women and children were ordered to sit on him. This both hid him, and, from the combined weight of those seated on him, pressed enough breath out of him so that any words the honest man might try to utter would come out as only inaudible little wheezes.

"Trust in God!" someone called out. "Jehovah will fight for us!"

Others joined in, but still faces were pale and eyes were

wide as the pounding of hooves and the clanking of the dragoons thundered ominously toward them.

Duncan and Fiona lay within earshot, hunkered behind a rock, peering through the heather. His breath coming in angry sobs, Duncan watched as the dragoons circled the meeting place with clipped precision. He scanned the ridges and depressions: no sign of Brodie. He took small comfort in the appearance of several of the men, besmeared with ooze from the bogs, and grass and mud stains streaking the white trousers of several others. A muddy pair of red-faced soldiers dog-trotted after, apparently unable to retrieve their horses and ordered to follow on foot.

"Present!" ordered the captain.

For a horrifying instant, Duncan thought he was about to order the men to fire down on the little congregation.

"Who's in charge of this motley band of psalm-singing traitors?" he barked, scanning the faces.

Duncan thought he detected the hint of a lilt and a rolled "r" here and there. He wondered if he might not be a Scot doing his best to put on an English accent and airs.

"I demand an answer!" the captain ordered, looking at each of the men in turn. A sneer of derision twisted his mouth.

No one spoke. A slight lifting of the seat on which several of the women sat, and a muffled grunt went undetected by the captain. "Perhaps a search of you who presume to call yourselves men," he went on, his chin extended in contempt. "Perhaps such a search might yield an ill-kept pistol or two. Not that any of you would be proficient at firing such—we have no fear of that, pathetic little band of gutter slime that you obviously are." He sniffed the air, wrinkled his nose in disgust, and held a lace handkerchief to his face, taking deep breaths of its scented folds.

"There, I am restored." Several of his men dutifully snickered at his mocking humor. "I say, if I were to uncover a weapon or two among you, I would feel justly threatened."

Here with brow lifted, he feigned a hurt expression and held his hand over his heart in mock offence. "And to threaten the king's man . . . is to threaten the king himself. I would naturally have to—well, to shoot you dead on the spot. Now then, come, who will be first in our little search?"

"He's baiting them," hissed Duncan. "Ian Troon's never a man for an insult. He'll stand up to them."

"And die on the spot if he does," whispered Fiona in return.

The captain looked at his lieutenant before continuing. The young officer nodded toward Ian Troon.

"You, with the red face, about to burst a button." He pointed his drawn sword toward Ian. "What is that wrapped up in your filthy plaid? Perhaps it's your coward of a minister. I demand an answer!"

More grunts came from where the women sat.

Duncan's father caught Ian's eye and defied him to vent his anger. A hothead like Ian could get the entire congregation shot. Ian ground his teeth together and turned a darker red. His eyes flashed in rage at the captain who taunted him.

"I wish I had a gun," hissed Duncan through gritted teeth. "A muckle big one."

"If ye were to shoot these," said Fiona, "more would come in their place, who would then shoot more of us. Father always says, 'Blessed are the peacemakers, for they shall be called sons of God.' That's what Father always says."

"That's from the *Bible*, Fiona," hissed Duncan, disgusted that she would attribute it to their father.

"Aye, I ken it, Duncan. But sometimes I worry that ye've forgotten that it's from the Bible."

Duncan looked at his sister in wonder.

The captain was speaking again.

"All right, then," he said. "If ye'll not give it up peacefully—" Here he broke off, and with a studied nonchalance, he gazed at his reflection in the polished blade of his sword. He breathed on the blade and slowly wiped it on his sleeve. Squinting critically, he moistened his finger, turned to one side for a better look, and smoothed his eyebrows. Coolly, and without taking his eyes from his reflection, he said to the young lieutenant at his side, "Shoot him."

SIR BRODIE

His oath, his covenant, his blood
Support me in the whelming flood;
When all around my soul gives way,
He then is all my hope and stay.

Edward Mote

Shoot him!" the captain repeated, raising his voice in annoyance. "Shoot him dead!"

The lieutenant hesitated for an instant. And in that instant Dame McBirnie stepped forward, goggling viciously with her one eye and wagging the knob of her stick threateningly.

"Aye, ye've gang and done a job of it, Eddie," she said, cackling with laughter. "This time it's an English dandy ye've become, is it?"

"Woman, what are you talking about?" replied the captain, looking up from his preening. He grew pale as he studied the old woman.

"Aye, I see it in yer eyes, Eddie," Dame McBirnie continued. "Ye ken who I am. Right well ye ken."

"Aye," the captain said weakly, now a flush of embarrassment rising on his face. "Is that ye, Auntie Morag? Aye, I ken the answer," he added, his feigned English accent fading. He seemed to wither under the old woman's one-eyed gaze.

"Aye, and ye're a shameful excuse fer a nephew, laddie," she said. "High-handed betrayer of the Covenant and oppressor of the Kirk, and a-leading these other wee lads along in it. I'm ashamed to own ye as my own kin. Shame, shame on ye!"

"Oh, Auntie Morag . . ." his voice trailed off.

"Now begone with ye, Eddie," she said, adding an even more vicious waggle of her stick. "Mend yer ways, and stop bringing grief to honest folk come peacefully to hear gospel preaching."

The unfortunate captain's company of dragoons looked on in wonder. Surely their commander would not give in to an old woman.

"Y-yes, Auntie," he replied meekly.

"See that ye do mend, then," she said, "or I'll be laying ye by the heels! Now begone with the lot of ye!" She dismissed the dragoons with a final shake of her stick.

The captain sheathed his sword, and with a yank of his reins, he spurred his horse into a gallop and disappeared over the ridge. His greedy company turned reluctantly and followed.

For a moment no one breathed a word.

"I'll lay him by the heels yet," said Dame McBirnie. "And to think I used to change his nappie."

"He's no Alexander Thomson or Corporal Deanes," said John Neilson to Laird Barscob. "Neither of that lot would have walked away—auntie or no auntie—and left us at peace to hear the Word of God preached."

"Praise be to God these dragoons weren't under the command of either of those monsters," agreed Barscob, stuffing a twist of tobacco into the bowl of his ivory pipe.

Grunts came from where the women sat on Mr. Crookshanks.

"Free the minister," called Neilson.

The women stood and Duncan's father and several others sprang to help the minister to his feet.

"We regret treating ye with such apparent disrespect," said Laird Barscob. "But, Mr. Crookshanks, ye must understand we did it for yer own good—and the good of yer flock."

Taking deep breaths of air, Mr. Crookshanks waved a reassuring hand at the men.

"Think no more of it," the minister said when he had recovered. "God moves in mysterious ways. He has granted us a deliverance beyond human explanation. Praise and glory be to him for it."

Duncan returned Fiona to his family. Then Mr. Crookshanks led the congregation in singing a psalm.

Duncan could not join them. With heavy heart he made his way down the hill to the spot where he last saw Brodie. Snatches of Psalm 105 drifted in his ears:

> Give thanks to God, call on his name;
> To men his deeds make known.
> Sing ye to him, sing psalms; proclaim
> His wondrous works each one.

He just couldn't sing. What had they done to Brodie? Now he ran. Still the words of the Psalm sounded in his ears.

> Think on the works that he hath done,
> Which admiration breed;
> His wonders, and the judgments all
> Which from his mouth proceed.

Duncan blinked back the hot, angry tears as a still blackand-white form came into view. He no longer ran. His feet felt like great curling stones as he trudged with heavy heart toward where his dog lay. Only faintly now came the strains of the psalm as he neared where Brodie lay sprawled in the heather.

> His cov'nant he remember'd hath,
> That it may ever stand:
> To thousand generations
> His word he did command.
> Yet, notwithstanding, suffer'd he
> No man to do them wrong:
> Yea, for their sakes, he did reprove
> Kings, who were great and strong.

He dropped to his knees beside his dog. The grass and heather surrounding the still form was stained crimson and still warm with Brodie's blood. A lead ball from the captain's pistol had crashed through Brodie's heart, killing him instantly. Duncan slowly ran his fingers through the velvety tufts of black-and-white fur on Brodie's cooling forehead. He stroked the long nose that had so often nuzzled him awake in the mornings, or had nudged him to attention while tending the sheep. There was no breath, no response. Brodie was gone forever.

For a long time Duncan knelt in the heather. He felt numb. He vaguely realized that the service must have ended by now and that people were walking silently past him. Jamie halted at his side, then moved on. Ancient Grier said something like, "Brodie's a hero, lad. He died a hero and he's to be remembered a hero." Duncan thought he heard a catch in Grier's voice as he said it. Mr. Crookshanks placed his hand on Duncan's head for a moment but said nothing. Laird Barscob drew his claymore, and Duncan heard the scraping of earth as the good man dug a hole. Duncan held Brodie's limp form in his arms for a moment, then slowly lowered his dog into the hole. He tried arranging the head, feet, and tail so they looked right. They didn't. He lifted the dog out of the hole. Lord Barscob handed Duncan his claymore. There're other things I'd rather do with this sword, thought Duncan. He gripped the hilt until his knuckles shone white through the brass pattern of the protective basket hilt. A tremor of emotion made the blade quiver. Then returning to the task at hand, he enlarged the hole to make more room for Brodie's head. Once more he lowered Brodie into the grave. He felt a choke in his throat as he scooped sod and earth into the hole, first littering the smooth black-and-white coat . . . then covering it entirely. A sob racked his frame as he placed the final stone on top of the cairn that marked the little grave.

It was a mournful family that sometime later made their way home. Fiona held Duncan's hand a good bit of the way. Several times his father placed his big arm across Duncan's shoulders. Brushing a tear from her eye, his mother planted a kiss on his cheek. Jenny wailed and sobbed in anguish until Duncan's mother threatened to give her no supper if she didn't stop. Angus tried reaching up and patting his big brother comfortingly. But there was no comfort for Duncan.

"'Tis a great loss, m'lad," said Duncan's father tenderly. "A great loss, indeed."

"Aye," was all Duncan could reply. "Aye, it is."

YE'LL HANG, SANDY

The wind sae cauld blew south and north,
And blew into the floor;
Quoth our goodwife to our goodman,
"Gae out and bar the door—"

Anonymous

D uncan remembered little about the next few weeks. It
rained. Not the Scottish summer drizzle that might
last for a few hours and stop. It rained for days and
days. And it grew colder. Sometimes at night the rain came
down onto the thatch pattering like icy bullets. And when
the wind moaned in the gnarled branches of the scattered
beech trees clinging to the hillside, it drove frozen rain
through the thatch and under the door. Winter had come.
Long dark months of bone-numbing wet and cold lay ahead—
an especially lonely cold for Duncan.

One evening as Duncan and his family huddled before the
peat fire, doing their best to keep warm while Duncan's father read
to them from Rutherford's Letters, a sharp knock came at the door.

Duncan's mother's eyes flashed as she looked up from her
spinning, and she caught her breath sharply.

"Who'd be out on a night like this?" said Sandy M'Kethe as reassuringly as he could. He rose and strode toward the door.

It burst open before he could get there.

Duncan's mother did her best to stifle a scream as the door banged against the wall, and a blast of wet cold filled the croft. But the expected red coat, brandishing sword and musket, did not enter. Ian Troon, eyes wide with enthusiasm, burst into the room.

"What's this all about, Ian?" Sandy M'Kethe boomed.

"Dalyell and Drummond are descending on all Galloway," he gasped for breath. "And they're starting with Glenkens."

"Slow down, Ian," said Duncan's father, closing the door against the cold. "Start at the starting place and tell us only what ye ken, on good authority, to be true."

"Aye, I've come for nothing else," said Ian eagerly. "Word is, Dalyell, the terror of the Russian wars, a monster and no man, is on his way to ferret out all traitors."

"Then we've nothing to fear," said Duncan's father, "for we're no traitors here."

"Sandy M'Kethe, hear me out," said Ian, his voice rising with excitement. "Dalyell's been given authority to hang every man at his own door. If ye're known as a Covenanter, ye'll be given no trial. Ye'll hang, Sandy, and what becomes of yer family after is of little doubt. He's on his way even as we speak, man. We must to arms and fight or all is lost."

"Hold, Ian." Duncan's father scowled at Ian Troon. "Where have ye heard such tales?"

"They're no tales, Sandy," said Ian. "Dalyell's hanged one hundred men in Glasgow already. What he'll do here in Glenkens if we don't rise and stop him is certain."

"But where did ye learn of this, Ian? Answer me straight."

"It's common knowledge in all Glenkens," replied Ian,

looking at Sandy M'Kethe as if he were the only one who hadn't yet heard. "Everyone in Dalry is talking of it and preparing theirselves against Dalyell. It's time to join up and fight, Sandy. In defense of the Covenant and yer family ye must fight. If ye don't, ye'll hang. It's certain."

"How many other crofters have ye told this to, Ian?"

"Every door from here to Dalry has heard the news."

"I'm wondering if ye're not the one responsible for it being common knowledge, then. Ye could be stirring up a pot that'll rise and boil over, and they'll be no stopping it when it does."

"I've delivered my warning to ye, Sandy," said Ian, rising to go. "And now ye'll have to be doing what's needed."

He turned on his heel and was gone.

"Father, is it time?" asked Duncan.

"I don't ken if it's time or no," said his father, returning to the fireside. "But what I do ken is this:

> Our sure and all-sufficient help
> Is in Jehovah's name;
> His name who did the heav'n create,
> And who the earth did frame.

"Hope in God who made the world," he continued, his voice steady with trust and confidence. "If God can only speak a word and bring into being this grand universe, his power is all-sufficient to care for his own in our trials. Fear not those who can only kill yer body, lad, but have no power over yer soul. Put yer hope in God, and I promise ye, come what may, ye'll never be lacking reasons for praising him for both his goodness and his greatness."

After praying with his family, Sandy M'Kethe locked the door and went to bed.

For a long time Duncan lay awake listening to the steady downpour outside. Was Ian Troon's report true? Would his father fight if they came to hang him? While thinking about these things, he reached his hand down to the cold, empty space where Brodie used to sleep at his side. He turned to the wall and tried to sleep.

THROUGH TO THE HILT

From every evil shall he keep thy soul,
From every sin:
Jehovah shall preserve thy going out,
Thy coming in.

John, Duke of Argyll

Tuesday morning, November 13, 1666, dawned wet and cold. Clouds, gray and heavy with moisture, slumped low over the hills. Rain fell in continuous sheets. Wrapping his plaid around himself against the damp, Duncan wondered if the rain would ever stop. He smiled ruefully. Maybe this incessant rain would serve as the best deterrent against the brutalities of the English soldiers. Surely even they, mad dogs though they were, wouldn't relish the idea of plundering on a day like this.

Peat smoke made a dull blue haze throughout the room. Some of the chill and dampness retreated reluctantly as the peat hissed and sputtered in the fire. Duncan's father laid out a row of cut peat near the fire in hopes that the small heat might dry out the other fuel and make for a better fire later in the day.

"Duncan, come with me up to check in on Ancient Grier. Cold and wet as it is, and with his years, we'd best be seeing that he's getting on all right. He's late threshing his corn. If this rain'll let be for the space of an hour, we'll thresh some of it for the old man."

Duncan inwardly groaned. But he pulled himself out of bed and began wrapping an extra plaid around his shoulders.

As he followed his father out into the cold rain, he snatched his breath in sharply at the drenching cold. The rivulets of rain water running down the path soon made his bare feet ache. As numbness set in, he slipped and nearly fell several times. No amount of digging his toes in seemed to help. He pulled his plaid up onto his head and blinked as he gazed after his father's broad back, partly obscured through the torrent of drips cascading off his plaid. Anyone who claimed that wool still kept you warm even when it got wet had never tested the theory—at least not in this kind of drenching downpour. Duncan shivered.

"Ancient Grier!" his father called, his voice partially drowned out by the rain. "Ancient Grier! Is all well with ye?" He knocked on the low door of the croft. No reply.

"With this rain it's hard to tell for sure," said Duncan in his father's ear. "But I see no smoke coming from his chimney."

His father lifted the latch, and Duncan, full of dread, followed him into the old man's croft. What if Ian Troon's report was true? What if they found Grier hanged in his own croft? Again he shivered.

"He's not here," said Duncan, his teeth chattering.

Furrows lined his father's forehead as he scanned the sparse furnishings.

"He's not here, but I don't think he's been gone for long," he said, crouching at the fireplace. "He's had a fire already today, though it's burned itself into nothing but weak smolderings."

"He's taken his claymore with him," said Duncan, eyeing the empty place on the wall where he had often seen Grier's sword hanging.

"Aye, so it seems," said his father slowly.

"Or someone else took it," said Duncan.

They stepped back out into the rain. Duncan sloshed to the far end of the croft. Something underfoot on the cold wet ground felt different. A warm, oozing sensation crept between the toes of his numb foot. He bent down and inspected his foot.

"Father!" Duncan called suddenly.

"What is it?" his father replied, striding toward where Duncan stood staring at the ground.

"Horse dung," said Duncan slowly. "Fresh horse dung . . . Ancient Grier doesnae have a horse."

"Aye," said his father, a grim set to his jaw. "That can mean only one thing."

He didn't need to say what it meant. Duncan followed his father back down the hill toward the village. The cold and wet seemed less noticeable as he tried equaling his father's stride without breaking into a run. As they came up on Thomas MacRoan's farm on the edge of the village, Duncan's father stopped at the farmhouse and pounded on the door.

Duncan ducked around the corner of the house while his father waited for a reply to his knocking. He hated the thought of farmer MacRoan remembering when Duncan took cover in his drinking pond. He wasn't about to be seen and risk hearing the man's mocking laughter again. And especially not in front of his father. He heard the door creak open.

"Sandy M'Kethe, what are ye doing out on a day like this?" asked the farmer.

Duncan heard his father ask after Ancient Grier.

"Ye best leave off searching for the old man, M'Kethe,"

said MacRoan. "Ye might find yerself a meddling in other folks' affairs."

"I ken ye've compeared at the kirk, Thomas," said Duncan's father. "And ye think little of our keeping the Covenant. But this is a matter of justice for an old man—for yer neighbor; ye can't turn a blind eye on old Grier."

"That's a funny thing, M'Kethe," snorted the farmer. "To my way of thinking, it'd be just for Grier to pay what he owes the king."

"And what is it he owes the king?" asked Duncan's father.

"Fines . . . fines they're forced to take out by threshing of his corn. That's justice. And I for one intend not to interfere with it."

"Ye ken they'll take all his winter food. And leave the old man to starve. There's no justice in that, man."

He'd heard enough. Duncan moved toward the barn.

Then he saw them. Four saddled horses stood tethered under a covered outbuilding next to the barn. Duncan peered in the window. Four of the king's soldiers appeared to be trying to light a fire on the floor in the center of the stone barn. In a wet heap of patched tweed and plaid lay Ancient Grier, his hands and feet tied so that he could not move. His face looked pale and strained, and his beard and hair were matted with mud. One of the soldiers spoke, and Duncan could just make out what he said.

"Old man, fall to your prayers," said one.

"You might think of it as praying over your last meal," said another. "Instead of seizing your pathetic corn in payment of your fines, we're going to strip you naked and roast you alive—and very slowly."

"Ye'll be popping and sizzling away until done to culinary perfection," said the first. The other soldiers laughed uproariously.

"Perhaps ye'd like to sing us a psalm or two?" jeered another.

"Aha! I've finally gotten the fire lit," said a fourth.

"In lieu of your many debts," intoned one of the soldiers, as if pronouncing the sentence of a court, "accumulated for your refusal to submit to your lawful king and sovereign, we extract the payment thereof in the form of—no, no, not corn this time—we extract payment in the form of your roasted flesh."

"This will make a merry funeral supper, indeed," said the first, who seemed to be the man in charge.

So intent on listening to the soldiers, Duncan did not hear his father come up behind him.

"What is it ye see, lad?" his father whispered.

Duncan nearly bolted out of his skin in alarm.

"They've g-got Grier," stammered Duncan, "and they say they're going to . . . to roast him alive. What are we going to do, Father?"

"God's commands make our duty to Grier clear enough, lad," said his father levelly.

"What?" asked Duncan.

"We do everything possible to save Grier. But four armed men against two without weapons . . ." Duncan's father seemed almost to be talking to himself. "Little we can do without help. Duncan, run like the wind to the Clachan Inn down at the village and gather what willing men ye find there. And Duncan . . ."

"Aye, Father."

"Tell them to come in arms. Without weapons we'll never force monsters like these to leave a poor old man alone. Now, off with ye, and haste ye back."

Twice Duncan slipped on the slimy mud as he raced down the steep main street of Dalry. Had he heard his father correctly? "Tell them to come in arms." He'd clearly said it.

Bursting in the door of the low stone inn, his face streaked with mud, Duncan looked around for someone he recognized. Four men sat in a corner, driven indoors by the cold and wet, pools of muddy rainwater at their feet. Duncan looked closer. One of the men looked up at Duncan. In an instant, he recognized John Maclellan, the fugitive Laird of Barscob.

"Dragoons—they've got Ancient Grier," Duncan cried, "and they say corn won't do. They're going to roast him alive for not paying his fines."

Barscob flew to his feet, his chair falling backward with a clatter.

"How many, and how armed?" he demanded.

"Four soldiers, with swords, pistols, and muskets," said Duncan.

"We've only three swords between us," said one of Barscob's companions. "And two pistols."

"Aye, but no lead for the pistols," said Barscob.

"There's no time to lose," said Duncan. "My father is there—unarmed. But they have Grier's claymore."

"We'll take them by surprise," cried Barscob, running out the door.

The others followed, Duncan bolting on ahead, worried now what his father might do in defense of Grier even without a weapon. And then what might the soldiers do to his father?

With relief, Duncan saw his father still peering in the window of the barn. Smoke now drifted steadily out an open window and partially opened door. Barscob and his companions joined them at the window. Laughter and shouting came from the soldiers in the barn, who now passed a crock of whiskey back and forth, taking long draughts in turn.

"Sandy M'Kethe, what think ye of our chances?" asked Barscob.

"I've got my eye on Grier's claymore, just inside the door," he paused. "But they have four pistols and at least two muskets."

"We have two pistols," said Barscob. "But no ball for either of them."

Barscob peered at the soldiers through the window.

"Looks to be Corporal George Deanes in command," said the fugitive nobleman, his eyes narrowing. "A tough monster and a great hater of the Kirk."

"They're drunk," said Duncan's father. "And they're not expecting us."

Two of the soldiers carried a gridiron into place over the fire.

"Roasting grid's ready for action, sir," one of the soldiers said. Then breaking into a ridiculous giggle, he suppressed a belch with the back of his hand.

"All right, men," said Corporal Deanes. "Pluck the feathers off the goose and ready him for roasting."

One of the soldiers swung his booted foot back and landed a vicious kick at Grier's middle. The old man groaned. Another soldier yanked off Grier's plaid, while another tore at his jacket and shirt.

"I've seen more than enough!" said Duncan's father, his teeth clenched in anger. "Weapons or none, we defend the old man, or betray the Law of God!"

With that he rose, and throwing the door of the barn open with a crash, Duncan's father snatched up Grier's claymore. He seemed to fill the entire barn, so fierce was his presence. Pointing the sword steadily at Corporal Deanes, Sandy M'Kethe boomed, "Touch the old man again"—he took a great stride toward the commander—"and in the name of God Almighty, I shall run ye through to the hilt."

The soldiers, though in a stupor from the whiskey, recovered themselves in an instant and drew their swords. By this time Laird Barscob and his followers, their swords at the ready, stood alongside Duncan's father, four ill-trained local men with swords but without even lead ball for their few pistols, against four well-armed and trained soldiers of the king.

"Why do ye use the honest man so?" cried Barscob.

"How dare you challenge the king's soldiers about their

lawful duty!" barked Corporal Deanes, his face growing red with fury.

Then with a sneer of derision, the corporal turned and deliberately gave Ancient Grier another vicious kick.

Just as Duncan's father prepared to throw himself at the commander, Barscob grabbed his tobacco pipe from his jacket pocket. Cramming it into the barrel of his pistol, he leveled it at Deanes and fired. Now in pieces, the ivory pipe shot through the air and found its mark, shattering against the corporal's chest. With a gasp of surprise and fury, Deanes groped at his chest. His knees buckled, and he sprawled in a heap on the floor beside his previous victim. Tearing apart the lapels of his red coat, buttons popping onto the stone floor, Deanes moaned as he withdrew his bloodied hand. In a voice high-pitched with panic, the corporal began reciting the Lord's Prayer.

"Our F-f-father, wh-who art in . . ."

Meanwhile, the soldier who had first kicked Grier lunged at Duncan's father. Duncan looked on in wonder as his father parried the thrust and came at the soldier like a fury. Though perhaps he was not as skilled as the soldiers, his father's movements were more fierce and rapid than Duncan's eye could entirely follow. The soldier gave way and backed toward the corner of the barn as Duncan's father came on. Barscob showed a skill with his sword in keeping with his breeding as a nobleman, but his companions, weakened as they were with cold and hunger, were no match for the third soldier. The big, sneering brute of a man spun and parried and stepped aside, enjoying the fight, as if playing with his prey before the kill.

Then, Duncan watched in horror as the sword of one of Barscob's companions clattered to the floor. Barscob's friend gripped his forearm and fell onto one knee, his face contorted in pain. Moments later, the big soldier spun on his heel and

121

brought his blade down on the shoulder of the other companion. He, too, fell to the floor. It was now three soldiers against two ill-trained defenders. Dismayed, Duncan watched the fray and listened to the clashing and scudding of steel against steel. If only he could do something.

While Barscob seemed to be getting the better of his opponent, Duncan's father landed blow after blow against the sword of his opponent. The man seemed to be weakening as he found himself pressed harder against the wall by the sheer strength of Duncan's father, fueled by indignation at the injustice done to Ancient Grier.

Duncan clenched his fists as he watched the big soldier turn. The man seemed to be sizing up the fight, weighing out the chances of his fellow soldiers against their opponents. He didn't seem to like what he saw from Duncan's father. Sandy M'Kethe had cornered his soldier and stood fighting with his back to the rest of the room. Lifting his sword, the big man made for the broad back of Duncan's father. Duncan stared, horrified: the soldier intended to cleaver his father from behind.

With fists clenched and howling with rage, Duncan ran toward the back of the soldier, his head lowered like a charging bull.

DUNCAN USES HIS HEAD

If it must be,
Warre we must see
(So fates conspire),
May we not feel
The force of steel:
This I desire.

T. Jackson

The rest of the fight was a complete blur to Duncan. He remembered vaguely charging at the big soldier, then nothing. Next thing he knew was a pounding headache and a pain so fierce that he feared his neck was broken.

"That was a noble use of yer pate, lad," came a weak voice from beside him.

He thought the voice sounded familiar, but when he tried to turn and look at the speaker, darkness closed in around his line of vision, and he felt a wave of sickness churning in his stomach.

"Lie still, lad."

His father's voice—he'd know that voice anywhere. His father's big hand caressing his forehead and cheek—he'd know that anywhere, too. He breathed a great sigh of relief. That brute of a soldier had not cut his father down after all.

Slowly his vision began to return.

"W-what happened?" he moaned.

"Ye only saved all our skin," this from John Maclellen of Barscob.

Duncan recognized his voice, and with that recognition, more of his memory of the fight returned. The fight was clearly over, but how much time had elapsed?

"Ye brought down the biggest and meanest of the lot," said Barscob again.

His father cradled Duncan's head in his hand and offered him a dram of something liquid. It made him gasp as he drank it, but it warmed him from inside, and his vision seemed clearer.

He smiled up at his father.

"He didnae get ye," said Duncan.

"God fought on our side, lad," said his father, gripping Duncan's shoulder. "Our times are in God's hands. My time hadn't come. Thank ye for what ye did, Duncan. Yer mother would have approved."

"Did they hurt Grier bad?" asked Duncan.

"Och, Duncan, Duncan," came from next to him. "Do ye think English brutes can prevail against the likes of Ancient Grier?"

Duncan turned and smiled at the pale drawn features of the old man. Wincing with the pain, Duncan struggled to a sitting position. Trussed in ropes along the wall of the barn sat the four scowling soldiers.

"Corporal Deanes isn't dead, then?" said Duncan.

"Unfortunately not," said Barscob loudly. "Though it was my best pipe, lead ball works much better on Englishman. It set him on his heels, scratched him a wee bit and made him bleed some, but, alack, there's been more harm to his pride than to his person."

"Ye'll all pay for this," said Corporal Deanes through teeth gritted in pain and rage.

"Paying's of two kinds," said Duncan's father firmly. "Aye, we may pay at the hands of ye English oppressors for defending our neighbor against yer brutalities. But, barring yer repentance, ye'll pay. Aye, ye'll pay on the judgment day. Make no mistake about it, sir, ye'll pay King Jesus for yer crimes against his Kirk and his bairns."

Deanes fell into a sullen silence.

Duncan's father and Barscob dressed his companions' wounds. When they were finished, they got into a heated discussion over what to do with the prisoners. Barscob's friends suggested hanging them then and there, but Barscob and Duncan's father refused to even consider it. Finally, it was agreed to give them quarter and free them, but without their weapons or horses.

Stiff and aching, Duncan rose to his feet and helped his father load Grier onto one of the horses. Though he protested at their help, after his ordeal, he lacked strength enough to walk on his own. Barscob and his men gathered the weapons and turned out the prisoners.

"Sandy M'Kethe," said Barscob when they'd gone, "ye ken that we've not seen the last of this?"

"Aye," answered Duncan's father.

"What we've begun, we must needs finish," said Barscob, gripping Sandy M'Kethe's arm. "We'll need the likes of ye and yer boy to finish it."

"Aye," was all Duncan's father said as they covered Grier, led the horse out of the barn into the drizzle, and headed up the lane toward home.

"Can we count on ye?" Barscob called after them.

"I'm a peace-loving man," Duncan's father called without

turning around. "I'll not say more until I've . . . until I've talked with my Father about it."

They walked on in silence for some time. Mercifully, the drizzle ended as they emerged from the forest.

"Father," said Duncan. "What made the difference?"

"The difference in what, lad?"

"Fighting. Ye ken—taking up arms."

His father sighed deeply before answering.

"God's Law tells us to love our enemies. But it also tells us to love God and our neighbor. It's not so easy to ken when those commands seem to come in conflict, Duncan. But I believe as God is my judge, it was a matter of loving our neighbor that made it necessary for us to take up arms against our enemy. And ye might say that restraining our enemy from doing evil by stopping them from roasting Grier alive was a way of loving them as well."

"But what happens next?" asked Duncan. "When Turner hears of it, he's sure to wreak vengeance on ye—on us. I wouldn't wonder if that vengeance'll make past plundering look like midges' pickings."

"That's why we go home, lad, and pray."

"Will there be a call to arms?" persisted Duncan. "And if there is—can I come?"

"Who'll care for yer mother and the wee ones if ye do?"

Duncan wondered if now was the time to tell his father all about the tunnels and passages below Dunfarg ruin. Instead he asked, "Father, will ye teach me to fight like ye did today, to fight with a sword?"

Duncan looked at the broad back of his father walking just ahead of him. His father made no reply for some moments.

Finally he said, "Duncan, if I can impart to ye strength and skill in fighting the battles of yer soul at the same time, then I'll teach ye."

***

"Whatever's happened to Ancient Grier?" called Duncan's mother as they neared the croft moments later.

Duncan's father explained briefly, leaving out, as Duncan perceived it, all the exciting bits of the fight with the soldiers.

"And though Turner's men won't like it," his father continued as he laid the old man down gently on a chaff-filled mattress in front of the fire, "we'll tend our neighbor just the same."

"We certainly will do," said Duncan's mother. "I've a hot broth simmered and ready for yer supper. It'll revive him. Now, then, Fiona, ye take this bowl of warm water and bathe Ancient Grier's bruises. And may judgment fall on those who gave them to ye."

"I've no bruises," said Grier, though faintly. "And I'll not submit to being hefted about like a sack of oats. Mind ye, the bit of broth sounds inviting, and if ye'd just add a morsel of oatcake with it, I'll be on my way back up to m'own croft."

"Now, hear this Grier," said Duncan's father firmly, but not unkindly, "ye're staying the night right here until ye gain some strength back. I'll hear no protest to the contrary."

"So ye say," grumbled Grier. "Well, then, after supper I'll tell the story of what really happened. Ye've gone and left out all the bits worth telling. Ye'd have been proud o' yer man today, Mary M'Kethe, aye, ye would."

"Drink yer broth, Grier," said Duncan's father.

Weakened and exhausted from his ordeal, no sooner did Grier drink the broth, the old man was sound asleep, much to the relief of Duncan's father. Grier's wheezing snores and worry over what the English might do in retaliation kept most of the occupants of the croft fitful throughout the night.

127

Next morning, Duncan heard his father steal from the croft when all was dark and make for his private place of prayer on the moor. Duncan knew his father would be confidently laying these latest troubles at the Almighty's feet in prayer.

When he awoke later that morning, Ancient Grier loudly insisted on being taken home to his own croft. He assured them that there was nothing wrong with him. So Fiona, Duncan, and his father walked with the sturdy old fellow back up the hill and saw him settled in his cottage. They threshed some of his corn for him, lit his fire, and Fiona prepared a pot of broth and some oatcakes.

"Ye can just leave my claymore here beside my bed," said Grier. "Aye, where I can reach it. I'll not go along so easy the next time. If they hadn't gone and taken me by surprise, strapping young fools, I'd have stretched each of them out on the floor without any of yer help, Sandy M'Kethe—not meaning to sound ungrateful."

Duncan's father smiled as they left the croft.

"Grier's a stout one, bearing up so through such troubles," said his father as he pulled the door closed against the November chill. He looked up at the churning gray and black of the clouds.

"More rain's coming," he said.

Duncan looked up at the menacing clouds, and as he did, his eye caught sight of his castle, its lone tower just visible over the rise to the north. There could never be a better time to tell his father his secret than right now.

"I'd like to show ye something, Father," he said. "And I think ye'd best be seeing it too, Fiona."

"Aye," said his father, following Duncan's gaze. "Up there, is it?"

"I found a secret passage under the old ruins of Dunfarg Castle," Duncan blurted. "Truth is, Brodie found it." Duncan fell silent for a moment. A flood of memories suddenly made him unable to speak.

"I'm thinking it might prove useful someday soon," he said when he'd recovered himself.

"Lead the way, lad," said his father.

Duncan set a brisk pace, leading his father and Fiona into the ruined walls of the castle. Halting near the concealed doorway, Duncan said, "Do ye see anything?"

His father studied the crumbled remains of the castle and turned and looked at Duncan.

"I see only rubble, lad."

Fiona looked at her brother, wondering what secret he was about to reveal to them.

"And if *ye* were looking for it and *didn't* see it," said Duncan, bending over and prying up the concealed door, grunting as he heaved the door open, "no English dragoon will ever find it." Duncan stood proudly next to the gaping entrance.

" 'Tis a clever find, lad," said his father, nodding in approval.

"It looks dark and . . ." said Fiona, peering into the hole. "And, well . . . dark."

His father made a light with his flint, and Duncan took him down below, showing him the gallery he hoped would work for the safekeeping of his family if war came. He explained how the passage seemed to continue, though he had never been all the way to its end.

For months, Duncan and Jamie had been stocking the passages with straw for bedding, old sheepskins for warmth, oats, corn, and tallow candles. Growing more excited, Duncan showed his father and Fiona where everything was. He even showed them how he and Jamie had rigged a way to close the concealed door from inside so that those below would be safe from detection.

"Does anyone else ken this place?" asked his father as they closed up the door.

"Only Jamie." He almost added, "and Brodie," but caught himself before he did. "Oh, and Ancient Grier. We told him all about it, though we didn't show it to him. I wonder if he didn't ken about it already, though."

"I hope we don't have need of it," said his father as they made their way back down the hill and to their croft. "But if it comes to that, Fiona, ye will bring yer mother and Jenny and Angus here. Aye, Duncan, Brodie has done us another noble deed in finding this passage, and ye and Jamie have done well in preparing it for use. I only wish times were such we had no need of it."

THIS IS NO PLAYACTING

If thou, Sharpe, die the common death of men,
I'll burn my bill, and throw away my pen.

James Guthrie

L ater that morning Duncan did his best to herd the
sheep to pasture. It was a lot more work without Brodie.
He scurried wide to the left flank trying to drive them
up the hill to the right—as Brodie used to do. All went well
until three lambs, now nearly as big as their ewes, bolted in
three separate directions—none, however, the direction Duncan wanted them to go. He hesitated, then ran back to try to
round up the stragglers. Meanwhile, the main flock began to
grow wider and meander this way and that. Then, one of the
upstart lambs plunged into the middle of the flock, sending
sheep, bawling and heels kicking, in all directions. Duncan
collapsed in the wet heather. Why did Brodie have to do it?
He felt himself getting angry at Brodie for dying. Then a wave
of loneliness and sorrow swept over him, and he buried his
face in the heather, a lump lodging tremulously in his throat.
No amount of swallowing seemed to get rid of.

With his face close to the ground, he suddenly felt, more

than heard, what sounded like a horse galloping up the path from the village. He sat blot upright and looked down the glen. His pulse quickened. Horse and rider were in sight now. It was no red-coated dragoon. John Maclelland of Barscob came into view, astride one of the soldier's horses and riding hard. He reined in, rocks clattering under the horse's hooves as he vaulted out of the saddle.

He spotted Duncan on the hillside and called, "Duncan, I must see yer father." He was breathing hard from riding, giving an added urgency to his voice.

"I'll get him," said Duncan, scrambling to his feet and running down the hill. But before he got to the door, his father, who had heard the riding, stepped out the door and closed it deliberately.

"What's afoot, Barscob? Ye'll forgive me for not having ye into my cottage, but I'd rather my wife and wee ones heard it from me first."

"So much has happened since yesterday's doings, M'Kethe," said the displaced nobleman.

"Begin after the fight," said Duncan's father. "I ken well enough the fighting part."

"We returned to the Clachan Inn, and fearing soldiers from the nearby garrison would soon hear from Deanes and take vengeance on the crofters throughout Dalry and all Glenkens, I thought it well to spread a word of warning. Word reached worshipers at a field meeting near Balmaclellan led by the young probationer, Alexander Robertson. Several young men, fearing violent reprisals if local soldiers heard the news first, decided to beat the soldiers to their vengeance by attacking the small garrison before they heard."

"They did what?" asked Duncan's father, hardly able to take in what Barscob said.

"One soldier was killed in the scuffle," continued Barscob.

"They seized valuables and, I fear, now necessary arms from the garrison. I fear the hand is played, and we must go forward in defense of justice for all those faithful to the Covenant—or be killed. Sandy M'Kethe, I believe it has come to that. We fight now, or Turner sweeps through with a bloody fury unimagined before now. All is lost if we don't fight—now. Too much has happened . . ." His voice trailed away.

Duncan looked at his father's steady eyes and furrowed brow. He saw no fear in his father's eyes. Duncan knew his father's hope was too firmly in the Lord to fear what men might do to him. Duncan watched the muscles of his father's jaw tighten and loosen. But he knew what question troubled his father's mind: what might Turner do to Duncan's mother and to the rest of his family while he was away fighting?

Right then John Neilson of Corsock rode up, followed by several other men mounted on farm ponies. They fairly bristled with pistols, swords, and muskets—most seized from the local garrison.

"Ye've heard all, then," said Neilson, seeing Barscob already there.

"I don't ken if I've heard all," said Duncan's father slowly.

"Word is Deanes will have arrived at Turner's in Dumfries by tonight," said Neilson, still astride his horse. "He'll tell a tale that will bring Turner in full fury down on us all. Like as not, he may be, as we speak, spinning some yarn about Barscob, here, shooting him for not signing the Covenant. Be sure there will be nothing told about the cruel provocation against Grier that started all this. We can expect no justice from Turner. It truly is fight or die, Sandy. I hope ye see that."

John Kilbride, his son Jamie, and many more of the fugitives living in the hills above Glenkens gathered around to listen.

"Might not we march to Edinburgh and seek justice from

the King's Council?" suggested Duncan's father. "If no justice is found, then we fight. At least then, as much as it depends on us, we'll have done all to live peaceably with all men."

"But the King's Council will never listen," said Barscob, "unless we have sufficient might to force their attention. Archbishop Sharpe, betrayer of the Covenant, hates our cause and will do all to crush what he'll, no doubt, call a revolt against the king. I fear the king's set up a cruel monster against the Covenant, a monster with Sharpe at the head and Turner at the tail. We must be in arms."

"And we must muster our forces near Dumfries first," said Neilson, "before Turner gathers his strength to oppose us. If we march to Edinburgh now, Turner will destroy everything in his path—including our wives and bairns left undefended here in Galloway. There's no time to lose."

"We need yer help, Sandy," said Barscob. "For the glory of God and the defense of his Kirk, we need yer help."

"Aye, and ye need ours," said Ian Troon, stepping forward, his eyes flashing eagerly.

"How's that?" said Duncan's father.

"I don't need to remind ye," replied Ian, "that yer exploits with the sword, a coming to the aid of Grier, is ken by all. And it'll be ken by Turner. Ye'll be one of the first to hang if we don't fight now."

"Like ye, Sandy, I don't share Ian's relish of the fight for its own sake," said Barscob. "But ye and I would be first on the list of those to hang for yesterday's rescue of Grier."

Duncan's father looked at Duncan. If Father and Barscob would be first to hang, thought Duncan, would Turner learn what I did—and hang me too? Duncan felt a constriction in his throat and swallowed hard.

Barscob took Duncan's father aside. They spoke earnestly together. On more than one occasion, Barscob gestured toward Duncan. Finally, his father turned and signaled for Duncan to join them.

"Lord Barscob needs a runner, Duncan." His father put both of his big hands on Duncan's shoulders and looked steadily into Duncan's eyes. "A runner who's fleet of foot, one who kens how to scatter to the mist when trouble's near, but who can spread the word to meet near Dumfries at the kirk in Irongray. This is no playacting, lad. Do ye be willing?"

"Aye," said Duncan, too excited to say anything else.

"What men do ye have?" asked Duncan's father.

"Fifty-four men—I hesitate to call them cavalry—but fifty-four men will ride with me," said Barscob.

"And with yer near thirty fugitives joining," said Neilson, "we are one hundred fifty strong on foot."

"We'll need more," said Duncan's father simply.

"And that's where Duncan can help," Barscob said, patting Duncan on the shoulder.

"When do I go?" asked Duncan.

"Ye must go now," said Barscob. "There is no time to lose."

For the next half hour, Barscob drew a map with the names of villages friendly to the covenanting cause in the thirty-some miles between Dalry and Dumfries. Duncan's father quizzed him on his knowledge of the route he would take until he was satisfied that Duncan knew where he was going and what he was to say when he got there.

"Remember, lad," said his father, "it's not a rising. We are in arms for a broken Covenant and a persecuted Kirk. We are loyal to the king as God's servant in civil matters, but loyal to Christ in all matters of the Kirk. We are in defensive arms only. This is not to be mistaken for a rebellion. Remember, lad, make clear—this is no rebellious rising. Our goal is peace with the English—not war."

After a tearful good-bye to his mother, Fiona, Jenny, and

little Angus, Duncan listened as his father prayed for God's mercy to rest on Duncan, on the family, and on his oppressed Kirk. Fiona would be responsible to take the family to the Dunfarg mines if and when they needed to flee. Duncan's father would march that very afternoon and well into the night to Irongray kirk where the Covenanters were to gather. Duncan, alone, would carry the word over moors and through glens to all friendly supporters of the cause.

Duncan watched Neilson and Robertson as they tried to form some rank and order out of the army of ragtag farmers. Some were armed only with pitchforks, scythes, and other farm implements. Precious few had any military experience. For a moment, Duncan thought of how disappointed Grier would be to find out he was left behind. He caught sight of Jamie's stocky frame, easily identifiable by the side-to-side rising and falling of his shoulders, as he made his way stoutly with his crooked leg. Jamie turned and waved.

"Godspeed, Duncan," he called with a grin. "We meet in Dumfries."

With a last wave at all in general, Duncan turned and ran off.

Once away from his family, that confusing lump in his throat dissolved, and in its place rose a thrill he could hardly contain. He finally had a part to play in striking back at the tyranny of the English king. He wiped the rain, now falling in steady sheets, from his face. It would help keep him cool as he ran.

His first stop came a few short miles away in the village of New Galloway where the River Ken flowed into the north end of Loch Ken.

"A defensive gathering of men loyal to the Crown rights of King Jesus in his Kirk," he called from the market cross, "meets in Irongray kirk tomorrow. They, like ye, seek justice and peace. All loyal Covenanters come join them—join together in arms."

Duncan swelled with importance as men riddled him with questions, but he was careful to say it was no rising.

From there he ran along the gray waters of Loch Ken, mighty Cairn Edward rising to the west above the loch. He delivered the same message at Airds of Kells, at Walbutt, then staggered into the market square in Knockvennie and gasped out the same message. The rain fell in torrents as night came on. Duncan could not remember being this tired—and hungry. His stomach rumbled, and his head felt light. But he knew he couldn't eat and still run. He'd be sick if he ate now. At Crocketford, he slurred out his message and collapsed at the foot of the market cross.

"Ye'll have to be trying that again, lad," said a kindly farmer. "Didnae understand a word ye said."

"A djefeshive ga—ing loyal t' Crown ri . . ." his voice trailed away.

"Where, lad, just tell us where to go," urged another man.

"Iron—kirk," stammered Duncan. "Dumfries . . ."

"When?"

"Now," was all Duncan could say.

"I'm taking ye to my wife, lad, for food and rest," said the farmer.

"No!" Duncan suddenly felt a surge of energy. Both food and rest sounded almost better than life itself, but he couldn't stop. The more men he called to arms, the more likely their success. And success meant safety for all Covenanters, but especially for his father and Jamie—and their families. So much depended on him continuing, no matter how exhausted he felt.

He drank a mouthful of water from the village well and staggered on. He no longer felt fleet-footed and invincible, but he must keep going. Barscob with his fifty-four mounted men would have arrived some time ago. He wondered how

Neilson's men—how his father and Jamie—faired tramping with heavy loads through all this rain and mud.

Sometime after midnight—now only with great effort putting one bare foot in front of the other—Duncan saw a row of fires burning, the light from the fires casting eerie shadows from tombstones against the stone walls and square tower of Irongray kirk. Men and horses moved in those shadows.

"Duncan!" Barscob's voice sounded above the rain and the din of horses and weary men. "Ye made it, but ye look a frightful sight, lad. Sit ye down here. By my calculations, ye must have ran some thirty-five miles since leaving Dalry over ten hours ago. Ye've done well, lad."

The kindly nobleman covered Duncan in a thick wool blanket, and within minutes he set a hot bowl of broth and a hunk of brown bread before him. Slowly at first, Duncan drank some of the broth. His face and lips felt numb, and warm trickles ran down his chin and neck as he tried to drink. But he couldn't remember when he'd tasted anything quite so good. Tired though he was, the food soon revived him enough to answer Barscob's questions.

"Do ye have any idea of the number of men that may come from the villages ye ran through?" asked Barscob eagerly. "And how well armed will they be?"

Duncan had no idea. He tried to listen to other questions fired at him by Barscob and others. Gradually, the warm broth seeped into every joint and muscle throughout his weary body. Soon all faded—the questions, the noise of horses and weapons, the fires sputtering as the rain fell on—it all faded into the welcome oblivion of sleep.

PRIMED PISTOL

It is impossible to give the details of the cruelties and
inhuman usage the poor people suffered from this butcher
[Sir James Turner], for so he was rather than a soldier.
Daniel Defoe

So much happened in the next hours, rising to such great
consequences, that Duncan could barely take it all in.

While Duncan slept, a mysterious fellow who called
himself "Captain" Andrew Gray made his way into their
camp, produced a military commission, and, during the
night's deliberations, effectively appointed himself commander of the company. Urged on by this Captain Gray, it was
decided that as soon as Neilson arrived with the foot soldiers, they would march to Dumfries, catch Turner by surprise, and do what might be done to ensure that no reprisals
would come from that quarter. The little army would then
march on to Edinburgh and seek redress for the grievances of
the Kirk.

As Duncan came fully awake and looked around at the
bustle of men and horses, he noticed the welcome presence of
several of the field preachers who had come for the spiritual

support and comfort of the men. Duncan had seen and heard some of them at conventicles he had attended with his family: John Blackadder, outed minister of Traquair; all Scotland had heard of Gabriel Semple, outed minister of Kirkpatrick of the Muir, who had been providentially delivered from prison at Edinburgh Castle after defying the king's bloody Counsel with the words, "My God will not let you either kill or banish me." It was widely known, and Duncan loved the story, that in a day when executions of covenanting ministers were all too commonplace, Mr. Semple was inexplicably set free ten months later. Large crowds gathered throughout the countryside to hear him preach. And there stood the fiery Alexander Peden, often called the Prophet of the Covenant, talking with Barscob and Gray, his claymore and pistol at his belt, musket in hand.

Then Duncan caught sight of Mr. Crookshanks reading Scripture with a small group of men nearby. The field preacher looked up. Signaling with his head, he invited Duncan to join them.

For an instant, Duncan hesitated. The last time he'd seen Mr. Crookshanks was the day the dragoon captain killed Brodie, he recalled, walking toward the group. He listened to the field preacher's reading: " 'Because ye have made the Lord, who is my refuge, even the Most High yer habitation, no evil shall befall ye . . .' "

While he listened, a scout rode up and announced that Neilson's men approached less than a mile away. Duncan's heart quickened. The news was heartily received, and when some time later the din of approving voices settled, Mr. Crookshanks resumed reading: " 'For He shall give His angels charge over ye, to keep ye in all yer ways. They shall bear ye up in their hands, lest ye strike yer foot against a stone . . .' "

"They've come!" one man called, excitement in his voice. "Neilson and the men of foot have come!"

Duncan clambered atop the tallest tombstone and peered eagerly at the haggard faces of the one hundred fifty men. In among the drooped shoulders and rain-drenched recruits, Duncan spotted Jamie. He'd walked all that way on his twisted leg. Then he caught sight of his father.

Elbowing through the sodden mass of men and supplies, Duncan made his way eagerly to his father's side.

"Ye've come safe, lad," said his father, smiling at him and running a big hand lovingly over Duncan's red locks. "With every step I took, I prayed for ye, Duncan. And God has sent his angels to guard yer feet from stumbling. Praise be to his merciful name."

Mr. Crookshanks joined them briefly and offered a prayer of thanksgiving with Neilson and all the men for safety through their long night march. Duncan noticed that the field preacher now wore a claymore at his hip.

Captain Gray ordered all the men to muster and prepare to march on to Dumfries.

"We'll set upon that monster while he's still in his bed," he barked. "Then we'll heap on his head a taste of the injuries he's dumped on yer kind these years. Galloway and the Lowlands will be avenged."

Duncan's father scowled at Gray.

"Who is this man?" he asked Mr. Crookshanks.

"I donnae ken," said the field preacher, eyeing the captain. "He claims to have a commission and military experience, as he claims to own the Covenant, though I ken nothing of the man before now. In any event, we'll not march out without committing our way to God."

Then the big field preacher boomed so all could hear.

" 'God shall arise!' And before we arise against the enemies of the Kirk, let us sing our confidence in God our Redeemer—and our true Captain!"

The weary marchers joined in the psalm, Duncan and Jamie lifting their voices with the rest. It is difficult to describe the collective voices of those faithful but desperate men that morning, rain washing down their faces, chilled and bone weary though they were. But Duncan thought that as they sang, so deeply flooded the sacred words into their souls, that from their lips sprang confidence and hope, the psalm giving inspired expression to that hope, sung with all the passion and vigor so characteristic of firm Scottish piety.

God shall arise and by his might,
Put all his enemies to flight . . .
In conquest shall he quell them . . .

***

Though Duncan's father made it very clear that Duncan and Jamie were along to guard the baggage, to carry supplies, to aid the wounded if it came to that, they were permitted to march alongside their fathers as the two hundred strong made their way over the Devorgilla Bridge and into the town of Dumfries. Of the two boys, Duncan had the most difficulty containing his excitement at being on the march and part of a real company of men in arms.

"This is the real thing, Jamie," said Duncan over the sloshing of feet in the mud, the tramp of horse, and the clangings and creakings of weapons and supplies.

"Aye," agreed Jamie simply.

"Halt!" cried Captain Gray from astride his horse. The word to halt was carried down the ranks of the little bedraggled company.

Somehow Gray already knew in what house Turner had quartered himself, and Gray had already forged a plan. He,

Barscob, and Neilson handpicked a small advance company of men to surround the house of Bailie Finnie where Turner still slept.

"I'd go anywhere with Sandy M'Kethe," Duncan heard Barscob say to the self-appointed Commander Gray as they walked along inspecting the rows of weary men.

Gray signaled for Duncan's father to fall in.

"Can I come, Father?" asked Duncan.

"Duncan, ken yer place, lad," said his father, his arm across Duncan's shoulder. "Ye and Jamie must do yer duty, small or great though that duty may seem to ye. Ye are not to do the fighting this time, lad. Do yer duty, and pray God to show ye how to love yer enemies—and give him glory in the doing of what ye must."

"Haste ye back, Father," Duncan called after as his father joined the advance company.

Duncan watched his father prime his pistol and draw his sword to check the blade. Duncan looked both ways, then inched away from the main body of men. He drew closer until he could just hear what was being said.

"The hour's still early for the likes of Turner," said Neilson.

"Aye, he'll not be at any praying," said Gray, "at least none directed to God above, of that we can be certain. Now then, men, we surround the house, muskets loaded. He's like to have only a few soldiers with him, and they lolling on their pillows, unprepared for any armed rising of this sort."

"With all respect, Gray," broke in Duncan's father. "This is no rising!" He looked steadily at the commander. "We are in defensive arms seeking peace and justice for Christ's persecuted Kirk."

The commander snorted. "Call it what ye will, man, Sharpe and Turner'll call it a rising—so will the king and his bloody Counsel at Edinburgh."

"They'll have a harder time calling it a rising," retorted Duncan's father, "if we leave off brutality and violence and conduct ourselves like Christian men seeking lawful redress."

"We're not here to murder Turner," said Barscob. "But we must stop him from leading his troops in a wide-scale plunder of all the south and west country of Scotland. That's what he'll do, make no mistake of it, if we don't stop him."

"Oh, I intend to stop him," said Gray, an evil sneer on his features.

"We'll not be a part of murder, Gray," said Neilson. "Sandy's right. If fight we must, that fighting must be in keeping with God's Word. It's of little use seeking justice if we set about it unjustly."

"Sorry lot," muttered Gray under his breath.

"Aye, no point in our claiming to defend the Covenant," said Duncan's father, "while breaking God's Law in the defending of it."

"Fine talk," snorted Gray. "This'll fire the blood of the troops, indeed."

"We'll not follow ye," said Duncan's father, "if ye're plotting evil in yer heart, even against a monster like Turner."

"Aye, give yer word they'll be no murder," said Barscob, "no robbery, no plundering of persons' belongings. Then we'll follow ye."

"So ye'll seize no weapons to arm my men?" asked Gray in a mocking, singsong tone. "Ye'd call that robbery, I presume."

"We must disarm Turner and his garrison," said Neilson, "and arm ourselves if we are to be heard. But we've no hope of being heard, Gray, if we do all with bloody intent."

"We're Christian men, Gray," said Duncan's father, "seeking peace and justice. And we will honor King Jesus in how we seek it."

"I'll not stand around talking when there is fighting to be

144

done," said Gray. "I, for one, am a man of action. If ye are to get yer justice, then we must act now. I'll try to bear yer scruples in mind. Now then, men, we surround the house. I give the orders. Follow me."

Duncan ran along, finding cover down the narrow passages leading off the main street, keeping his father and the dozen or so men as near in sight as he could manage. They halted at what must be Bailie Finnie's house. Gray gave a silent signal with his arm to surround the house. He pointed his musket in the air.

Duncan jumped as a shot shattered the silence of the morning, its retort rattling off the stone walls of the houses lining the street.

"You dog, Turner!" barked Gray. "Your house is surrounded with angry Covenanters—from Galloway. They're all armed and itching for your blood. Come out peaceably, and I'll do what I can to hold them off."

What? thought Duncan. It was Gray who seemed to be itching for Turner's blood, not the other way around. And Gray had as much as named them.

"Ye may have fair quarter," Duncan heard Neilson call out.

A voice answered from inside the house: "I was unaware there was a war on, and if no war, how can I be a prisoner and in need of quarter?"

"Suit yourself, Turner," barked Gray again. "Be a prisoner—or die!" To back up the threat, Gray flourished his sword in the air and banged the hilt sharply against the door. "And be quick about deciding which it'll be."

From where Duncan squatted across the street, he watched the door open slowly and out stepped Sir James Turner into the drizzly morning. The terror of the Covenant, oppressor of the Kirk, the man who had made himself feared throughout the Lowlands, stood in a puddle of water before

145

the door, lifting and shaking first one stocking foot and then the other. He reminded Duncan of a cat that has just stepped in water. The rain began soaking his loose-fitting nightshirt, and his nightcap drooped over his extravagant curls. Face red with rage, he stared defiantly at Gray and the little company of men.

By this time the remainder of the band of Covenanters, as planned, gathered around the house, blades drawn and pistols primed. So many of these men and their families had suffered so much at the hands of Turner, Duncan held his breath, wondering what would happen next.

"With a word, I could turn them lose on you, Turner," said Gray, a swagger in his tone. "They'd tear you apart, slowly and deliberately, one popping joint at a time—and ye'd deserve it all."

Turner looked around at the mass of haggard men closing in around him. His face grew pale.

"However, merciful man that I am," continued Gray, sauntering up close to Turner. "I will simply dispatch you with one quick, relatively painless shot." He raised his pistol to Turner's trembling head and cocked the hammer. Turner, though an expert on cruelty to others, grew pale. His eyes pinched shut as he waited, and dribbles of rain fell from the tip of his prominent nose.

SHOOT THE MONSTER!

As pants the hart for cooling streams
When heated in the chase,
So longs my soul, O God, for thee,
And thy refreshing grace.

Scottish Psalter (42)

Y e shall as soon shoot me!" cried Neilson. "I'm a man of my word and I gave him quarter."

"Put down the pistol, Gray," said Duncan's father.

"Monster that Turner is," said Barscob, "we'll none of us stand by while ye murder him in cold blood. We'll all hang for sure if ye shoot him."

Gray snorted in disgust and lowered his pistol.

"Clear the house. Make prisoners of all within," ordered Gray.

"I'll march my men to the garrison and seize what weapons we find there," said Barscob.

"We need arms—" said Gray. Duncan heard him add under his breath, "and men willing to use them might help."

"Here and now we must pledge our allegiance to the Crown rights of our Redeemer," called Mr. Crookshanks.

"Aye, to the market cross, to pledge the Covenant," called out the young field preacher Alexander Robertson.

"I've some business to attend to," said Gray. "But I'd be most honored, Sir James Turner, if ye'd ride astride my noble steed and join the rest at the market cross."

Duncan scowled at Gray. Something wasn't right about him. It seemed to Duncan that Gray might actually be playacting through all this. It even seemed to Duncan that Gray spoke somewhat differently now that he had seized Turner.

Turner looked in disgust at the bony Galloway nag Gray offered. "I'd rather crawl."

"But ride you shall," said Gray, nodding for assistance and hoisting Turner onto the bare back of the pathetic beast.

Turner's nightshirt was soaked through, and rainwater dribbled from the limp toes of his stockings. In the drenching cold, Turner's teeth chattered, making his fleshy, dimpled chin quiver pathetically. For a fleeting instant, Duncan actually felt sorry for him. He watched as Turner was led away, the most reluctant of participants in the proceedings that would follow.

All this time, Duncan had stood just around the corner of the house where Turner only moments ago had slept. When the men cleared off down the street, Duncan peered around the corner and watched Gray closely. Sneering back down the street at the disappearing mob, the commander then turned and deliberately entered the house. Duncan moved to the window and peeked through a gap in the curtain. He watched as Gray drew his sword and in a single stroke bashed open what must be Turner's chest. Then Gray bent over and ransacked the contents, scattering papers, lace collars, and stockings about the room. After a moment he stood up with a smaller chest in both hands, pried it open, and threw his head back in laughter. Duncan caught sight of the contents as the man turned. Gold coins overflowed onto the floor.

Duncan hardly believed what he saw. While his father and

the small band of Covenanters pledged their loyalty to uphold the Crown rights of the Redeemer, this self-appointed scoundrel was busy robbing Turner's money, and in the process making all of them look like common thieves. It probably wasn't even Turner's money in the first place, more likely the skimmings of fine money plundered from the faithful in Galloway. But it wasn't Gray's money. That much Duncan knew for sure.

The cracking of musket fire abruptly broke in on his thoughts. Gray spun around. He'd heard it too. Duncan jumped back from the window, turned, and ran down the street toward the market square as fast as his weary legs would go. He heard more musket fire as he neared the square.

The solemn men pledging their loyalty to the king in matters political and to the King of kings over all stared down the street from the direction the shots came. Turner looked hopefully down the street.

"Barscob's engaging the garrison," called Neilson. "We'd best muster to his aid."

"Wait, here he comes now," said another.

"And he's got wagons and horses," said still another.

"Loaded with weapons," said a voice in the crowd.

Duncan thought it sounded like Ian Troon's voice.

"Is there food in those wagons?" one man called.

"Is all well?" asked Duncan's father, as Barscob rode nearer.

"Aye, ye heard the shots," said Barscob. "They put up a fight, not wanting us to walk away with their guns . . . We killed one of theirs," he added quietly.

"Better get used to killing," boomed Gray's voice. He now sat astride Turner's big charger and had just ridden up and heard the news.

Duncan scowled. He wanted to blurt out all he'd just seen.

"What do we do now?" someone gave voice to the question in everyone's mind.

A mangle of voices rose in reply. Some, fearing reprisal from Sharpe and the King's Counsel, wanted to disband. Others insisted that they must finish what they'd begun and march forward to Edinburgh.

"What about Turner?" called one.

"I say we shoot the monster and be done with him," called another.

"Aye, he'll not eat up our supplies of food, then," agreed another.

"We'll kill him over my dead body," called Neilson.

"Now that you have arms enough," said Gray, "we march direct to Edinburgh and seek redress. All will be well."

"Are ye daft, man?" cried Barscob. "We must gather more support if we hope to be heard at Edinburgh. We need more men—men in arms."

"I say we return to Galloway," Neilson said. "And march through the friendliest villages there and in Ayrshire seeking all who will join us."

By this time, Duncan had worked his way through the mass of men and horses and had rejoined his father. Jamie stood nearby and greeted Duncan with a grin.

"Father!" said Duncan urgently. He told his father the whole story of what he'd seen Gray do back at Turner's house.

"Scoundrel as I thought," said Duncan's father grimly.

"Many more will join us in Galloway," Neilson continued urging above the din.

"To Galloway!" Duncan's father and John Kilbride called loudly.

If they returned to Dalry, Duncan thought, they could see that all was well with their families.

"To Galloway!" Duncan and Jamie joined them.

"To Galloway!" More joined in the cry.

CHOSEN FEW

Let the world deride or pity,
I will glory in thy Name.

John Newton

Thursday, November 15, 1666, descended into darkness and night as the weary men marched the thirty-two miles back over the sodden moors to Dalry. Exhausted from having run all that distance only hours before, Duncan wanted to give up and collapse facedown in the mud and sleep many times throughout that long night. However, the sight of Jamie forging on ahead of him kept him on his feet. They talked little.

He overheard his father and John Kilbride, in guarded tones, discussing Captain Gray.

"For all we ken he's a Royalist, hired to stir things into a rebellion," said John Kilbride. "Then the English would feel just in wiping out the lot of us."

"If he'd had his way, Turner'd be dead," said Duncan's father. "And we'd all be to blame for it, with all possibility of a peaceful resolve with the king lost forever."

"But why would a Royalist kill another Royalist?" asked Kilbride.

"I donnae ken," said Duncan's father. "Maybe Turner's out of favor with Sharpe, and this is a way of killing off two birds with but one stone—we Covenanters being the other bird."

"But how to go about exposing Gray for the thief and scoundrel that he is?" said John Kilbride.

They marched on in silence.

***

"Now then, lads," boomed Gray as they neared the village of Dalry. "I turn you loose to plu—, that is, to gather supplies from the surrounding crofters. Remember you fight in a good cause, and for any you meet who might think otherwise and show themselves reluctant to contribute . . . You have my permission to compel them," he said, patting the hilt of his sword. "Ye'll be helping them do the right thing for the cause. Now be off with you."

"Hold!" cried Barscob. "We'll have no plundering of another man's goods. Aye, we'll need supplies—food, drink, and all the wool blankets ye can spare from yer *own* homes," said Barscob to the men. "But we'll none of us stoop to plundering our neighbors."

"Aye, no sense in our fighting for justice against the oppressors of the Kirk," said Duncan's father, eyeing Gray levelly, "if we're behaving just like them—*robbing* others of what's not ours."

Gray grumbled and looked darkly at Barscob and Duncan's father.

"Reassemble west of the river in the field just north of the village—well before nightfall," said Neilson to the weary men. He stationed men to guard Turner and dismissed the rest with, "And God be with ye."

***

Duncan and his father, along with the other fugitives from the remoter hills around the Glenkens, marched off, more eager to see their families and plan for their safety than to gather food and warm clothing. As they passed by the river near the kirk, Duncan and Jamie slipped away and hailed the widow Ferryman.

"What have ye heard, Mrs. Nothing?" asked Duncan.

"Tables have turned on Turner," she said with a smile.

"How'd ye ken that?" he asked.

The old lady winked at the boys. "Speak less; hear more," she said knowingly.

"Mrs. Nothing," said Duncan, an idea occurring to him. "If ye heard that dragoons were coming, and we men were away fighting"—he liked the sound of that—"we men were away fighting, could ye get word up the brae to our families— so they could scatter? If ye could get word to my sister Fiona, she kens where to go."

"I'll hear all I can, and I'll do all I can," said Mrs. Nothing.

"Thank ye," called Duncan as he and Jamie hurried off to rejoin the men.

Duncan and his father spent the next two hours with Duncan's mother, his sisters, and little Angus. His father assured his mother that there had been little danger, though what lay ahead was unknown to them.

"We rest content to ken that if we honor the Lord by seeking justice with just means," he said soothingly, "God will honor his bairns. He honors those who honor him. He goes before us, Mary, m'love. Fix yer hope on him alone—come what may."

Meanwhile, little Angus had fixed his eyes on his father's claymore and pistols.

Clutching his little bow in his fist, he said stoutly, "Father, I'm big enough to come fight." He almost tottered over as he stretched himself up to his full height, his chin jutting upward.

Duncan's father assured Angus that he was needed at home to help and care for his mother and sisters. Much more was said, and tears were shed when it was time for Duncan and his father to be off.

"God be with ye, Duncan," whispered Fiona.

As they descended the hill, Duncan wondered what lay ahead and when he might see them all again. He was grateful for the drizzle that fell on his face as he turned for one last look at his mother, Fiona, Jenny, and wee Angus standing at the door of their croft, looking anxiously after them. Oh, how he wished Brodie were there to help care for his family.

Word spread rapidly throughout the region of the seizure of Turner, and when all the men had gathered that evening, twenty or thirty more eager men had joined the ranks. Neilson had dispatched several scouts to watch the hills around the makeshift encampment along the river. While the men took stock of weapons, food, and other supplies, a mounted scout came galloping into the camp. He bolted from the saddle.

"Red coats—" he gasped for breath. "Red coats spotted, approaching from Loch Howie."

"Prepare to march!" called Neilson.

"We ride ahead to find a more defensible position," said Barscob.

"Head for the wilds north, hard by Carsphairn," said John Kilbride. "We'll find cover there."

"To Carsphairn, then," called Neilson and Barscob together.

Only later would any of the men learn of the ruthless retaliations already set in motion by the English. The redcoats just spotted near Dalry would prove only to be men from the local garrison, small in number, and with Turner held prisoner, there was little a handful of redcoats could hope to do against the growing numbers of Galloway Covenanters.

However, word of all that had transpired had reached the vindictive Archbishop Sharpe in Edinburgh. Since Turner, his commander, was taken, Sharpe promptly chose Lieutenant-General Dalyell as his new commander in chief, and the notorious Drummond as his assistant. Sharpe declared the desperate Galloway farmers incorrigible traitors, and their deeds he dubbed a rebellious rising. He further ordered that all involved were to be put to death without mercy or pardon.

Meanwhile, another bone-numbing night march lay ahead for the hopeful Covenanters. They headed this time north to Carsphairn, where the troublemaker Captain Gray disappeared, never to be heard of again. Nor was Turner's gold ever seen again. After an anxious night camped out on the barren moors, the men made their way to the village of Dalmellington, where they encamped November eighteenth—the Sabbath.

On that same day, two thousand five hundred Royalist foot soldiers and six troops of dragoons under Dalyell and Drummond left Edinburgh and marched west with orders to hunt down and crush all rebels.

***

With the blessing of the locals, the inn at Dalmellington became an impromptu headquarters for Barscob and Neilson, and a place where they kept Turner under guard.

Duncan and Jamie had been ordered to be on hand to carry messages for Barscob and Neilson. Though relieved to be rid of Gray, neither of these good men felt capable of the military leadership required for success. They commissioned two others, Ross and Shields, to go and search for more recruits—and for military leaders sympathetic with the covenanting cause. Ross and Shields did not return. Unknown by the rest, they were captured, speedily tried, and hanged as rebels at Kilmarnoch. The search for a leader would go on.

Duncan and Jamie, glad to be indoors where a warm coal fire burned cheerily, waited on the needs of Barscob, Neilson, Mr. Crookshanks, and other field preachers as they scanned maps and debated over strategy. For the last hour Duncan stood at a table in the corner of the inn, the assistant to Turner's guard. Turner sat brooding at the table, his guard eyeing him with pistol ever at the ready. Duncan's job was to be the secondary to the guard, keeping his eyes on Turner, who might try to disarm the guard. It was Duncan's job to nudge the guard if his attention waned or if his head nodded in weariness.

Duncan shifted from one bare foot to the other, for the last several minutes Turner had kept eyeing him. Duncan couldn't help hating the man, but the seed of pity had been sown when Turner was first taken, and Gray *had* robbed and humiliated him.

"Lad," Turner spoke.

Surely not to me, thought Duncan, looking over his shoulder for Jamie or another of the boys who had recently joined the march.

"You, lad," said Turner again. "What think you of my circumstances? You look an intelligent enough lad. What would you do in my place? Speak, lad."

Duncan swallowed. "What circumstances is that . . . sir?"

"Come lad, look at my bonds," said Turner. "I'm a prisoner of desperate men—you among them—and more than once they've threatened to kill me. What think you, I ask?"

Duncan looked warily at the long defiant nose and haughty eyes, the dimpled chin and the sneering mouth. But behind it all, Duncan thought he detected a sincerity in the man's expression. Duncan thought of what his father would say to any man—hell-hound or otherwise—who asked such a question.

"James Turner, sir," began Duncan, "ye're like to die sooner than later, sir."

"True enough, lad," said Turner. "But what ought I to do?"

"Repent," said Duncan simply.

"Repent?" said Turner, a smile playing at the corner of his mouth. "Of what?"

"Breaking God's Law, sir."

"And, tell me, lad, how have I—loyal subject of his Majesty the King—how have I broken God's Law?"

How would his father reply? He thought of Turner's great evils against the Kirk. But what of those who had never done such great and public evils? Did only those who did great crimes need to repent? Duncan knit his brow in thought.

"We all of us are violators of God's Law," he began. "We are proud, and we think more highly of ourselves than of Christ and our neighbor." Duncan listed more sins that all men commit, but as he spoke he began to think more of his own sins. "We . . . that is, I am impatient and walk by sight rather than by faith. I am vengeful, not waiting for God to avenge in perfect justice . . ."

"This is a merry list of sinning, lad," said Turner when Duncan finally paused for breath. "Tell me, how ever is one to be rid of such heinous offenses?"

Duncan recalled something he'd heard his father say. Mr. Crookshanks and other field preachers said it often, too.

"There is nothing ye or I can do to be rid of our sins, so great are they," said Duncan.

"Then my case is hopeless?" said the prisoner.

"Only when ye truly believe that it is hopeless—will ye have hope," said Duncan. "God has extended his mercy widely—on all his elect."

"Aha," said Turner, slapping his palm on the table, "but how do I know if I am one of the chosen few, lad?"

"As things stand just now," said Duncan, "neither ye nor I ken whether ye are elect or no."

"Then who does know?" asked Turner, looking slightly more sober.

"God who did the electing," replied Duncan.

"Then I simply sit back, do as I please, and let God move the pieces about the cosmic chessboard. That's it, is it? Well, if that's it, what good is my repentance?"

"Like King Charles of England, sir, ye're wanting to stand in the place of God," said Duncan. What was it his father often quoted from Mr. Rutherford? "Ye must understand," continued Duncan, warming to the discussion. "Duties are ours, but events are God's."

"Hold on a moment, lad. You are leaving me behind. What does that mean?"

Duncan frowned in thought before replying.

"It means God chooses, but no man who doesn't humble himself, turn from his sins, and seek repentance is among the chosen."

"Ah, lad, ye've done well—for a Presbyterian, that is," laughed Turner. "But it's hard to turn a Turner!"

Whatever hint of sincerity Duncan thought he had detected in the man vanished. Turner threw his head back and laughed heartily. Duncan felt the fire come into his face.

"While ye laugh at this young lad's witness to ye," boomed

Mr. Crookshanks, who had been listening in, "ye forget yer original question, man. Ye are like to die for yer heinous crimes and oppressions against Christ and his Kirk, for which God is angry and will judge ye in hell. And this lad's been telling ye how to repent and leave off all yer sinning. Shame on ye, Turner. Shame on ye for persecuting those who've made conscience to keep the Covenant, and shame on ye for the mocking of this lad—and the gospel."

Turner sneered at the minister.

"But think of all the enjoyment I shall provide you whilst I burn and crackle in hell fire," he laughed once again. "Now then, bring me a pint of ale and some food. Whereupon, I'd be most appreciative if one of you ministers might offer a prayer of blessing and thanksgiving for it—this being the Sabbath, or had you all in your frenzy to rebel against his Majesty the King, God's anointed, had you forgotten it was the Sabbath? Now then, we must have some praying here, and perhaps a sermon and some psalm singing thrown in for good measure."

Duncan ground his teeth together. He wanted to grab the pistol from the guard and use it on the monster.

Just then, Mr. Welsh of Irongray entered the inn.

"I'll not cast my pearls before swine," said Mr. Crookshanks, looking fiercely at Turner. "But perhaps Mr. Welsh here, since ye haven't had to listen to this man's most recent blasphemies, perhaps ye'd do the honor of leading us in a prayer of grace for the meal."

"Turner, I regret to hear that a man so deserving of death for his crimes against the Kirk," said Mr. Welsh, holding his Bible near the fire, doing his best to dry out the pages. "I regret that ye'd no room for repentance. Ye shall surely die, sooner or later, and do ye desire to join the ranks of those already in hell whose peculiar crime was the persecuting of

Christ's Kirk? Ye'll not find them merry company, man, of that I assure ye."

Mr. Welsh continued with his urgings before praying with Turner. To Duncan's great relief, he and Jamie were sent on an errand and so left Turner and the interior of the inn behind.

The damp November air struck Duncan full in the face, bringing some cooling to his temper.

"Ye spoke well, Duncan," said Jamie, ambling through the camp at his friend's side.

"But I can't help hoping Turner pays for his crimes," said Duncan. "I find myself hoping, Jamie, that he's not one of God's elect—that he burns in hell!"

"I understand, Duncan. But think more of yer own sins—sins committed in defiance of God's covenanted mercy to ye, and ye'll find more place for the loving of yer enemies."

"Aye. Loving yer enemies . . . That's no easy thing, Jamie."

DUNCAN'S FALL

That soul that on Jesus hath leaned for repose,
I will not, I will not desert to his foes;
That soul, though all hell should endevour to shake,
I'll never, no never, no never forsake.
Rippon's Selection on Hymns

Two more days of weary marching over the barren and lonely moors found the little army in south Ayrshire. They followed the rising waters of the River Doon to where the high-arching stone bridge—the Brig o' Doon—crossed, and the road led north to Ayr.

Barscob, Neilson, and Crookshanks, looking anxiously at the darkening clouds, deliberated for several moments, then called a halt.

Mr. Crookshanks lifted his voice in heavenly petition for God's hand to guide and keep them in their distress. He specifically prayed that God would grant them a leader worthy of his cause, to which request Barscob and Neilson were first to offer a hearty "Amen." When the prayer ended, men collapsed in exhaustion on both sides of the bridge.

"I like Mr. Crookshanks," said Jamie, his legs dangling

center-arch on the bridge. Duncan lay in a heap next to his friend and only grunted in reply.

After Duncan had thought about this for a moment, he sat up, looking puzzled.

"Crookshanks," he said slowly, looking a little shyly at his friend. They almost never talked about Jamie's leg. "Crookshanks. I'd never put that together before now," said Duncan. "It was just a name."

"Och, Duncan, it's not so much his name," said Jamie, looking at the bend in his leg as he spoke. "It's his faith in God and his love of King Jesus and his Kirk. That's what makes me like Mr. Crookshanks the most."

"Aye," said Duncan, joining his friend in dangling his legs over the bridge. With growing interest, he watched the waters flowing past, and for one moment he wished he had some hooks and a line. There'd be salmon in this river this time of year, he thought—big, fat ones, maybe.

Jamie shuffled in his shoulder bag and pulled out a book.

"Let me read ye something, Duncan," he said.

"What is it?" asked Duncan, eyes searching the water for fish.

"The Letters of Mr. Rutherford. He especially got it right just here," said Jamie, flipping pages as he spoke.

" 'All Christ's bairns go to heaven with a broken brow—' " he paused. "Now listen to what he wrote, Duncan."

"I am listening," said Duncan.

" 'All Christ's bairns go to heaven with a broken brow—and a crooked leg . . .' It's that part about the crooked leg that I like most," said Jamie, smiling as he looked down at his twisted leg.

"What's he mean by it?" asked Duncan, following his friend's gaze.

"We all of us," began Jamie, "well, we all of us have troubles—flaws, I suppose ye'd call them. He doesn't mean everyone's actually got a crooked leg like I do. But, do ye ken something, Duncan? I no longer think of my crooked leg as a curse. Though it is a curse to my body, it's a boon to my soul. God's ordained my crooked leg—my crookshank—so I might give him glory in my weakness. That makes it a great gift given to me by my Lord, that it is, Duncan."

Duncan looked in wonder at his friend's face. It was all lit up with gratitude as though someone had just made him a clan chief. Then, for an instant, Duncan almost envied Jamie his crooked leg. If it came along with that much contentment, I'd take one too, he thought, still looking at Jamie's face.

A sharp cry from a sentry stationed north of the bridge broke up the conversation. Both boys were on their feet straining to hear the cause of the alarm.

"Approaching at full gallop," the sentry called, relaying what a scout had just told him. "A small well-armed company."

"Redcoats?" many men demanded, clutching for their weapons.

"Nay, they carry a banner declaring themselves on the side

163

of—Christ and Covenant!" the sentry replied, his voice cracking with excitement. "We are reinforced!"

Speculation about who it was that came to their aid flew throughout the enthusiastic men.

As every man strained to see who came, Jamie and Duncan nearly had an argument about who would climb on whose shoulders so they might see the reinforcements first.

"Duncan, I'll brook no argument on it," said Jamie.

"Nor will I, Jamie Kilbride," retorted Duncan.

"But I have over ye in weight. I ken I outweigh ye by at least a stone."

Duncan just couldn't let Jamie lift him on his shoulders, not with his leg.

"Oh, it's m'crooked leg, is it?" said Jamie. Then with a great howl and amidst much laughter, Jamie tackled Duncan, finally wrestling him up on his shoulders. Giving in, Duncan sat atop his friend's shoulders and craned to see the approaching men.

Suddenly, round a bend, and breaking out of the forest, rode as stout and well-equipped a company of men as Duncan had ever seen—outside of redcoat uniforms.

"Who is it?" panted Jamie, the strain of Duncan's weight sounding in his voice.

"I donnae ken," said Duncan, awe in his voice. "But the man leading them looks as capable a leader as ever I've seen."

"Reminding ye, Duncan," grunted Jamie, staggering a little under Duncan's weight, "veteran that ye are of less than a week—ye haven't seen many leaders of men."

"Aye, there's that," agreed Duncan. "But who is this man?"

"James Wallace," said Alexander Peden, the field preacher, overhearing Duncan's question. "Aye, 'tis James Wallace, indeed. His lands lie hard by Dundonald Castle, a few miles to the north of here."

"Wallace?" said Jamie. Duncan wobbled precariously as Jamie's attention was drawn away from holding him steady. "Any relation to William Wallace, ye ken, the one from the history books?"

"Aye," laughed Peden. "James Wallace springs from one and the same heroic stock, and that's a fact."

"Is it so!" said Jamie, forgetting that Duncan was perched on his back. Then it happened. Completely distracted by this new information, Jamie unintentionally let go of Duncan's legs.

"Hip, hip, hey, ho! Hey!" gasped Duncan in surprise. Jamie staggered in a circle clutching at his friend's legs. It was too late. Duncan flipped backward off of Jamie's shoulders— and plunged headlong over the mid span of the Brig o' Doon. His arms and legs flailed the air desperately as he fell. "Ooooooh!" he yelled, a cry that ended in a gurgle, and an enormous splash, as he plunged into the deeps of the River Doon below.

The black water closed over him.

Then, spluttering and splashing, and blowing water from his nose and mouth, Duncan surfaced.

"Are ye all right, Duncan," called Jamie anxiously from atop the bridge.

"C-cold," sputtered Duncan. "And w-wet. And, Jamie Kilbride, I'll b-be g-getting ye for this!"

BETRAY 21 AND LIVE

Scots wae hae wi'Wallace bled,
Scots wham Bruce hae often led,
Welcome to your gory bed,
Or to victory!

Robert Burns

D uncan finally made it to the bank of the river and wrung out his plaid and kilt. He looked darkly at his friend.

"I do hope yer not hur—hur—hurt—" Jamie broke into a spasm of laughter.

Duncan waggled his head and half grinned as he watched his friend's amusement.

"Ye should have seen yerself a-flailing off the brig like ye did—" Jamie fell to his knees, weak with laughing. "And then—ga'sploosh!" He roared on, tears now streaming down his face. The men who'd seen the show laughed with him. And, finally, unable to help himself, Duncan soon joined in the fun.

Then, with the sound of champing bits and the blowing and snorting of horses, Wallace brought his company to a stand near the bridge. His keen, sober eyes scanned the scene.

Duncan froze. What would Wallace, who'd come to bring order and discipline to the bedraggled army, what would he do when he saw Duncan soaked from his swim?

"Fine weather for taking a wee swim off the brig," roared Wallace, swinging down off his horse. "And I'm glad to see ye all in such good spirits. It's only the toughest Scots who make bold to go for a swim in late November."

Duncan drew himself up at the compliment. Grinning, Jamie slapped him on the back.

Barscob, Neilson, and Mr. Crookshanks looked the picture of relief at the sight of the veteran commander, James Wallace. They took him into a nearby barn and began briefing him, several sturdy and well-armed military aids never far from his side.

"Tell us more about Wallace," urged Jamie to Mr. Peden.

"Aye, the best of commanders," said Peden, resuming his story. "He was lieutenant colonel in the Parliamentary army and fought in good faith for Christ and Covenanted Presbyterianism under Charles Stuart. Made prisoner, he was, at Dunbar, and there is no Christian soldier alive his equal in piety, patriotism, and love of God's Law and justice. But mind ye, he's a stickler for discipline and drill. He and his officers will have this rag-tag lot marching and maneuvering to the fear and admiration of our enemies."

"Who are the men with him?" asked Duncan.

"That'd be Major Learmont," said Peden. "And no better cavalry commander alive. Next to him stands holy Captain John Paton—bold as a lion, he is. And there's the godly soldiers Captain Arnot and Major M'Culloch. How they'll turn this lot into an army while we're shivering from moor to moor, our enemies closing in, I donnae ken. But if anyone can do it, Wallace is the one."

"He'll not be like Gray, then?" asked Duncan, wringing water out of his red locks.

"Nor like Turner," said Peden with a snort. "Wallace and Turner used to fight on the same side. But unlike Turner, Wallace and these Christian soldiers continue to fight for justice and truth." Then the field preacher added, "Not for money and fame, like Turner."

"We're in good hands, then," said Jamie.

"Will they teach us, me and Jamie, to use a gun and the claymore?" asked Duncan eagerly.

"Aye, if yer the least bit keen," said Mr. Peden.

"But, Duncan," said Jamie, "ye've no need for Wallace or anyone else to teach ye to use the claymore. All the Lowlands kens what yer father did with his claymore. I say, learn from yer father."

Over the next two days Wallace did just as Peden said. After praying and singing a psalm with the men, he promptly set about putting everyone through the most rigorous military drill and training any of them had ever experienced. Duncan's father put his claymore in his son's hand and taught him how to parry the blows of an enemy—and how to return those blows. Duncan wished he had his own claymore, but for now he'd have to be content with sharing his father's.

In between training, they managed to make short marches east to Coylton and Ochiltree. As they passed through every village, their ranks swelled as more joined their cause. Duncan and his father often collapsed in a heap and fell asleep at the end of their training, exhausted but hopeful. Even spiteful Turner couldn't help recording in his journal, "I never saw lustier fellows than these foot [soldiers] were, or better marchers."

Then, Friday night, November 23, as they searched for shelter from the rain near the village of Cumnock, an alarm shrilled throughout the camp.

"Dalyell, Sharpe's new commander, approaches!" went the cry. "To arms!"

"This is no place to make a stand," called Wallace above the din of voices. Though his army now numbered near seven hundred men, Wallace secretly harbored a deep concern over the lack of powder and weapons among his troops. They never shot real rounds in drill because they could so ill-afford to waste precious ammunition. A pitched battle here with the likes of Dalyell would be short indeed, and most certainly end in disaster for his men.

"We take to the wilds and reassemble—" Wallace paused, consulting a sodden map. He deliberated with Major Learmont and Captain Paton for several minutes. "Reassemble up the River Ayr at Muirkirk," ordered Wallace.

That night march, hammered as they were by howling winds and driving torrents of near-freezing rainfall, was the worst yet. Sometime around midnight, Duncan became aware of several young men who joined and marched with the Galloway men. But with the wind tearing the words from their lips, few even tried to speak.

When they arrived at barren windswept Muirkirk, worried about detection from Dalyell's scouts and snipers, they shivered out the remainder of that miserable night without food or fire. Duncan and his father huddled together for what slight warmth they could lend to each other. Duncan seldom had any feeling in his toes.

Next morning, having retreated before the foul weather, Dalyell was nowhere to be seen. Duncan, stiff and cold, reentered the world of consciousness with a sneeze that made his head throb. He lay in a pool of water, and his right hip, leg, and foot were completely numb. As he reached down and massaged his foot, trying to regain some feeling, he overheard a conversation. He blinked several times to see through the mist and rain. It was the young probationer, Alexander Robertson, and another field preacher who'd joined them from Ireland.

"I fear, Andrew M'Cormick," said Robertson, pouring water out of his boots. "I fear our cause is hopeless."

"Aye, and I've been thinking the same," said the Irishman as he worked at scraping rust off his claymore with a handful of fine gravel.

"I spoke with Mr. Peden on the subject last night," said Robertson. "He's for scattering and fighting another day if it comes to it."

"This stinking weather may be God's way of telling us it's time to scatter," said M'Cormick.

"Aye, we'll take it up with Commander Wallace," said Robertson.

There was no time for such a conversation with the intrepid Wallace that morning.

He slogged among his men, giving encouragement and advice. Duncan could see from Wallace's wet clothes and mud-bespattered armor that he'd slept no dryer or more comfortable than his men.

"Ye've had a hard go of it, men," he called out for all to hear. "But remember that yer sacrifices, God willing, make for peace and justice for yer wives and bairns—and for the Kirk. It is for God's name we march and seek lawful redress before the king's Counsel. Remember yer Covenanted vows. Now then, on yer feet, and let us up and quick march to Douglas!"

As Duncan rolled over, about to scramble to his feet, he felt something hard poking his side. He reached down and yanked his plaid aside. It was a claymore! And there was a note attached:

Dear Duncan,

    Ye may think me a coward, but I fear our cause is hopeless, and I've made my decision to scatter and fight another day. But I wanted ye to have my sword—

I'll get another. Wield it like yer father for the Crown rights of the Redeemer in his Kirk!

Yours sincerely,
Alexander Peden

Duncan turned the blade over and over in his hand. Peden's claymore! Now, his claymore!

"I heard him come in the night," said his father, smiling as he watched Duncan admire the sword. "Mind ye, in yer admiration for it, Duncan, my lad, don't forget that a patient man is better than a warrior. And don't neglect the Sword of the Lord—the Word of God."

The storm raged on throughout the day as they dragged themselves into Douglasdale. From the sodden hillsides shaggy highland cattle watched the procession. Then with an indifferent toss of their wide-spreading horns, they resumed grazing. Duncan lifted his head as the mud under his bare feet gave way to stone pavement. Water ran steadily off the scabbard of his new claymore, sometimes trickling down his leg.

He looked dully at the narrow, winding street of Douglas village. Rain poured in sheets off the slate roofs of the dreary cottages that hemmed them in on either side. The wind whistled down the main street, as if through a tunnel, and the smells of burning peat and coal smoke whipped enticingly past Duncan's nostrils. The thought of collapsing before a warm peat fire consumed his mind. All the better if it was the fire at home in his own croft, his mother serving him hot broth, roast lamb, oatcakes—maybe haggis.

"Steady, lad," said Duncan's father at his side, as if reading his thoughts. "We none of us would rather be anywhere but home—home before a cheering fire, home surrounded by our loved ones, and surrounded by peace and justice, surrounded

171

by freedom to worship God and bow unhindered before his sovereign rule. Aye, but for all that, lad—we march on."

"Father, I never imagined that fighting would be like this," blurted Duncan through lips chattering with the cold and damp.

"Aye, but things worth having come at a cost. Sometimes at great cost. But ye make freedom to worship God yer goal—and not the fighting itself. The just cause, when ye own it justly, will drive ye on when nothing else will."

Wallace called a halt at the far end of town at the ancient church of St. Brides. Duncan looked up at the stout octagonal tower rising above the narrow nave and into the dark glowering clouds. In this weather, the little stone building looked cold and uninviting. Streaks of rain left dribbling stains on the sturdy stone walls, and steady torrents fell from the mouths of gargoyle downspouts around the eaves. Nevertheless, a slate roof covered the church and would afford some protection from the relentless storm.

But it was too small to shelter everyone inside, and men began erecting makeshift tents over the red sandstone tomb markers that filled the churchyard. The faithful minister of the parish welcomed Wallace and gave him the use of the church for a place of refuge from the storm and a place to worship—and to hold a council of war.

"We halt tonight, men, among the tombs of the warrior Douglases," he stood at the west entrance and called as loudly as he could above the storm. "Rest well, and pray God give us wisdom, and success to this, his enterprise."

Duncan and his father, along with Jamie and his father, were among those given a place inside the kirk. The faithful among the villagers brought peat and some coal, along with large pots of steaming hot broth, oatcakes, and slabs of mutton to cut up into the broth. While Duncan wrung out wet plaids and hung them, like damp shrouds, over the stone effigies of the honored dead of the ancient house of Douglas, his father coaxed a small fire into life in their corner of the west transept of the kirk. Peat smoke hung in the air, but with it came some hint of warmth. Duncan sat rubbing his feet as close to the fire as he dared. He had not felt so alive for days—days that seemed like a thousand years.

" 'Tis grand to feel some warmth again," said one of the newcomers Duncan had noticed the night before. He spoke to no one in particular, but then he turned to where Duncan sat still rubbing his feet.

"Are yer shoes hurting yer feet, lad?" he asked.

Duncan grinned at the man. Surely he was joking.

"I thought shoes were for helping yer feet," said Duncan, "not for hurting."

"Aye, they're for helping. I'm a shoemaker—shoes are for helping ye."

Duncan's father introduced himself to the kindly shoemaker and asked his name.

"The name's Matthew Paton," he replied, "from the village of Newmilns. Let me have a look at yer shoes, lad. I'll do what I can to make them not hurt ye."

"Shoes just get in the way," said Duncan.

The man studied Duncan for a moment.

"Let me have a look at yer feet, then. I might just be able to make ye a pair of shoes that'll help ye."

"God gave me tough feet instead of shoes," explained Duncan as the man sized up his feet.

"Aye, he did. Now my guess would be that ye're a runner," said Matthew Paton when he completed his inspection. "And I be thinking ye're a fast runner. As such ye live under the apprehension of shoes because ye be afraid they'll get in the way of yer running. Am I right, then?"

"Aye," said Duncan simply. He couldn't help liking the shoemaker.

"Well, I intend to be disabusing ye of such a foolish notion about shoes," said Matthew. His eyes narrowed and a playful grin spread across his face. "At least about my shoes," he added with a wink. Then he turned and dug in his sack. "Besides that, shoes are biblical," he continued as he selected a piece of leather. "Ye need yer feet shod with the preparation of the gospel of peace, so says the apostle. And what's good for the feet of yer soul, I'll be bound, is good for the feet of yer body."

After everyone finished their meal, James Wallace called them to attention.

"God has given us a kirk with walls and roof in which to invoke his name, pledge our loyalty to his cause, and hear his voice."

"Let us worship God!" called Mr. Crookshanks.

Prayers were offered, psalms were sung, and then Mr. Crookshanks introduced another newcomer.

"We are blessed to have in our midst the fugitive minister, Mr. Hugh M'Kail. For his sermon wherein he declared 'That the Kirk and people of God had been persecuted by a Pharaoh upon the throne, a Haman in the state, and a Judas in the Kirk,' he has lived a marked man."

Duncan watched the pale-faced young man as he stepped into the pulpit and opened his Bible. " 'Whosoever shall confess me before men, him shall the Son of Man also confess before the angels of God.' " He closed the Bible and looked about the packed congregation. Gazing intently back at him behind the windblown faces and weary eyes, he saw, in the main, peace-loving, God-fearing men driven to desperate measures by oppression. The honest smells of men on the march for more than a week, of wet and drying wool, of

174

soaked leather mingling with the rising steam, hung in the air with the pinching smoke of their little fires. For an instant, Duncan's mind ran back to the parish church in Dalry and the incense George Henry swung all around the place. How different this smelled.

"Very soon," began the young minister, "some of us will face the enemies of Christ's Kirk who will present us with what might appear to be a most tempting offer: deny Christ and his cause, betray the lovers of the Kirk—and we shall let ye live. So they will say. On the other hand they will say: reaffirm the Covenant, confess yer faith in Christ, stand by the cause of Christ and his Kirk—and we shall make certain ye die in the most agonizing ways human hatred can devise."

Duncan stole a glance at his father as Mr. M'Kail continued his sermon.

"James Wallace has given ye the best of training for the temporal fighting, and it looks as if fighting it will come to, but each of ye be certain ye are standing fast against the enemies warring against yer soul. Make certain that before God Almighty ye are owning the Covenant from yer heart . . ."

Duncan's father put his hand on Duncan's shoulder as the sermon ended and they all prepared for sleep. As was their daily practice, Duncan's father read to him from Holy Scripture: " 'My son, keep sound wisdom and discretion: so shall they be life unto thy soul, and grace to thy neck. Then shalt thou walk in thy way safely, and thy foot shall not stumble. When thou liest down, thou shalt not be afraid: yea, thou shalt lie down, and thy sleep shall be sweet.' "

Then with heads huddled close together, father and son committed their way to God and prayed for the safety of their dear ones far away.

Duncan and his father lay side by side, each in the half of a man-shaped depression of a stone-vaulted casket that lay opened like a book, and that had not yet been employed for its intended use. His father arranged his plaid so that much of it covered Duncan. After heaving a great sigh, Duncan rolled on his side and slept.

Meanwhile, Matthew Paton the shoemaker did not go to sleep. He sat up, humming to himself as if it were a spring day and he at home in his little workshop in Newmilns making shoes for Lady Loudoun. All around him came the heavy breathing from men so deeply exhausted that not one was disturbed by all Matthew's cutting and tapping—and humming.

THE SHOEMAKER

From Covenanters with uplifted hands,
From remonstrators with associate bands,
Good Lord, deliver us!

Anonymous Royalist Rhyme

Wallace ordered a piper to arouse the men at first light for the march onward to Lanark. The piper marched through the kirk, stepping over the bodies of slumbering men, the stone walls and timbered ceiling giving extra penetration to the jolting melody. Many of the reclining forms groaned and covered their ears. Not all Scots like piping, and early in the morning the ranks of those who don't swells considerably.

Duncan thought of Ancient Grier as the skirling of the piper startled him back to life. He thought of the sword dancing Grier had taught him. He thought of his mother, of Fiona, of Jenny and Angus. He thought of Dunfarg Castle and the secret mines. Had dragoons scoured the countryside? Had they found his family in their hiding place? He thought of Brodie. He thought of the English. He wondered, if it came down to it, would he confess his faith before men—and be brave under torture?

"Now, then, lad," came the bright voice of the shoe-maker, as if resuming a conversation left off only moments ago. He held out to Duncan a pair of well-oiled leather shoes. "I've gone and made these for ye, and I'm hoping they fit ye just so, lad."

Duncan was speechless. He slipped his feet into the soft fleece interior and felt the warmth seep into his toes.

"Ye'll notice I sewed these wee ridges into the soles," continued Matthew, "so as ye can keep yer footing while running. And they'll be keeping ye a wee bit warmer."

"That's most kind, indeed, of ye, Matthew," said Duncan's father. "But I have no money to pay ye for them."

Matthew looked offended. "I donnae want yer money."

"They're f-fine shoes, Matthew," stammered Duncan. "And I thank ye for them."

"Well, lad, ye'll be needing all the warmth ye can find in the days ahead. I feel a cold snap in my joints—" Matthew nodded confidentially and pressed his face against the stained-glass window, "—maybe snow."

***

The piping stopped, and while men rose stiffly and began packing their things, Duncan overheard James Wallace's firm voice talking near the front of the kirk with two men. Duncan strained to hear and recognized the voices of Mr. Robertson and Mr. M'Cormick. He knew what they would be saying. Soon other voices joined in the discussion.

"We march onward, men, in defense of the faith!" This from Wallace, his voice rising above the others firmly.

"Then I say," came another voice, "we be rid of Turner, here and now. His wrongs are great enough, that no one doubts. And he costs us in ale and meat at every inn we pass."

"We none of us would have lasted this long under his promise of quarter," added another voice.

"True enough!" boomed Mr. Crookshanks's voice. "But we gave him quarter, and if we act unjustly and break our word and bear falsely with that quarter granted the man, why should we expect that God will be our secondary and fight on our side if we act as unjustly as Turner?"

"Hear, hear!" said Neilson.

"But they started it!" whined another voice.

"God calls us, if war we must wage, to wage that war according to justice and honor," added Mr. Crookshanks. "Their dealing falsely with us makes no head to wipe the crime out of our behaving falsely with one of them—though he be the devil himself."

"Aye, but he is!" said one.

Laughter filled the kirk.

"Turner lives," said Wallace, "for now. And I'll brook no abuse of the man. Now up, and onward to Lanark where we shall renew our oaths to God."

***

Monday, November 26, from the steps of the Lanark Tollbooth, Mr. John Guthrie preached a stirring sermon to the infantry, while Mr. Gabriel Semple gave a biblical charge to the men of horse. At the conclusion, both ranks gathered, and with arms uplifted and glad hearts, they with one voice swore their loyalty to the Covenant:

"I do bear my witness to the National Covenant of Scotland, and Solemn League and Covenant betwixt the three kingdoms. These sacred, solemn, public oaths of God can be loosed or dispensed with by no person, or party, or power, upon earth, but are still binding upon these kingdoms, and will be so for ever hereafter . . ."

Their voices grew louder, and Duncan felt the water stand in his eyes as he professed his faith along with the fighting men. " . . . Jesus Christ is my light and my life," they cried, "my righteousness, my strength, and my salvation, and all my desire . . ."

Wallace, Captain Paton, Mr. Crookshanks, Barscob, Neilson, and others framed a manifesto formally explaining the origin and goals of the little army, declaring their actions just and in self-defense against cruel plunder and ill-usage by Turner and others of his ilk. This declaration they sent ahead to Edinburgh in desperate hopes that it might help them seek redress. Then Wallace ordered them to march north to the capital.

Only hours later, Commander in Chief Dalyell, followed by ranks of well-armed redcoat troops, rode into Lanark. His second in command, Drummond, pressed hard after Wallace through the pitiless Gladsmuir Hills. Wallace and his men were forced to march on without rest through the bleak and broken moors.

Night fell, and still Drummond came on, his Royalist snipers firing their muskets at any stragglers.

Then it hit. In the blackest part of night, the wind swept down on the exhausted band, driving icy blasts of bone-numbing sleet into every joint. When their frantic way dipped down a valley in the moor, the sleet turned to drenching rain. When they were forced to scramble to the higher wastes, it turned to snow.

"Yer shoes don't hurt ye, I trust?" said Matthew Paton in Duncan's ear.

Duncan looked up in wonder at the grinning face of the good shoemaker. How could he be so cheerful in this weather, hounded as they were by Drummond?

"No, they help me," replied Duncan, doing his best to return the smile.

"Aye, and I'm glad of it," said Matthew. "Glad of it indeed."

Duncan thought he heard the shoemaker humming the plaintive psalm-tune *Martyrs* above the howling of the wind and the tramp of weary feet, but he couldn't be sure.

The desperate men marched on, drawn to the Loadstone Rock at Edinburgh. But not all of them remained so fixed. Ranks that had grown to nearly one thousand now shrank by twos and threes. Some men unwillingly halted, like frail Hugh M'Kail, too sick and unable to continue. Others vanished because they feared the worst.

As the storm raged on and they passed through Bathgate and Newbridge, most of the men felt wretched in the extreme. Finally, valiant Wallace called a halt in the now snow-covered Colinton churchyard, the grim towers of Edinburgh rising ominously only four miles away.

Making themselves as comfortable as they could in the wet snow, Duncan and his father read from the Bible and prayed. They tried to sleep. Duncan could not stop shivering. What would the morning hold?

BATTLE!

It was a Januar or December,
Or else the end of cauld November,
When I did see the outlaw Whigs
Lye scattered up and down the rigs.

Anonymous

Thursday, first light, November 28, 1666, Duncan woke with a start. Musket fire, though muffled by the snow, broke the stillness and soon had all the men on their feet.

Dauntless Wallace quickly sized up the situation and ordered the men to march south into the wilds of the Pentland Hills. Drummond was in hot pursuit as the men skirted the foothills of the Pentlands and began their ascent. Edinburgh Castle and the hill of Arthur's Seat defied them to the north. And the Bass Rock rose dark and foreboding from the sea.

Duncan climbed for his life, sometimes slipping back on the layer of wet snow that shrouded the slopes. His father unsheathed his claymore and rammed its point into the hillside for support. Duncan did the same. They made more rapid progress this way, and others soon followed their example.

"I say we make our stand here," one of the men called, gasping for breath as he rested on his hilt.

"We make our stand where they can get no cannons," yelled Wallace. "We must choose our ground carefully. March on!"

"Wallace kens this country from the Parliamentary Wars," explained Mr. Crookshanks, marching near Duncan and his father. "Cromwell and Leslie had it out near here. And ye can be sure of it, Wallace kens what he's doing."

Wallace scanned the hills, then led his men to the base of Turnhouse Hill, where iron-gray clouds pressed down on its 1500-foot summit. Duncan followed the commander's gaze. A trenchlike ravine bordered the base of the snow-covered hill to the northwest, and an old sheep drover's road followed the tree-lined burn that poured through the narrow glen. Rising more gently to the south stood Lawhead Hill. Where the two hills came together lay a centuries-old market green. On this green Wallace chose to make his stand.

Though greatly outnumbered by the king's forces, and sorely lacking in weapons and ammunition, Wallace was a clever old campaigner and not easily beaten. He chose to divide his force into three battle units. He ordered Major Learmont, one of his advisors, to ride out and establish a cavalry position on the left wing of the green. Barscob and his Galloway horsemen, Wallace positioned on the right. With Neilson and the Galloway footmen, including Duncan's father, Wallace took his stand in the middle. A hasty inventory of all weapons and ammunition yielded only twenty pounds of loose gunpowder, to be used in a mere sixty muskets and forty pairs of pistols—precious little if they were to hold out against the muskets and artillery of the Royalists. Only half the foot soldiers carried swords, a few had pikes, and the rest wielded only scythes and other farm implements.

Wallace studied the trees along the burn. He directed the men to cut branches and shape them into poles. He then ordered all those without swords to lash their scythes onto the poles, turning them into deadly pikes.

While the soldiers transformed their farm tools into weapons, Wallace scanned the surrounding hills. Where were the Midlothian reinforcements? He'd sent others ahead to drum up more troops. Where were they? Oh, if only the King's Counsel in Edinburgh had received their declaration sent from Lanark. If Sharpe and the Counsel would only hear their petitions and render justice. He looked at his troops. They looked like hunted sheep that had somehow escaped shearing, "ragged in pelt and dirty in cloot," he thought. "And I've led the poor rag-tag rullions to this." For a fleeting moment he was tempted to call a general retreat and order the men to scatter in twos and threes. Most—perhaps all—might be saved if he gave the order. But what would become of their petitions? Few of these men could simply return home and resume life after coming this far in a rising such as this. Though Wallace desperately hoped for a peaceful last-minute resolve, he feared it had come to this: fight or die.

Wallace looked at the two well-armed men guarding Turner, his old comrade-in-arms. He frowned. He had to have absolutely every man and every gun for the fight. But who would guard Turner? Maybe it was time to pistol the monster and be done with him. Wallace dismissed the idea: we gave him quarter. Then his eyes fell on the two sturdy lads with the Galloway men. He had an idea.

"I need two capable young men to guard Turner—with their lives," boomed Wallace. "Do I have volunteers?"

"Draw yer sword, Duncan," said his father. "There's a noble task with yers and Jamie's name on it."

"But, Father—" began Duncan, pleadingly, "—I'd rather be with ye, Father."

"And I'd be honored to have ye at my side, lad," said his father, stroking Duncan's head. "Dear lad, as things stand, we donnae have a hope against the fire power of the redcoats. But we'll fight for Christ and Covenant with all we have and leave the end result where it belongs, safely in the Lord's great hands. But yer duty lies out of the main fray of this battle. I may need ye to care for yer mother, God bless her—" He broke off for a moment. "And for yer sisters and wee brother. Guarding Turner's an important and honorable duty, lad. Play the man, but keep him bound and never take yer eyes off him."

"God be with ye, Father!" called Duncan as he and Jamie escorted Turner, at sword point, up the hill. They halted fifty yards behind and uphill from Wallace's footmen. From here they could view the whole sweep of the battlefield stretching below. Duncan checked the leather straps wound around Turners wrists. They looked good and secure.

"It is the young Presbyterian preacher," said Turner, eyeing Duncan, a mocking lilt in his voice. "We meet again."

Duncan's face grew red, and he was about to say something he knew he shouldn't.

"Sir, if ye would kindly sit," interjected Jamie, politely.

Duncan frowned at his friend. Wasn't that like Jamie to be so all polite and kind, even to the monster that was the cause of this whole rising.

"We're under orders, sir," continued Jamie almost apologetically, when Turner was seated, "to bind ye well." Jamie wrapped a leather strap round and round Turner's ankles.

The boys decided that guarding Turner in shifts would work best. While one held Duncan's claymore and kept his eyes fixed on their prisoner, the other would watch the battle and report what he saw. Duncan locked his gaze on Turner, his claymore at the ready. He was determined not to look over his shoulder at the battlefield, not even for an instant.

Turner lifted an eyebrow and tilted his head. His eyes narrowed. He seemed to be sizing Duncan up. Duncan shifted from one foot to the other.

"What's happening, Jamie?" he said impatiently, his eyes never leaving Turner's mocking features.

"Nothing much," said Jamie.

Duncan shuffled his feet. If only he knew that no one, especially his father, would be killed. If he knew that—then nothing would be nearly so exciting as a battle. If only he knew.

"What now, Jamie," he said. "At least tell me what's not happening."

"Ah, wait, there's Mr. Crookshanks," called Jamie, his eyes on the left wing and Major Learmont's cavalry.

"And?" said Duncan, moving from side to side in his impatience.

"And, Duncan," said Jamie, this time with more excitement in his voice, "Drummond's ordering a charge—a charge into Learmont's cavalry! There coming on like hell kites!"

Duncan felt his throat go dry. Keeping his back to that charge was one of the most difficult things he'd ever done in his life.

"Tell me everything ye see, Jamie, everything!"

"Great puffs of smoke rising from Drummond's horsemen.

They're thundering toward the left wing. And now great puffs of smoke are rising from Learmont's men."

Duncan heard muskets cracking and rumbling as they echoed off the hills.

"More smoke," said Jamie.

Duncan heard the sound of more musket fire. He sniffed the air. The first acrid smells of saltpeter reached him. He blinked.

"Did we get any of theirs?" asked Duncan, imagining real redcoats toppling backward off their horses and lying still in the snow.

"Aye," said Jamie quietly. "And another."

More muskets fired. The smell of gunpowder grew thicker.

"Well, what now?" asked Duncan.

Jamie was silent.

"Jamie, I cannae bear this! What do ye see?" called Duncan.

"They got thr—no, four—of ours," said Jamie, his voice sounding hollow.

"No, donnae tell me that, Jamie."

"And, Duncan"—Jamie's voice was barely audible now—"I ken one of them was Mr. Crookshanks. I'm sure of it."

Duncan did not know how to reply.

"Too bad, lads," said Turner, shaking his head in mock grief. "Tut, tut, tut. Too, too bad, lads."

"But now Drummond seems to be retreating," said Jamie. "Duncan, I'll take over for ye."

"Now that all the actions over ye will," said Duncan, handing his claymore off to Jamie.

Drummond did retreat, but only for a time. He rallied his cavalry at Castlelaw Hill and waited in frustration for Dalyell to arrive with the main body of the Royalist force.

"Can ye hear our lot?" Duncan asked Jamie.

"Aye," said Jamie. "Tell me only what I can't hear."

***

The Covenanters grew restless as they waited. The field preachers, led by Mr. Welsh and Mr. Semple, called loudly on the Great God of Jacob, the Lord of Hosts, to come to their aid and fight for them against the enemies of the Kirk. Next they sang from the Psalter.

Jamie could hear it clearly. Duncan needed no words to describe the music that rose and reechoed off the steeps of Turnhouse Hill that day. Seven hundred desperate men sang as they had never sung before, crying out to God with the ancient prayer:

> O Lord, my hope and confidence
> Is placed in thee alone;
> Then let thy servant never be
> Put to confusion.

Though Turner looked derisively down his long nose at them, Duncan and Jamie joined the singing.

> And let me, in thy righteousness,
> From thee deliv'rance have;
> Cause me escape, incline thy ear
> To me, and me save!

Turner interrupted their singing with a snort. "Look around you, lads! God's not going to deliver the likes of you. My men will grind your faces in the mud, and not even God in heaven can save you."

Duncan and Jamie ignored him and sang on with the men.

> They mock, "God leaves ye; he'll pursue
> And take: none he will save."

189

Be thou not far from me, my God:
Thy speedy help I crave.

The frigid November day ground on toward evening. The boys guarded Turner in shifts throughout the afternoon. Then, just before sunset, Dalyell arrived with the Life Guards of the king's army, three thousand strong. With their redcoats they looked like a rushing river of blood, pouring up the glen and fanning out, rank on terrifying rank, against them.

It was Jamie's turn to guard Turner.

"There's so . . . so many," stammered Duncan.

"What do ye see?" asked Jamie.

"Dalyell's troops," said Duncan, awe in his voice, "thousands of them."

"It's about time," said Turner, yawning nonchalantly. "Now if I'd still been in command—"

"Look at his beard!" Duncan cut Turner off. "I've never seen anyone so grim—he looks like a bear."

"He hasn't my chin," said Turner, sniffing as he jutted his dimpled chin for Jamie to see. "So, you see, he must keep it covered. Actually, he's taken something of a vow, loyal monarchist that he is. He has refused to cut his beard since the beheading of the first King Charles nearly twenty years ago."

"I hear drums," said Jamie. "What's happening?"

Duncan watched as a squadron of Drummond's cavalry advanced cautiously uphill toward Learmont's men.

"They're about to fire!" called Duncan.

Then musket fire boomed, far louder than before, as both sides simultaneously poured rounds into each other's ranks. Duncan wondered how much of their precious gunpowder they'd used up in that enormous volley.

"How many?" asked Jamie.

"How many what?" replied Duncan, squinting through the growing walls of smoke choking the air.

"How many are down?"

"Men are down on both sides," said Duncan. "But the smoke is so thick I can't tell how many. But Wallace and our fathers are not yet in the fray."

Dalyell's footman rushed down as the battle became more engaged.

"Jamie, ye should see Captain Paton with his claymore!" called Duncan excitedly. "He's giving grief to one of Dalyell's captains—their blades are flashing faster than I can see. Paton's driving him back. Oh, Jamie, next to my father, I've seen no one fight with a sword like Captain Paton. Ye really should see him, Jamie."

"That's too cruel, Duncan," called his friend, still keeping his back to the battle and his eyes on Turner. "Too cruel."

"Now it looks as if Wallace has ordered men with muskets to take up positions along the dry stane dyke along the burn," said Duncan. "That's smart. That'll give cover."

The air was tense with anticipation, but for several moments nothing seemed to be happening.

"Oh, Jamie!" groaned Duncan. "Dalyell's added his dragoons into the fight! They're charging uphill on Wallace, trying to make a breach in our defenses."

"Twill soon be over now, lads," said Turner, smugly.

"Aye, it won't!" called Duncan. "Wallace—and my father and Jamie's—are charging down on Dalyell's horse and footmen. Those pikes Wallace had the men make—they're driving back Dalyell's men with them!" Duncan threw his head back and hooted with glee. "English dragoons and footman—redcoats all—running down the hill like scared rats when my mother's after them! Oh, Jamie, this is a sight! And I wish ye could be seeing it!"

KILL HIM, OR FREE HIM?

24

Horseman and horse confess'd the bitter pang,
And arms and warrior fell with heavy clang.
Pleasures of Hope

"Ah, but, lads," said Turner, now more soberly. "Watch the field closely."

Duncan no longer felt ecstatic. He frowned at what he could see of the battlefield. One moment the Royalists were on the run. But not anymore.

A smile tugged at Turner's mouth. "Pity, lads. Your Covenanters have o'er leaped themselves. It's an age old problem in warfare."

Duncan grabbed a handful of his hair in each hand and pulled. Something was going desperately wrong down there.

"Most troublesome problem, indeed," continued Turner in the tone of voice a dull sort of professor of history might use in a classroom. "When you have gained what appears to be the upper hand over your enemy, just how far do you pursue them when they seem to flee before you. It is a most annoying problem. Pursue too little and lose your advantage. Pursue too far, as—tut, tut—your lads have clearly done here—ah, there's the rub, indeed—pursue too far, and your retreating foe turns and strikes both sides of your line into utter confusion. Case in point just there," he nodded down at the broken ranks and growing chaos below.

"Now then, if I were commanding just now," Turner continued in his cool detached manner, "I would be compelled to hammer your flanks into—raw flesh. I would, naturally, feel most grieved about it all, but nevertheless would press my advantage—until not one of your rabble remained standing."

"Jamie, can ye shut him up?" asked Duncan.

"What is Wallace doing about it?" asked Jamie in reply.

"He's ordered men from his right wing to assist," replied Duncan. "But it looks to me like the right wing is already too weakened. . ." His voice trailed off. "It's getting so dark I can hardly make things out, but it looks now like Dalyell is leading a fresh regiment of horse into the center. I see Barscob—he's boldly leading our Galloway men against the fresh charge. But there's just so few. . ."

"God be with ye, Father," said Jamie.

"Aye, and amen to that," said Duncan, biting his lower lip until he tasted blood. "I wish we could do something," his voice trembling as he said it.

Dalyell's men lit fireworks to illuminate the field. Gleefully the Royalist troops began mopping up: taking prisoners and killing those who fled. The boys watched the eerie scene below. As one bright burst of flame hung longer in the air above the melee, Duncan saw the snow stained with blood where Wallace and his men made their stand. Trumpets blared and drums thundered in through the darkness.

"What do we do now?" said Duncan, hoarsely, his eyes wide and unblinking. He wanted it all to stop, and at the same time he was unable to look away.

"Well, now perhaps I might make a suggestion," Turner's voice came from the darkness. His mocking tone was gone. Even Turner had been moved by the boy's reaction to the great defeat. He spoke with more tenderness than he had likely used for years. "I am sorry to tell you, but all is lost for your side. But if you will release me unharmed, I will rejoin my men and do what I can for you."

"We donnae just let him go, Jamie," said Duncan.

"I think we have no choice," said Jamie.

As Duncan was about to cut through Turner's bonds with his claymore, he suddenly remembered that it was Turner's cruelties in Galloway that had led to all this bloodshed. And if his father now lay dead or dying in that bloodstained snow, it was Turner's doing. Moonlight shone on the bare blade of his claymore. He looked down at Turner. The flesh around the cleavage of the pathetic man's chin quivered. Duncan wondered if he could drive his blade into the man—no, he's not even a man, he's a monster. Then he halted. What would please his father? Killing him or freeing him? Duncan's breath came in hot blasts. He knew the answer. He lowered the blade and cut through the bonds. Jamie helped the man to his feet.

"But ye'll remember," said Duncan, "that more than once when others wanted to kill ye, it was my father who spoke in yer defense, sir."

"I shall remember," said Turner, briskly. "And I shall do all I am able to grant the favor in return—for you lads and for your fathers."

Stiff from his bonds, Turner hobbled down the hill and soon was lost from their sight.

"Well, what now?" said Duncan.

"We pray God has delivered our own," said Jamie. "And we do our best to find them."

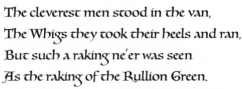

I SMELL THE DEVIL!

The cleverest men stood in the van,
The Whigs they took their heels and ran,
But such a raking ne'er was seen
As the raking of the Rullion Green.

Anonymous Ballad

I f Turner were still with Duncan and Jamie, he might have gone on to further their education about warfare. He might have told them how very often more men fell in the aftermath of a battle than in the pitched fighting itself. So it was at Rullion Green. Those who fell in the battle were surprisingly few. But as the moon rose higher and Covenanters fled into the hills, Dalyell and his men scattered in pursuit, determined to wipe out as many of the rebels as possible.

But the looming question in Duncan's mind was whether or not his father and Jamie's were still alive. As men ran past them in flight, they searched battle-weary faces. Most were too frantic in their eagerness to be as far away from that place as they could get to notice the boys. But one of the men suddenly stopped.

"Jamie, lad!" he cried.

"Father?" Jamie called hopefully into the darkness. "Father, is that ye?"

"Aye, it is, Jamie, my son," said John Kilbride, embracing Jamie.

"Ye're alive and unhurt, then?" said Jamie, looking at his father's blood-streaked face.

"I've only a wee saber scratch from one of Dalyell's dragoons," he replied, touching his cheek. "Oh, but blessed be God Almighty who's brought us together after such a rout."

Here John Kilbride noticed Duncan, still studying every face that flew past them.

"I donnae ken where yer father is, Duncan," said John Kilbride, his hand on Duncan's shoulder. "Last I saw him he was fighting as lustily as ever a man fought in a just cause. I can give ye the hope that I never saw him fall, but more than that, I cannae tell ye. But, Duncan," urged the man, "there's no time to lose. Dalyell's horsemen will be on us any minute. Ye must flee with us—for now."

Pistol shots came from down the hill, lending more credence to Kilbride's words.

"Ye ken if it were Jamie in my place," said Duncan, anguish in his voice. "He'd not leave the field without ye. While there's any hope that my father might be alive, I must search for him. He might be lying somewhere down there, hurt but living. I cannae leave him."

"I ken ye'd see it that way," said Kilbride.

An idea suddenly occurred to Duncan. "But ye'll fly on home to Dalry, won't ye, and care for my mother and family while I search for my father? If he's hurt it may be some time before I can get him back. If they've taken him prisoner, it may take me a wee bit longer, but I'll bring him back. God helping me, I'll find him and bring him back."

John Kilbride looked closely at Duncan's eyes. He wasn't sure that Duncan fully understood what he was talking about. He even feared that Duncan might have gone a bit daft from the shock of the battle. Covenanter prisoners only came out of prisons for the short walk to the nearest gallows. But how could he urge the boy not to do all he could for his father?

"Ye'll be careful, lad?" said Jamie's father, after promising to care for Duncan's family as his own.

"God be with ye, Duncan," said Jamie.

"I'd say ye'd be best to skirt around the foot of that low hill to the south of the green," Kilbride said as they turned to go. "They'll not be expecting ye to go there. But keep yer head low, and watch yer back."

Having no better plan, under cover of night, Duncan made his way toward the foot of the low hill. It had the added advantage of giving him a position near the battlefield. And he knew he must begin his search there. He had to know if his father had fallen and lay dead in the field. If he found his father there, his search would be over.

Turner might have further instructed Duncan in another feature of war and battles: small skirmishes can sometimes continue for hours, even days, after the pitched battle is ended. And in those skirmishes the vanquished may prove more valiant than the victors.

As Duncan scrambled across the snow, one hundred yards southwest of the cluttered battlefield, in the light of a flare, he witnessed one such skirmish. Captain John Paton, burly, keen-eyed hero of the Protestant cause in the German wars, and veteran of the battle of Worcester, came face-to-face with fierce Dalyell himself.

"Halt, filthy traitor!" bellowed Dalyell. "I've got you now!" he barked in triumph.

Duncan dropped in the snow and lay still. Not twenty yards away stood Dalyell with several redcoats at his side and Captain Paton.

"Ye'll not find me so easy to kill," roared Paton defiantly, "as ye've found it to turn coat and fight against the cause of Kirk and Covenant."

Both men drew their pistols. "Crack!" Duncan jumped as they fired at each other at point-blank range. Dalyell's shot missed Paton altogether, but in the moonlight, Duncan watched Paton's lead pistol ball hop down the front of Dalyell and land on his boots. Stunned but unhurt by the blow, Dalyell struggled with the reloading of his pistol.

"I smell the devil in ye, Dalyell!" yelled Paton.

He quickly reloaded one of his pistols, pointed it at Dalyell, and fired. Dalyell dodged to one side and lost his footing in the snow. Paton's shot found its mark on the redcoat soldier next to Dalyell. The soldier fell dead on the spot.

"Seize him, you cowards!" Dalyell ordered his men.

There was no time to reload. Paton drew his claymore. It was four to one. With a cry, the bold captain brought his claymore down on the skull of the closest advancing redcoat. The others halted.

"I'll roast the man alive!" screamed Dalyell. "Paton, I'll see you and all Whigs exterminated! Now, men, seize him!"

"Take my compliments to yer master," Paton called as he turned into the night. "And tell him I cannae come to supper tonight!" And with that, he disappeared into the night, leaving Dalyell empty-handed, cursing, and berating his soldiers.

If only the whole battle could have gone like that, thought Duncan as he inched his way toward the battlefield. There were still too many soldiers about. He dared not go any closer. He huddled in the cold and snow, waiting for an opportunity to begin the grim search for his father.

As the night wore on, Duncan heard fewer and fewer pistol shots. Sometime after midnight the dragoons halted their bloody hunting, and the last of them rode into the camp Dalyell had established near the battlefield. Even victorious English soldiers get tired and cold, thought Duncan. And not even they wanted to sort and bury their dead that night. A battle-weary sentry was posted. Then, the whooping and laughing of drunken soldiers celebrating victory rose mockingly from the camp.

If he could only get to where they held the prisoners. He would rather search among the prisoners. It somehow seemed more hopeful. And the thought of tramping throughout the night over the bloody snow, searching for his father among those who died, sent a shiver of dread that racked Duncan's whole frame. Gradually, quiet descended over the camp, and with it a grim, lonely silence hovered so thick over the battlefield Duncan could almost feel it.

Moonlight cast eerie shadows over the littered field. Duncan didn't actually remember walking down to the battlefield. He just found himself in the midst of it all. Claymores and pistols, makeshift pikes and here and there a musket; the tattered rags of coats and plaids; blankets and fleeces carried for bedding. Duncan shivered. A large warm fleece might not do much against the cause of that shivering. Nevertheless he gathered one up and tied it into a bundle. And there were Bibles and Scottish Psalters, most sodden now with snow—and some with blood. Duncan found a Bible and a Psalter that were not yet ruined and tucked them in his plaid. As an afterthought, he snatched up a pistol, and then another with a leather pouch of powder and ball. They might be useful to him somehow as he searched for his father. He walked on. Horses had died that day and lay in grotesque heaps where they fell.

And bodies lay strewn about the field, not as many as Duncan had feared, but bodies of men who only hours ago had lived and breathed—and hoped. A few were redcoats, but most wore the rullion rag uniform of the fugitive Covenanter.

Duncan turned and trudged back up the hill. His stomach churned and he felt numb. How could war seem so glorious—even exciting—until you saw it like this, at first hand? But an even more troubling question had been in the back of his mind for hours: what about the God of Jacob . . . what about him fighting for them? What had they sung just before the battle?

Cause me escape, incline thy ear
To me, and me save!

Had God not heard them? Was the cause of the Covenant not a just one? Why had God abandoned them—and him?

He didn't know how long he marched that night, but while most of his comrades had fled south, Duncan doggedly plodded north, as in a dream, toward Edinburgh.

There had been no sign of his father among the dead. He had no idea if his father had been chased down and killed and lay dead somewhere on the lonely moorland. He clung to the hope that his father was among the prisoners—surely he was. And the prisoners the Royalists would march to Edinburgh and trial. Duncan refused to think of what would follow those trials. He had to get to Edinburgh. From there he might learn where his father was. And if he was alive—he would rescue him.

FRIEND 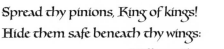 OR FOE?

Spread thy pinions, King of kings!
Hide them safe beneath thy wings:
William Cowper

ometime in the wee hours of the morning, Duncan had
staggered over a farmer's dyke, near the village of Hillend, and collapsed in an exhausted heap against the
wall and slept.

He awoke to the nuzzling of a dog. For an instant he
thought that everything that had transpired in the last
months had all been a bad dream. Brodie had not been killed;
his father was not dead or a prisoner of the English; and he
was home among his family, his sheep, and his dog.

The dog nuzzled him again. There was something different
about this kind of nuzzling. This was not that fine-tuned, per-
sistent, but gentle prodding as Brodie used to do. No, this was
slobbery and jerky, with excited breathy squeaks intermixed.
Duncan cautiously opened his eyes.

Looming large, an inch from his face, was a very wet black
nose, its nostrils flaring excitedly, and dark smiling eyes. And
a slobbery pink tongue coming at his face—Slurp! Slurp!

It worked like magic. Duncan did what he had begun to wonder if he could ever do again: he smiled. And he didn't stop smiling. He sat up and coddled the plump body of a black-and-white puppy. Shivering with carefree puppy enthusiasm, its whole body waggled rambunctiously with the incessant beating of its tail.

And then in an instant all motion stopped. The puppy lowered its nose to the ground and crouched, every mysterious nerve tuned and alert.

Sheep.

"Aye, ye're a keen one," said Duncan, who'd sensed them too. And now he heard their bleating and the sound of their light hooves pattering on the sod just over the wall.

Duncan's heart suddenly lept into his throat. Sheep at this time of the morning, moving close together could mean only one thing: a shepherd.

And would that shepherd be on the side of the Covenant or the oppressors of the Kirk? He'd heard stories while on the march of how locals after a battle often joined in the plunder and even sometimes in the bloody mopping up.

He heard a shrill whistle: the shepherd, sending a dog to flank the sheep on the left. What if the shepherd spotted him? He had to get away—to Edinburgh. Maybe he should bolt and run for it. He was fast—that is, he was fast when well fed and rested. The farmer would not likely be armed, and he wouldn't want to leave his sheep to chase down the likes of Duncan. But then, maybe the English had offered a reward for every Covenanter captured and turned over to Dalyell and Drummond. In which case a poor sheep farmer might think it worth his while to bring him down.

Hesitating, Duncan shifted his weight. As he did so his claymore clattered loudly down the stones from where he had propped it against the stone wall. The racket made by the sword seemed much louder to Duncan than it actually was. But it served as a signal to the puppy, which now, at all costs, wanted at the sheep. Whining and scratching, the young sheep dog clambered its way up and stood precariously atop the wall.

The shepherd, only a few yards away, heard all and saw one of his pups perched on the wall. He strode over to the dog.

"Aye, and what have we here?" he said, picking up the pup.

He must have spotted me, thought Duncan. He liked the sound of the old farmer's voice and made his decision.

"I-I'm a fugitive from the fighting in the Pentlands," he blurted. "And I'm obliged to ye for letting me sleep by yer wall. I'll just be on my way, then."

The farmer nearly dropped the puppy. He hadn't seen Duncan and had been speaking only to the young dog.

"Ah, so!" the farmer replied, leaning over the wall and surveying the boy. News of the battle had swept through the region. He saw the hollow emptiness in Duncan's eyes, the tattered clothes, the pale cheeks, the claymore, the lines of weariness in the boy's face, and he knew it must be true.

"Ye look hungry, lad," said the farmer kindly.

"Aye, but I'll just be on my way, then," Duncan repeated.

"Ye have no cause to fear me turning ye over to the tyrants, lad," said the farmer, reading Duncan's thoughts in his wary eyes. "I almost wish yer lot had been successful up there." He nodded his head back up at the Pentland Hills.

"Aye," replied Duncan with feeling.

"Come into my croft and warm yerself," said the white-haired farmer. "Ye'll be needing nourishment before ye go on yer way."

As Duncan gathered his things, the farmer signaled his dogs and finished moving the sheep to pasture.

Duncan fell in dutifully behind the stooped old farmer as

he led Duncan to his home, and the black-and-white puppy fell in dutifully at Duncan's heels.

"Now then, I've found a young lad, cold and hungry," the farmer said when he entered the croft.

An old woman stood no taller than Duncan. She studied her husband wordlessly.

"Whatever we think of the Covenant," he said firmly, "we ken Sharpe and the English are the real tyrants."

"Do ye like hot broth?" she said to Duncan, her voice quavering with age. "And oatcakes?"

"Aye," said Duncan.

"Now, then, laddie," said the old woman, "sit yerself down by the fire and rest. Ye look a lonely, grieving sight, ye do, poor lad."

Duncan collapsed into a chair before the fire, and the puppy curled up at his feet and began snoring. The farmer went back outside and closed the door behind him.

The warmth of the fire and the nourishing goodness of the broth seeped into his bones. He wasn't entirely sure about the farmer and his wife. They didn't like the English, nor did they seem to be a part of the covenanting cause. Were they going to turn him over to Dalyell? If they were, why feed him? Maybe they were just fattening him for the kill.

"Did ye fight alongside yer brothers and father, up on the green?" asked the old woman. "Ye look a lonely, sorrowing lad, that ye do."

Duncan found himself blurting out the whole story, and once he started, it came like a flood. He told about Brodie, about Grier, about the mines and his family, about Turner, about the march, about the battle—about searching for his father among the dead on the battlefield. He couldn't stop it. Pretty soon he was holding his face in his hands, and the old woman had her arm around his stooped and convulsing shoulders. She patted and cooed comfortingly. Duncan heard the puppy whimper and felt its warm tongue on his hands.

"There, there, lad," she said, rocking him side to side. "Ye've had a hard go. But we'll not deal falsely with ye."

"Now that runt of the litter has gone and attached hisself to ye, lad," the farmer said as he came back inside.

"Aye," sniffled Duncan.

"I've gathered what information I could," continued the farmer. "Word is, James Wallace and ye Galloway Covenanters fought so gallantly against such odds that Dalyell with four times yer numbers had to resort to stratagem to finally defeat ye. If ye'd been reinforced, all would have been lost for the tyrant's side. They say Dalyell took some forty prisoners—there's different stories as to how many for sure. They're to march right past here to Edinburgh later today."

"Maybe the lad can catch a sight of his poor father," said the woman. She filled her husband in on Duncan's story.

"The innkeeper told me they're bound for Haddo's Hole within the walls of St. Giles," he went on. "That is, as many of the unfortunates as they can cram into the stinking place. The rest they'll send to other prisons—who kens, maybe even the Bass Rock."

"But how will I ever get to my father if he's held at the Bass Rock?" asked Duncan in anguish. "I could see it from the battlefield. It's away out to sea."

"Aye, it is," said the farmer. "I do wish I could get yer father back for ye," he added, but with little hope. "I ken ye won't like me saying this, lad. But ye'd best to content yerself to bide here and take yer leave of yer father as he marches past in bonds. For there's little hope after such a rising that the king'll free a man involved such as yer father."

"Ye should see him fighting with his claymore," said Duncan, as if to crowd out what the farmer said. "But he doesnae like fighting and killing," he went on, almost in despair now. "He always taught me to love my enemies. He didnae like taking his claymore to the field meetings. He said it somehow didn't seem right when he went to worship the Prince of Peace to have a weapon at his hip." Duncan paused, stroking the puppy's head absently. The farmer's wife dabbed her eyes with her apron. They waited for him to continue. "He only fought to defend our neighbor, Ancient Grier. He told me that loving my enemies sometimes meant stopping them from doing evil to my neighbor."

The old man and his wife exchanged glances. Five years ago they had reluctantly bowed to the bishop and compeared at the episcopal service in Hillend. But even though they were not Covenanters, they both knew that for just feeding their neighbor—this forlorn young man—and taking him into their croft they could be fined, imprisoned, and if things got any worse, hanged for it.

"Yer father sounds like the best of men," said the farmer's wife. "And it's an honor to render what little we can to his son."

"Aye, it is, indeed," said the farmer, nodding decisively.

"Ye've been most kind," said Duncan. "But I'd best be on my way to the capital."

"Only after ye've rested and had more nourishment, lad," said the old woman, firmly.

"And if ye sit here at the table and keep watch from this wee window, ye may catch a sight of yer good father," said the old farmer. "Then, off ye go to do yer all for him, and a good son ye are for it," added the old man.

The little croft filled with the savory aromas of roast lamb, boiled turnips, oat porridge, and ale served for the midday meal. As he chewed, Duncan felt the nourishing juices of the roasted meat as it delighted his taste buds and invigorated his blood. He hadn't tasted anything so good for days and days.

He glanced frequently out the window between helpings. The kind farmer's wife seemed to derive a special pleasure as she heaped more food on his trencher and watched Duncan put it away with such youthful relish. Duncan was more than happy to give her that pleasure.

During the meal, he felt a nudging from under the table. A warm tongue licked at his leg. Two paws worked eagerly up and down on his knees. Duncan looked both ways and slipped a morsel off his trencher and held it under the table. He felt the eager tongue of the puppy lapping it out of his hand.

"Ye're looking more alive with every bite, lad," said the farmer. "They'll not be along for a wee while," he said as Duncan again glanced out the window. "Why don't ye lie down and have a rest."

"I couldnae do it," Duncan said, his cheeks now bright red from the warmth of the croft and the good food. "What if I missed him?"

"We'll do yer watching for ye, lad," the farmer said.

"No, I just couldnae," said Duncan, fighting back a yawn.

Duncan pushed his trencher away. He could eat no more. He heaved a great sigh of satisfaction.

The farmer and his wife smiled at each other as they watched his head bob up and down. Within minutes, still sitting at the table, his head lolled forward and he lay on the table. One hand stretched out beside his reclining head, and the other rested on the head of the now-sleeping puppy who had crawled up on his lap.

How long he slept, Duncan could not be sure. But he awoke to the farmer's voice.

"The harbingers of Dalyell's army just rode by on their way to the capital," he said, his hand on Duncan's shoulder. "The main body of the army will not be far behind."

207

"And ye're sure I'll be able to see from here?" said Duncan, pressing his face to the window.

"Aye, ye will," said the farmer.

The puppy clambered its way farther up as if trying to see out the narrow window with Duncan.

"Down ye go, fella," said Duncan, laughing.

"The runt's taken a rare liking to ye," said the farmer's wife.

"Do ye like dogs, lad?" asked the farmer.

Duncan pretended to be busy looking out the window. He didn't like dogs—any old dogs. He had liked Brodie—he had loved Brodie and only Brodie. And there was no dog that was ever going to take Brodie's place. He reached over and deliberately pushed the puppy off his lap. It landed on the packed earth of the floor with a thump and a whimper.

"No, I don't like dogs," said Duncan shortly.

"Too bad," said the farmer. "They can be a lad's friend."

"I ken that," said Duncan.

Then, Duncan thought he felt the ground shaking. Outside, he heard the noise of a great company of horses and men approaching.

"They're coming on, lad. Me and the missus, we'll step to the door. They'd be expecting that and wonder if we didn't."

Would his father be among the prisoners? Was there any hope if he was? Duncan watched closely as the proud redcoats marched by, Dalyell with his grizzly beard leading the victorious procession into Edinburgh.

After the first rank of cavalry rode by, a long company of foot soldiers followed. Redcoat after redcoat, marching in precision. But no prisoners among them. More cavalry, Drummond riding proudly at their head.

Then, Duncan's heart quickened. Flanked by dragoons, and led at gunpoint by infantrymen, a line of weary, bloodied prisoners marched—or rather stumbled. They looked the most dejected of men Duncan had ever seen. One of the dragoons kicked a prisoner who staggered and nearly fell. Other soldiers laughed.

Duncan searched faces anxiously. He recognized some of the prisoners: there was Neilson who granted quarter to Turner, and they had saintly Hugh M'Kail in tow. They must have captured him earlier and brought him to the main body of prisoners after the battle. Duncan caught his breath: they had Matthew Paton from Newmilns. Duncan wiggled his toes in the shoes the ever-cheerful shoemaker had made for him. Maybe he could rescue him, too. Maybe he could rescue them all—and throw in for good measure the ending of all of this tyrant king's injustices. How many of these men would be alive in two days—in a week? And what horrible tortures and cruelties must they endure before the end? He felt so helpless. If only he could whisk them all to safety. If only he could.

NOT MUCH TIME

Arise thee youth!—it is no human call—
God's church is leaguered—haste to man the wall;
Haste where the Redcross banners wave on high,
Signal of honour'd death or victory!

James Duff

N ear the end of the line of prisoners Duncan spotted him. Broad, strong shoulders stooped forward in weariness, his father walked amid the abuses of the soldiery.

Inflamed with that invincible but irrational determination of youth, Duncan gritted his teeth and said out loud to himself, "I've got Peden's claymore, and with it and my pistols, I could charge the rear of the prisoners, hack my way through, free my father, and disappear in the mist!"

The puppy looked up at Duncan and yawned.

"Ye're right, Paton," said Duncan to the puppy. "It's a crazy plan, I ken it is."

"Ye've gone and named a dog ye don't even like?" said the farmer, smiling, as he and his wife rejoined Duncan inside the croft.

Duncan reddened. Why had he called that puppy Paton?

"I . . . I suppose I was thinking of Captain John Paton who I watched have it out with Dalyell himself," stammered Duncan, trying to explain. "And I was thinking of my friend the shoemaker, Matthew Paton." He nodded his head out the window. "They have him too."

"Too?" asked the farmer's wife. "Did ye see yer father, then, lad?"

"Aye," said Duncan, not trusting himself to say more.

He reached down and gathered his bundle up and slung it over his shoulder. He strapped on his claymore.

"I cannae thank ye enough for all yer kindness to me. I'll tell my father of it. He'll be grateful to ye."

"Hold on, before ye go, lad," said the farmer's wife. "Ye'll be needing food." She wiped a tear from her eye as she packed up some of the roast lamb and oatcakes.

The farmer and his wife looked sadly at Duncan as he prepared to march out after three thousand soldiers and take on the entire Royalist city of Edinburgh—determined to rescue his father.

"Ye cannae go alone, lad," said the farmer.

"Aye, ye cannae," agreed his wife.

For a brief moment Duncan thought they were both going to come along with him.

"Ye must take Paton with ye," said the farmer. "He's keen on sheep and has taken to ye. And he'll be good company for ye on yer mission."

"I ken he's not yer Brodie, lad," said the farmer's wife earnestly. "But ye take him along—he's yers."

Duncan thanked them and made his way along the sheep wall toward Edinburgh—and his father. Paton waddled along at Duncan's heels.

"We've done right by the lad," said the farmer, as they watched him go.

"Aye, and do ye ken what I ken about him?" said his wife.

"Aye," said the farmer, simply. "If any lad of his years could do it—it'll be this lad who does it. That much I ken."

Duncan didn't want to overtake the army. Only a few miles lay between him and the capital, so he walked rather than ran, conserving his strength. It gave him more time to work out a plan.

As he approached the city, he paused at the summit of Blackford Hill. Sprawling before him lay the imposing towers and spires of the great city. And dominating all, Edinburgh Castle stood solid and defiant in his path. From his vantage point he watched the army draw near the city. I have to arrive before them, he thought, breaking into a run. In the city he could blend with the crowds, keep his ears open, and come up with a plan. But he'd have to hurry.

A persistant yapping came from behind him.

He halted and turned around. It would be some time before Paton would have Brodie's speed, Duncan thought with a smile as he watched the puppy tearing after him, tail wagging for all it was worth.

"Come on, Paton," he said, crouching down and scooping up the little dog and slinging him around his neck, as he did with new lambs when they got tired.

In his haste, Duncan began overtaking more people on the road as he neared the city.

"Now there's more claymore than a lad has a right to be wielding," said a man, herding a goat. "My guess is ye stole it off a corpse after the skirmish at Rullion Green. I have half a mind to cry 'thief' on ye."

Duncan was about to retort, then he checked himself. Edinburgh was crammed with Royalists. Any one of them returning from a battle might eagerly seize him and have him thrown in with the other prisoners. A lot of help he'd be to his father then.

He ducked behind the next sheep wall and rearranged his bundle so that the claymore was wrapped in the fleece and invisible to the next inquisitive person he met. He hid his pistols deep in the folds of his plaid.

Duncan entered the city by the West Bow, near the grass market. A festive atmosphere buzzed through the city. News of the rout of the Covenanters at Rullion Green had spread rapidly.

"Aye, I hear Dalyell left not a single man alive," Duncan heard one idler say.

"Then what do ye call that lot?" asked another, pointing to the procession of soldiers and prisoners.

" 'Twas a manner of speaking only," said the idler defensively.

"Fact is," said another, "I heard that seven hundred Covenanters, armed only with scythes and a sword or two, had Dalyell and the Life Guards of the Court of High Commission—three thousand strong—running for their very lives."

Suddenly, Duncan heard, and felt in the pit of his stomach, the rumbling of the great cannons mounted around the battlements of the castle. Smoke rose above the castle. The cannons roared again and again.

They're celebrating our defeat, thought Duncan bitterly. He ducked into Covenant Close, one of many dark narrow corridors off the Royal Mile, the main street of the capital that connected Edinburgh Castle at one end of the medieval walled city with Hollyrood Palace at the other. He peered out the passageway at the masses of people cramming the street and shouting gleefully at the soldiers as they passed in triumphal review. Their shouts turned to jeers and taunts as the exhausted prisoners staggered by.

"Cursed Whigs!" screamed one man, hurling a rotten turnip at the prisoners. "Hanging's too good for the lot of ye!" He hurled another turnip. It landed with a sickening splat on the back of Neilson's head. The doomed lord of Corsack plodded on, ignoring the insults.

Hugh M'Kail looked weak and sickly as he staggered by. The prisoner in front of Matthew Paton nearly collapsed with weariness. The shoemaker attempted to help the dispirited man, but the nearest soldier struck him hard in the back with the butt of his musket.

"Get a move on, villain!" growled the soldier.

Duncan wanted to scream that it was the soldier who was the villain. But then he knew he could never save his father if he did.

As his father marched heavily by, Duncan had an idea. If only he could somehow let his father know that he was in the crowds without drawing attention to himself. It may be useful for his father to know that he was near.

He had it! His father had taught him a series of whistles for signaling Brodie to do certain things with the sheep. Most farmers had a small arsenal of signals unique to their way of communicating with their sheep dogs. Duncan's father was no exception.

Duncan whistled: one long, one short, one long, at just the right pitch and inflection, the way his father had taught him. He did it again. To most everyone it would sound like a songbird, or maybe a jackdaw trying to imitate a thrush. But if his father could only hear it above the screeching and jeering of the crowds, he would recognize that whistle, and he would know that there was not another person alive who could whistle that way—except Duncan.

Duncan held his breath, his eyes glued on his father. Then, almost imperceptibly, his father stole a glance in the direction of the whistle. Duncan, with the puppy still on his shoulders, caught his father's eye for an instant, an instant of recognition and silent communication both would cherish for some time to come.

After that the crowds surged behind the procession and grew so heavy that Duncan could not see what happened to the prisoners. A halt was called when the prisoners came alongside the great crownlike spire of St. Giles, High Kirk, now a cathedral. Duncan remembered what the old farmer had said: most prisoners would be thrown in Haddo's Hole— at St. Giles.

"St. Giles is where we begin, Paton," said Duncan, turning his determined steps toward the Gothic church.

As Duncan approached the great arches of the entrance, the last redcoats passed under the menacing spikes of the portcullis guarding the entrance to Edinburgh Castle. Crowds choking the Royal Mile gradually dispersed. There would be no hangings that afternoon.

"And what does a heather rat like ye," barked the warden of the cathedral, when Duncan and Paton reached the top of the steps, "want to come into our grand cathedral for? Come, lad, speak up!"

Duncan hadn't expected a challenge at the church door. He couldn't exactly tell them that he was looking for his father, a prisoner taken at Rullion Green, and ask the man if he'd be so kind as to make inquiries.

"To pray?" said Duncan, hesitantly. "Can I pray here?"

The man leaned over and narrowed his eyes at Duncan as if he'd asked some strange request.

"I suppose the dog's here to pray, too," growled the man.

After assuring the warden that he'd hold Paton in his arms and not let him down, the man impatiently waved Duncan to enter.

Duncan stared around the church. Rows of massive dark stone pillars held in place the ribbed vaulting of the ceiling rising high above. And pointed arches that looked like huge doorways ran between the pillars. High above him stood rows of pipes—the kist o'whistles Grier had told him about.

Noise from the left wall of the nave caught his attention and echoed throughout the stone sanctuary: muffled shouting, keys clanking, and chains rattling. Duncan shivered.

He walked forward. Then, frowning, he halted. Kneeling toward the altar was a girl, her head bowed, and she appeared to be praying. Ah, he remembered what Grier had said about King James making Presbyterians kneel in church. On tip toes, he stepped nearer. Finding a place near the girl, he sat—then looking at the girl again, he knelt.

He did pray—he prayed as he had never done before. And soon he prayed, just as he'd heard his father pray, as if no one else could hear him but his Father in heaven. Paton curled up on the back of Duncan's legs and went to sleep. What he did not realize was that sometime in the course of his praying, he began actually praying out loud.

When he could think of no more to say, he stopped.

He looked around the now quiet cathedral—and

caught his breath. Staring at him with two very wide and very blue dancing eyes was the girl. Duncan couldn't help noticing her bright red hair and the freckles that decorated her rosy cheeks and slightly upturned nose.

Duncan rose quickly from his knees and sat down. Paton woke with a loud squeak as he landed on the stone floor. Duncan felt his cheeks growing hot.

"Ye were praying, indeed!" she said.

"Well, so were ye," Duncan retorted.

"But ye were kneeling," she said accusingly. "I thought Covenanters didn't kneel for anything."

Duncan looked hurriedly around the church to see if anyone had heard. How did she know he was a Covenanter?

"Kneeling's for papists," hissed Duncan, warming to the debate.

"Is it?" the girl said, cocking her head. "How so?"

Duncan tried to remember what he'd heard about why Presbyterians didn't kneel.

"Papists do it," he said lamely. "A-and it's . . ." He had it! "It's idolatry. That's it. Kneeling means ye might be worshiping the elements."

"Elements? Air, water, fire? Speak sense, boy."

"The bread and wine at the Supper," explained Duncan in exasperation.

"But everybody kneels when they pray in the Bible," she went on.

"But that's . . ." he started to reply. "Aye, but that's . . ." he stammered. Maybe she had him. "Well, but Jesus is the only King over the Kirk," he replied, attempting to steer the conversation to safer theological waters.

"But, 'the powers that be are ordained of God,' " she snapped. "That makes King Charles God's ruler by divine right."

"Hmph!" said Duncan, eloquently.

"Which makes anyone who disobeys the king," she continued, "a rebel against God. That'd be ye—and yer father."

Duncan stared wide-eyed at the girl. How did she know about his father? What had she overheard him praying?

"What does yer father do?" she asked.

"Sheep," said Duncan shortly. "He's a farmer, and we keep sheep."

This girl infuriated him. And the last thing he had time for was to sit talking with a silly girl. But he did need information, especially information about the prisoners. He looked again at the girl and let out a short sigh. He'd rather take on a company of dragoons. But no matter how great the cost, he would find out where his father was.

He tried putting on his best smile.

"So what were ye praying for?" he asked, mustering as sweet a voice as he could.

"I was praying for the new prisoners. I always pray for the new lot that come in. Rebel prisoners are so bad, ye ken."

Duncan now turned an entirely different shade of red. Her eyes danced in merriment as she looked at him. He wondered if the girl was baiting him. What had she heard him praying? He clenched his teeth together.

"Ye're a liar, ye are," she went on, as if it were a widely known fact.

"Am I?" said Duncan, staring hard at her. She reminded him of his sister Jenny.

"Aye, ye are," she went on with a toss of her red hair. "Either ye were lying to me—or ye were lying to God—and on yer knees."

"How's that?"

"Ye were praying for yer father who was taken in the rebel Whig fighting," she said. "And that makes him a soldier not a sheep farmer. So there it is, then."

Paton laid his ears back and growled at the girl.

"Ye donnae ken anything," Duncan said, shaking his head in disbelief.

He tried to explain, and before he knew it, he was blurting out the whole miserable story of the rising.

"And now he's a prisoner," he concluded, gazing at the fading light illuminating the blues and reds of the stained-glass windows at the east end of the church. "And I am going to find him—and get him free," he concluded, saying each word slowly and deliberately.

When he finished, the girl extended her hand and said, "My name's Lindsay."

"Mine's Duncan," he said, taking her hand briefly.

"My father's the jailer," said Lindsay conversationally, as if she were telling Duncan that her father sold cheese in the grass market. "Maybe I can help ye," she offered in her carefree manner.

"Yer father's *what?*" asked Duncan in disbelief.

"Jailer to the Court of High Commission," she replied matter-of-factly, her head bobbing side to side as she recited his title.

Duncan suddenly saw her in an entirely different light. "Yer father's the jailer?"

"Aye, he looks after prisoners, mostly here at Haddo's Hole—that's what most folks call that." She nodded toward a low Gothic arch at the northwest end of the cathedral. She looked around the arches and pillars of the church. "Seems an odd place for a prison—a church, I mean."

"Aye, it does," agreed Duncan. "I . . . I would be grateful for all the help ye can give me. If I could be certain where he is—that would be a good start."

Suddenly, he wondered if he'd told her too much. She seemed to be an episcopalian, loyal to the English, and she was the jailer's daughter. A word from her to her father, and all would be up for Duncan—and for his father. He looked pleadingly into her eyes.

"I can trust ye not to breathe a word of this to anyone?" he said.

A ray of golden light from the stained glass sparkled on her curls as she tossed her head back. A merry laugh broke the stillness. Was she mocking him?

"Ye can rest assured, Duncan, I'll not be the cause of ye failing to find yer father and doing what ye can for him." She grew sober. "But I've never heard of any rebel getting free from one of the king's prisons. I ken these things."

"Could ye stop referring to them as rebels?" said Duncan. "I ken ye've only heard one side of things, and maybe I'll be explaining the other one to ye sometime, but 'til then, I'd be most obliged if ye'd not refer to my father as a rebel!"

"I'll try, then," said Lindsay. "I've never heard of any . . . of any Covenanter getting free from one of the king's prisons. It's just not done."

"What happens to them?" asked Duncan, afraid to hear the answer.

"The gibbet," she said shortly. "Hanging 'til dead, then for the really bad ones, dismemberment."

"What?"

"Head and hands chopped off and spitted on pikes over the Nether Bow," she explained, "for all to see."

"When for these?" asked Duncan, his voice hushed with emotion.

"A week," she said. "Maybe a bit more for the ones they'll be hammering for information."

A week. That didn't give him much time.

THE HANGING SHOW

When dangers gather round,
Oh, keep me calm and fearless;
Help me to bear the cross
When life seems hard and cheerless;
                    Johann Heermann

After again promising him information about the prisoners held at Haddo's Hole as soon as she could get it, Lindsay left Duncan in the darkening cathedral. He and Paton curled up in a small chapel near the south transept. They slept at the foot of the marble effigy and entombed remains of Montrose, the great scourge of the Covenanters who had years ago driven Duncan's grandparents and his father and uncle from Inverary in the civil wars.

The next week went by far too quickly. When he was not searching for food at night in the grass market after the last venders went home, he walked the streets of Edinburgh hoping to catch bits and pieces of news of the fate of the prisoners. When nearly overcome with despair, he climbed the barren slopes of Arthur's Seat. Flopping onto the springy heather, he stared dejectedly at the great city, the seat of royal power in Scotland. He had to have a plan—a real plan that would work. But first he had to find his father. And very little time remained.

Lindsay seemed to have done all she could: his father had spent that first night in Haddo's Hole but was transferred sometime during the week to another prison. Soldiers under orders from Archbishop Sharpe dragged in fugitives accused of participation in the rising, and more room was needed for these new prisoners. His father could be in the dungeon of the castle. He might even be at the Covenanter prison at Grayfriars where the National Covenant was read and signed in 1638. Or he might have been moved to the Glasgow Tollbooth, or even a prison in Dumfries—or he might be at the Bass Rock.

Duncan overheard snatches of the Counsel's proceeding against the Covenanters. Some effort was made to argue that the prisoners were granted quarter and should thus be honorably freed.

"I heard tell," said a turnip vender, "that Sir James Turner himself even spoke on behalf of the argument for honoring the promise of quarter to the prisoners. Now, that strikes me like nothing I ever heard coming from the likes of Turner."

Duncan moved closer and made as if he were looking over the man's turnips.

"Aye, but in defense of the rebel Whigs," said another, "they honored their promise of quarter and freed Turner, so why shouldn't Turner do the same for them?"

"Aye, and that makes the charges of rebellion against them," said a customer next to Duncan, wagging a turnip with each word, "a wee bit harder to swallow, now doesn't it?"

"Now, laddie, if ye're not buying," barked the vender, slapping at Duncan's hand, "ye be moving along, then!"

But the fate of the prisoners was on everyone's lips. At the very next stall Duncan overheard more.

"Sharpe's a-calling the rout at Rullion Green, so I heard,"

said a man dressed like a page, apparently on an errand from the castle kitchens, " 'a seasonable mercy of God for the furtherance of his Majesty the King's service in the Kingdom.' His worship spoke like that, he did."

"The King's Court thinks it was all a planned rebellion to overthrow his Majesty," one man said, nodding knowingly.

"Aye, they planned it all for months," said another. "It was bringing down the monarchy they was after. They was plotting like Guy Fawkes, they was."

"And like Guy Fawkes," chimed in one, "they'll hang fer it."

Duncan wanted to blurt in that they had it all wrong. To explain how it really began, neighbors defending an old man. He knew it was no use. He walked on.

"They have two of the ringleaders in their grip," he heard one woman say confidentially to another. "Neilson of Corsock and a rebel preacher, Hugh M'Kail. And they're using—the boot!"

"W-what's the boot?" asked Duncan.

The women looked at Duncan narrowly.

"The boot," said one, "is an iron case clamped tight about the knee of the prisoner."

"The executioner," joined the other, "jambs an iron wedge betwixt the condemned man's knee and the iron encasement—"

"—and then the executioner lifts his mallet," rejoined the first woman, "and on a signal from the judge—"

"—he drives the wedge home with his mallet," interrupted the second woman, "over and over again until the knee is little more than a pulpy mass of flesh, bone, and blood."

"T-they're doing this to the prisoners?" stammered Duncan.

"Not all," said one.

"But word is Hugh M'Kail suffered eleven blows of the mallet before they finished with him," said the other.

"Why are they doing it?" asked Duncan.

224

"They want information about who started the rising," said the first.

"Did he tell?" asked Duncan, his eyes wide.

"I heard," replied a man, passing by, "that Mr. M'Kail only said that James Turner started it with his plundering and wasting of Galloway Covenanters."

He called him Mr. M'Kail, thought Duncan, studying the man's face. In reverent tones, the man spoke on.

"He betrayed neither man nor Christ, nor did he revile his tormentors."

Duncan walked away in a daze. He remembered the last sermon he'd heard Mr. M'Kail preach at Douglas. The text was about not betraying Christ or his Church.

***

Duncan and Paton slept wherever they found a place: in the cathedral, among the gravestones at Greyfriars Abbey, or in the dark corridors of one of the many closes that gave access to the Royal Mile on the main street of the ancient city.

Friday, December 7, Duncan awoke to a rib-crunching kick to his middle. Paton yapped savagely at the intruder.

"Up and be gone, ye gutter filth," said a coarse shopkeeper, waste sloshing from a bucket he carried in his hand.

Duncan scrambled to his feet, grabbing at his things as he did. His side ached, and his stomach growled as he and Paton walked past Cowgate and neared the grass market. Maybe someone would toss them a crust of bread or a piece of pickled vegetable—anything to fill the gnawing cavity in his stomach.

The grass market was alive with activity. People crammed the streets. From the windows in the tall houses lining the

market and facing the West Bow of the walled city, three and sometimes four faces stared out on the square.

Duncan saw with horror that a giant cross-tree gallows had been erected in the marketplace. A black-hooded hangman slowly knotted coarse rope into a noose. Duncan stared. He couldn't move. He felt as if he wore shoes made of lead. The man mounted a ladder and secured the noose to the far end of the gallows. Number one. Over the next hour the methodical hangman, sometimes whistling as he worked, knotted and secured hanging nooses until a row of stout head-sized loops dangled ominously from the cross-tree timber. Ten in all.

Duncan forgot his hunger. He wanted to run far away and hide. But if his father was to be one of those hanged today—oh, he just wished he could do something to stop it all. Standing in the cold and wet, he waited.

"Duncan, I've been looking all over for ye." It was Lindsay's voice. "I've found out some good news," she said. "Yer father is not among the ten who hang today."

He breathed a deep sigh.

"Thank ye," said Duncan, never taking his eyes off the scaffold.

"And I ken he's not at Greyfriars," she said, "nor is he held at Glasgow. Isn't that good news, Duncan?"

He turned and gave her a half smile.

"Thank ye, Lindsay," he said, turning back to the scaffold. "I've just got to find him before . . ." his voice trailed off.

"Aye, I'll do what I can," she said.

Midday came and went. More people crowded the market: soldiers, drummers, and squealing children who marched around imitating the soldiers and whacking at one another with toy pikes and wooden swords. They laughed and called to one another expectantly, as if waiting for a parade.

Then sometime after two o'clock, the drummers beat a slow ominous roll. Duncan's head swam as he watched the ten condemned men escorted roughly, each to his noose.

" . . . for treasonable crimes aforesaid . . ." Duncan only half heard the reading of the sentence against the men. He recognized all of them: Captain Arnot and Major M'Culloch, advisors and leaders under Wallace; the Gordon brothers, Robert and John of Knockbreck. . . . Though numbed at what those men were about to face, he felt a wave of relief. Lindsay's information had been right: his father was not among them.

He couldn't bear to watch—not to watch the way most people had come to watch. He looked around at the crowds. Most gathered for the entertainment, but he also saw sober faces, tears, and anguished looks among the mob. But somehow he felt it his duty to watch.

The Gordon brothers reaffirmed that it was in defense of religious liberty that they resisted the oppressors of the Kirk, to which they all agreed. The captain of the guard on duty ordered a drum roll to drown out any other dying words any of them hoped to say.

The order was given, and the hangman went about his civil duty with a rapidity that made for a virtually simultaneous hanging of the faithful men.

Duncan felt the tears streaming down his face. The English practiced slow-drop hanging with the victim's arms left untied: it prolonged strangulation and satisfied the cruel bloodlust of the crowds as they gawked at the clutching convulsions of the dying. Robert and John Gordon clung to each other and died in a brotherly embrace.

"Is it over?" he heard himself asking, when the ten limp forms were finally taken down.

"Aye, this hanging show is," said a man next to Duncan.

"But have no fear, lad," the man went on with a grin. "The prisons are jammed to the rafters with Whigs. We'll see more like this lot. Aye, there's good entertainment ahead, mark ye, within the week."

MARTYR'S BIBLE

O may my soul on thee repose,
And with sweet sleep mine eyelids close;
Sleep that may me more vig'rous make
To serve my God when I awake.

Thomas Ken

Duncan wandered through the dispersing crowds at the market. He wanted at all cost to avoid the Watergate where he'd heard the head of Captain Arnot was to be spitted and left for ignoble display indefinitely. The tyrants sent the ten grizzled right hands to be fixed on Lanark Tollbooth where the men had reaffirmed their loyalty to the Covenant. The remaining hands and heads were sent to the villages where the men had lived to serve as a deterrent to anyone else who dared resist the absolute power of Charles over the Church.

His mind so distracted by all he'd seen, Duncan suddenly stumbled into the side of a cart. And the next thing he knew, he found himself almost nose to nose with the grinning face of a haddock. Paton growled at the fish.

"Now then, lad," said a not unkind voice. Paton turned

and growled at the voice. "Ye must be watching where ye're going."

Deep in the back of Duncan's mind he sensed a faint hint of familiarity in the man's voice.

The man spoke again.

"Are ye well, lad?"

Duncan looked at the speaker. And for a fleeting moment his heart leaped with joy. It looked so like his father. Surely somehow it had all been a dream after all, and it was his father.

"Father?" said Duncan, uncertainly.

"No, poor lad, I'm not yer father," said the man kindly as he sorted out the few fish left in his cart. "Yer brains been a wee dimmered by the hangings, is it?"

Duncan's heart dropped. He was growing used to disappointments. He turned to go.

"Wait, lad," said the fishmonger. "Ye look hungry, and I've had a good catch this morning. Take this along." He handed Duncan the haddock.

Duncan gathered sticks as he tramped outside the walls of the city toward the open country of nearby Arthur's Seat. The idea of waking up to being kicked again did not appeal to him, and he needed to build a fire. Bringing a rock down hard on a few grains of the gunpowder from his still unused pistol created more spark than he needed. Soon he had a crackling fire. And after arranging the large fish on his claymore, he slowly turned it first one side and then the other over the fire. His stomach roared in desperate anticipation: he'd eaten nothing all day.

Roasted fish never tasted so good, thought Duncan as he took another handful of white flaking fish, the steam rising from the layers, and put it into his mouth and chewed. Paton seemed to enjoy it, too. Duncan ate all he could and saved the rest until morning.

Lying back against the soft heather and his bundle, plaid wrapped around him, he sighed. He shifted places. There was a lump in the bundle. Digging around inside he pulled out the Bible he'd saved from the battlefield. In the dim light of the fire he opened it. He read the name on the inside cover: John Ross of Ayrshire. One of those who died that day was named John Ross. Duncan wondered how it came to be left in the field. Perhaps when Ross asked for quarter in the field and was taken prisoner, the English searched him and threw it aside. He'd never know for sure, but he would cherish it all the more because it was a martyr's Bible. He let it fall open and put his finger on the page: Revelation twelve, verse eleven.

"And they overcame him by the blood of the Lamb, and by the word of their testimony; and they loved not their lives to the death."

Duncan reread the verse. It was perfect. He read it through again.

After praying for his father's release, he curled up in his plaid. If only tomorrow he could find his father.

He slept.

THE SMELL OF FISH

Blows the wind today, and the sun and the rain are flying,
Blows the wind on the moors today, and now
Where about the graves of the martyrs the whaups are crying
My heart remembers how!

Robert Louis Stevenson

Duncan!" yelled Lindsay, running toward him where he waited for her in front of St. Giles. "I've found him!"

"Lindsay, are ye a daft limmer, lass," said Duncan, looking side to side.

"Aren't ye glad to ken it?" she said indignantly. "Ye ken it's no easy thing finding these things out."

"Aye, and I'm most grateful to ye. But if ye announce it to the world, I'll be found out and never get him free anyway. Now, where is he, lass?"

"He's held in the Tollbooth," she said, holding her hands palms up and shrugging her shoulders. "Simple as that, the Tollbooth."

"Can I get a message to him?"

"I donnae ken about that. There's only so many risks I can take before being found out."

They walked past the somber dark stone front of the Toll-booth near the Nether Bow. Duncan pulled Lindsay by the arm and ducked into a close. He studied the place. Soldiers with muskets and swords patrolled the gated entrance.

"But just how am I going to get him out?" he said, more to himself than to Lindsay.

"Aye," said Lindsay.

"Don't take those risks that will get ye found out, Lindsay," said Duncan earnestly. "But do what ye can. Find out how long they'll be keeping him there; if he's had a trial; if they'll be moving him to another place. Moving him's good, if we ken it ahead of time. Find out what ye can. And I'm grateful to ye."

She turned to go, then she spun back around, her red curls flashing.

"Duncan," she called.

"Aye," he said.

"Ye smell like a haddock." With a laugh she turned and was gone.

Duncan wandered through the marketplace, his ears tuned to any information about what lay ahead.

"They've fixed a date for the next round o'hangings," said a wine merchant to one of his customers.

"So they have," replied the customer. "Do ye ken who and when they'll swing?"

"I donnae ken who," came the reply. "But December the fourteenth's the day for the swinging."

Duncan hurried on. He must find out who was to hang that day.

Then he spotted the kindly fishmonger, haggling with an old woman, one hand on her hip and the other clenched with a finger wagging at the fishmonger.

Duncan drew closer.

"If I sell it to ye for that, I'll not be able to go a-fishing ever again. And ye then won't have any fish to eat!"

Grumbling, the woman paid for her fish and left.

"Ah, it's my young friend what took me for his father," said the man, smiling warmly at Duncan.

"I've come to thank ye for yer kindness to me."

"Ye're looking a sight better, lad."

"And 'twas yer fish that made the difference."

"The hanging's troubled ye," observed the man. "Ye didnae ken one of them, did ye?"

Duncan was silent. He remembered the account of Peter and the servant girl, and how easily Peter betrayed the Lord. He looked at the man more closely. There could never be a man who looked as much like his father but wasn't.

"Aye, I kent all of them," said Duncan.

The man looked hurriedly side to side. He motioned Duncan closer.

"So do ye be one of them, then?" he asked in a whisper.

"Aye," Duncan said without hesitation. "I own Christ and Covenant, and so did—so does my father. He's in prison at the Tollbooth."

Slowly at first, and only after repeated urgings from the curious fishmonger, Duncan told his story.

An odd look began coming over the man's face.

"And what is yer father's name, lad," he asked urgently, "his name, what is it?"

"He's Sandy M'Kethe of Galloway," replied Duncan, puzzled by the man's insistence. "But he was born near Inverary—"

"I ken the rest," said the fishmonger, his hands on Duncan's shoulders.

"Lad, I am yer father's brother," he said, "yer Uncle Hamish."

Duncan stared open-mouthed at the man.

"No wonder ye thought I was yer father in yer dazed condition."

A flood of relief swept over Duncan. Surely this man, his own flesh and blood, his father's brother, surely he would help.

"Will ye help me free him?" asked Duncan.

An odd look came over Hamish. He stroked his chin and frowned without replying for several minutes.

"Duncan, yer father and I," he began slowly, "we don't see eye to eye, shall we say, on Presbyterianism. Even a fisherman doesnae last long as a Covenanter here in the king's Edinburgh. And I have no influence over any one in Court, even if I did share yer father's convictions. I'll do what I can for ye, lad, by way of a fish now and then. But I can't see my way clear to hazard all, against my chosen path, and follow ye in some half-cooked scheme to free yer father from the Tollbooth—donnae look at me that way—lad, it's never been done! And any man fool enough to try it will be the next one thrown into the stinking place."

Duncan was speechless.

"Now, donnae go a-looking at me like that, lad," said Hamish. "Ye must understand, Duncan. My wife is daughter to a vicar—yes, lad, that'd be *Anglican* vicar. She hasnae got the family connection I have with ye, and if she ken ye were scheming like ye are—well, let's us just say, expect no help from that quarter. I dare not take ye home with me. But I'll see ye're well fed."

FAREWELL, THE WORLD

Sing with me, sing with me!
Blessed spirits, sing with me;
To the Lamb our song shall be
Through a glad eternity.
Scaffold Song, James Hogg

S o though I've found my own flesh and blood in this place," Duncan concluded after explaining all about his Uncle Hamish to Lindsay, "he'll not help us."

"Well, ye don't need him, then," said Lindsay, crossing her arms, her mouth set in a firm pout.

"I don't?" said Duncan. "I wish ye were right about that. What did ye find out."

"The next men to hang," she said, "will be a laird by the name of Neilson, a young probationer named Alexander Robertson—and Mr. Hugh M'Kail. Everyone's been talking about Mr. M'Kail. He sounds like some kind of saint or something. Have ye met him?"

"Aye, and heard him preach the gospel like no other. I wish I could save him."

"From what I hear, he's almost eager for dying," said Lindsay.

"But maybe it's not the dying he's eager for, but the going to heaven."

"That'd be it," said Duncan. "They're all great lovers of Christ, and I want more than anything to be like them."

"Duncan, three days after Hugh M'Kail is scheduled to hang, they're moving several of the strongest of the prisoners—yer father's to be the first—by boat to the Bass Rock. My father says they have plans to make it into a prison for Covenanters and need strong labor to hew more dungeons out of the rocks."

"So they're going to make them build their own prison?" said Duncan. "A place where future generations will rot away?"

"But, Duncan, the point is, they'll be moving yer father," she said. "And we ken it ahead of time."

"Aye, but what can we do," said Duncan.

"Yer uncle is a fisherman," said Lindsey. "Which means he has a boat."

"But have ye not been listening to what I've been trying to tell ye?" said Duncan. "He won't be helping us."

"Ye must try again, Duncan," said Lindsay. "If ye want to save yer father, ye must try again."

***

Thursday, December 14, Duncan and Lindsay stood at the grass market and watched as Neilson, Robertson, and several others met their end. Duncan's Uncle Hamish tried to go about business as usual, selling fish to the crowds gathered for the hangings.

Neilson, who had lost all his lands and wealth for his loyalty to Christ's Crown and Covenant, spoke boldly before the drums drowned him out.

"If I had many worlds," the condemned lord's voice rose clearly above the din of the onlookers, "I would lay them all down, as now I do my life for Christ and his cause."

Three days later, Duncan read a public notice posted on the door of St. Giles announcing that in Glasgow two days hence the following rebels taken at what was now dubbed the Pentland Rising would hang for treason. With dread in his heart, Duncan scanned down the list. The mist came to his eyes as he read:

"Matthew Paton, shoemaker, Newmilns."

Duncan leaned against the door and sobbed. Lindsay looked the other way until he stopped.

"He made these for me," he explained, pointing to his shoes. "After a long day of marching over the drenching moors, he stayed up through the night making them. I never met a more cheerful man when things went hard."

December 22, crippled and so broken by the boot he could barely drag himself to the gallows, Hugh M'Kail made his way to the scaffold—and death.

In the presence of such a one as M'Kail, even the usually jeering rabble fell silent as he passed. He offered encouraging words to those he recognized. "Trust in God, lad!" he called cheerfully in Duncan's direction. The soldiery treated him with a respect seldom seen at the scaffold, and no drums drowned out his final words.

The pale young minister, assisted by his doctor cousin Matthew M'Kail, paused at the foot of the scaffold, and after declaring that he had seen in this his earthly woe, "a clear ray of the majesty of the Lord," he sang the thirty-first Psalm:

Into thy hands I do commit
My spirit; for thou art he,
O thou, Jehovah, God of truth,
That hast redeemed me.

Crushed and broken as his knee was, as he mounted the first step of the scaffold he said, "I care no more to go up this ladder, and over it, than if I were going to my father's house." At the next agonizing step he paused, "Every step is a degree nearer heaven."

When he finally reached the top, after wiping his pale forehead with the sleeve of his hair cloth coat, he took out his Bible and read from the last chapter.

"And he showed me a pure river of life, clear as crystal, proceeding out of the throne of God and of the Lamb . . . and his servants shall serve him: and they shall see his face . . . And the Spirit and the Bride say, Come. And let him that heareth say, Come. And let him that is athirst come. And whosoever will, let him take of the water of life freely . . . Surely I come quickly. Amen, even so come Lord Jesus."

After more encouraging words for the faithful, he prayed.

"Now I leave off to speak any more to creatures, and turn my speech to thee, O Lord. Now I begin a conversation with God, which shall never be broken off. Farewell, Father and Mother, friends and relations! Farewell, the world and all delights! Farewell, meat and drink! Farewell, sun, moon, and stars!"

Here the weakened man's voice grew stronger.

"Welcome, God and Father! Welcome, sweet Lord Jesus, Mediator of the New Covenant! Welcome, blessed Spirit of grace, God of all consolation! Welcome, glory! Welcome, eternal life—!"

His prayer was cut off as the noose tightened around his neck. Tears streaming down his cheeks, Dr. Matthew M'Kail clutched at the convulsing legs of his martyr cousin until life was gone and he became still.

Though the Royalists hoped to destroy Covenanting Presbyterianism by killing the likes of Hugh M'Kail, the tables turned, and by his death many would be drawn to living faith in the Christ of the Covenant.

Duncan looked at his uncle. Tears streamed down the man's cheeks.

"I almost think my father might envy Mr. M'Kail his death," said Duncan, watching as the martyr was taken down. Petitions had already been granted, ensuring that there would be no dismemberment of Hugh M'Kail's body, no hands or head cut off and exposed to the elements.

His uncle looked at Duncan.

"Which my father's soon to face," said Duncan. "If it comes to it, I ken my father's martyrdom will be no less an honor to King Jesus. Will ye be watching his, then?" asked Duncan.

"His what?" asked Uncle Hamish.

"Well, his hanging, then?" replied Duncan.

"Not if I can help it," said Uncle Hamish, passing his hand over his brow.

"Ye can!" said Duncan. "And I'm so glad ye're willing!"

"What?" asked Uncle Hamish.

"To help us rescue him," said Duncan.

They stepped into a close, and Duncan outlined his plan, with Lindsay adding suggestions as he went.

"And all we need is a boat," concluded Duncan.

"A boat, is it? When?" asked Uncle Hamish reluctantly. "I can't see as ye'll be letting me out of it. And how could I be living with myself if I didn't do what I could to stop my own brother from facing that scaffold." He shuddered as he said it.

"December twenty-fifth," said Duncan.

"What about it?" said Uncle Hamish.

"That's when they move my father," said Duncan.

"Aye, Christmas morning first light," confirmed Lindsay. "So says my father."

"Fathers, shmathers!" retorted Uncle Hamish in frustration. "And who's yer father?"

"Jailer to the Court of High Commission," she replied simply.

"Och, and for my part in this plan, lassie," said Uncle Hamish, shaking his head, "I'm like to be seeing a good deal of yer father someday soon."

A CHRISTMAS SWIM

Our soul's escaped, as a bird
Out of the fowler's snare;
The snare asunder broken is,
And we escaped are.

Scottish Psalter (124)

Duncan's scheme demanded a great deal of careful planning if ever it was to work. Lindsay did her part by finding out that Duncan's father would not be bound, because they wanted his strong back, first for rowing the boat, and when they left the harbor, for sailing it out to the Bass Rock. She also had the ingenious idea of helping the woman who prepared the scanty meals for the prisoners. Duncan wrote a note to his father outlining the scheme, and Lindsay coated it in wax and buried it in Duncan's father's gruel. It was a big risk, but they would need his father's cooperation if the plan would work. They could only hope he'd received it.

Uncle Hamish, meanwhile, learned from a drunken soldier on sentry duty at the pier at Leith that there would only be two soldiers with Duncan's father in the boat, a small yawl, sailed by two local fisherman. Uncle Hamish knew them. For a crock each of Loch Lomond whiskey, they asked few questions, and Duncan's uncle secured their cooperation with the plan.

Duncan's uncle explained to his wife that he had some important seasonal fishing to attend to that would keep him away for several days. He could only hope that if she caught wind of the escape, an unlikely event given the English reluctance to broadcast military blunders, she would not connect his absence with it and go tell the vicar, her father. If word of the escape did seep out, he felt confident that he would have time to return before she found out.

A great many things had to happen as planned, or the rescue would be worse than a failure. They met often over the next days to discuss those plans. Duncan's uncle more than once had to break up impromptu skirmishes between Duncan and Lindsay over kings and kneeling. And at other times he nearly despaired, so impossible seemed the rescue plans. One such time Uncle Hamish held his head in his hands, shaking it from side to side in despair.

"I'm yoked with daft limmers all," he would say.

"But it's desperate plans that often work, in the end," insisted Lindsay.

"By that line of reasoning, this plan must succeed," said Uncle Hamish, "for it's the most desperate I ever heard of."

"Aye, but we have no other choices," said Duncan.

On the late afternoon of December 24, 1666, a dank fog lay thick over the harbor at Leith. Fogs like this had, over the centuries, made the Edinburgh port at Leith a favorite place for smuggling. Duncan surveyed the clinging gray mass and hoped that it would serve them well for the kind of smuggling they had planned.

Lindsay stood on the pier at his side, but almost unrecognizable. She'd disguised herself in boy's clothes, a ragged kilt and plaid, and it looked like she'd rubbed dirt into her face.

Duncan frowned at her. He thought she looked pretty ridiculous and told her so.

"It makes me look more like ye," she explained, with a laugh, when he asked her why she'd smeared dirt on her face and littered her curls with wee bits of heather. "Only I donnae have a claymore." She laughed again.

He scowled at her. Duncan had given up trying to figure Lindsay out. Why was she helping him? Sometimes he thought she seemed to be enjoying it all as if it were just some game—and not a matter of life and death for his father. But she was helping, and his plan would never work if it hadn't been for her.

"All right, get yer things on board," said Uncle Hamish. "We've a big fish to catch today."

Duncan stepped down into his uncle's fishing boat, a seaworthy double-ender, stout of frame and wide at the beam. Long sweeps lay at the ready amidships, and his uncle had lashed the mast, spars, and sails down the starboard side of the craft out of the way for easier rowing until they needed them.

Carefully Duncan laid his claymore under the middle thwart, where he'd be sitting. He checked the pistols and rewrapped them in his fleece. Lindsay handed Paton down to Duncan.

"Ye'll take good care of him, now won't ye?" she said, speaking to the puppy.

"Aye, ye ken I will," Duncan replied as he arranged the rest of his bundle in the boat.

Paton scurried around the floorboards and sniffed every rib of the vessel. His tail wagged in approval.

"And, Duncan, it being Christmas and all," she sounded almost shy, "I've made ye this." She handed him a basket.

"What is it?" he asked.

"Christmas dinner," she called. "Enjoy it with yer father tomorrow. And may God go with ye!"

He stood up to look after her. His uncle pushed away from the dock, and with the sudden movement, Duncan plopped onto the seat. He hadn't even thanked her. He gripped the oars in his hands and pulled. Duncan felt a strange sensation come over him as he watched the fog slowly enfolding Lindsay where she stood on the pier. Then he couldn't see her at all.

"Ye were right about the kneeling, Lindsay," he called in a hoarse whisper between strokes. "God be with ye!"

"Aye, I was," she called, followed by a confident little laugh. "And ye're right about the King of kings," came her voice through the grayness.

"Don't ye two start in," said his uncle. "Not here."

"Aye, Uncle," said Duncan hoarsely. "We'll do nothing of the kind."

"Now then, it's the Black Rocks for us," said Uncle Hamish. "Ye man the oars, and I'll steer." He stood at the stern, tiller in hand; listening, he peered into the wall of gray.

Duncan did his best at the oars, but his experience on boats had mostly been on Mrs. Nothing's chain ferry over the River Ken. No rowing or sailing there. His uncle offered whispered instructions as they made their way across the harbor to the natural breakwater of the Black Rocks. In moments the entire pier was lost in fog and the rapidly descending darkness. Duncan glanced over his shoulder into the blackness.

"How do ye ken where we're going?" asked Duncan.

"It's sure not by seeing," said his uncle. "Not on a night like this. I've been sailing these waters for many years, lad. And ye develop a sense of where ye are, even when ye can't see anything at all."

Duncan rowed on, trying to pull evenly. He listened to the lapping of the water against the hull.

"That sounds like how my father describes faith, Uncle,"

said Duncan. "Knowing where yer going even when ye can't see with yer eyes."

His uncle only nodded in reply. He moved the tiller, keeping them on that unseen course in spite of Duncan's uneven strokes.

"I hope we'll be able to see them," said Duncan. "In this fog and dark we could pass a few feet away and never ken we'd passed them."

"Aye, but if they leave at first light tomorrow morning, we'll hear them," said his uncle. "Besides, I ken right where they'll pass us. And we'll be lying in wait, and they never suspecting a thing—if all goes well, that is."

"Aye, if all goes well," repeated Duncan.

Several moments later Duncan rested on his oars.

"I hear something," he said.

"It's the water washing on the point of the Black Rocks," said his uncle. "We tie ourselves up just here—and wait until morning."

The gentle motion of the boat had rocked Paton into a sound sleep. But Duncan was too excited to sleep. Every wash of water on the rocks, he sat up, certain that it must be the boat his father was in.

"Duncan, lad," said his uncle in irritation. "Lie still, or we'll never hear it."

A light breeze began to blow just before dawn. Duncan shivered and clutched his plaid around him more tightly. His stomach churned in apprehension. What if they failed?

As the gray light of dawn crept slowly over the horizon, Duncan stepped onto the wet rocks and scrambled to the top of the ridge and listened. The fog had thinned. Looking closely, he thought he saw the shadowy outline of the harbor. And what was that? The shape of a yawl broke through the mist. Two soldiers, two fishermen, and one man at the oars—his father. It had to be.

"They're coming!" he hissed to his uncle as he climbed back into the boat.

"Prime yer pistols, lad," said Duncan's uncle, softly. "Remember, ye don't need to shoot at the boat. The sound of those pistols will rattle and crackle around so off the rocks here, they'll think they've been set upon by a first-rate ship of the line."

His uncle stepped the mast and readied the gaff-rigged main and jib for unfurling and, with a following wind, a rapid escape down the coast.

Duncan checked and rechecked the pistols. He fingered the hilt of his claymore. He hoped he wouldn't need it. It would be an unequal fight, indeed, if he had to take on two trained soldiers.

"With the whiskey in their bellies," said his uncle, "we can hope the soldiers won't offer much resistance."

They waited. With each moment the tension mounted. What took them so long? Duncan shielded the pistols under his plaid. He had to keep the powder dry in this mist. If the pistols misfired all was lost. A flash in the pan just wouldn't do. A dull-gray light now lit the scene. Duncan's uncle readied the mooring lines so they could slip away at a moment's notice.

"They'll pass right there before us," whispered his uncle, nodding toward the rocky point only fifteen yards away. "When ye see the bow of their boat, I'll slip our lines and hoist sail, and ye let loose those pistols. First one, then on the count of one, two, three, fire the next. Yer father and the fishermen will do the rest. While the redcoats are thrashing about in the drink, we'll come alongside and pick up Sandy—I mean, yer father. Wait! That's oars I hear! Ready yerself, lad."

Paton sat up, a low growl rumbled in his throat.

So much could go wrong, thought Duncan, fingering the pistols. He realized as he looked at them that he'd never actually shot a pistol in his life. While drilling them on the march, James Wallace had shown all the men how to shoot, but they had been so short of powder, he'd only pretended. They had to work now, or all was lost.

The bow of the fishing yawl came slowly into view.

"Now, lad!" called his uncle as he slipped the lines.

Duncan scrunched up his face and pulled the trigger.

"Blam!" and then its retort ricocheted off the rocks. "Crackle, crackle, crackle!"

"Blam!" he fired the second pistol. It too echoed off the rocks.

So far so good, thought Duncan. Sails snapped in the breeze, and his uncle steered toward the yawl.

As soon as the pistols sounded, both guards jumped to their feet and readied their muskets to fire on Duncan and his uncle. The yawl racked violently. Duncan caught a glimpse of one of the fishermen pretending to panic and jumping side to side at the stern.

Then, Duncan's father took up one of the long oars and, gripping it in the middle, he knocked the musket out of the first soldier's hands and into the water. With a sloosh, it sank out of sight. Then, like a flash, he brought the other end around, and with a thwack behind the knees, he sent the unfortunate soldier headfirst into the icy water.

Duncan's uncle sailed nearer.

The second soldier turned his gun toward Duncan's father. But he was a split second too slow. Again Duncan's father swung the oar. Thwack! He caught the man in the small of the back. The soldier's musket went off as he hit the water.

Duncan grabbed the gunwale of the yawl as his uncle brought them alongside. The soldiers flayed in the water near the rocky point.

"I . . . I can't swim!" one called out, gasping with the cold. With boots and heavy coat, the other soldier did little better.

"Now'd be a fine time to learn," called Uncle Hamish.

The fishermen, meanwhile, pretended to surrender, holding their hands high in the air.

"Hop on board, Father," said Duncan, extending a hand toward his father. He couldn't stop grinning. It had worked! His plan had worked!

"I cannae do it, Duncan," said his father in frustration.

Duncan couldn't believe his ears. "Why not?" he called back.

"They've chain locked me to the keel," he called. "And I ken one of those lads has the key." He pointed toward where the two soldiers splashed in the water.

"Oh no," said Duncan, looking at the black iron chain shackling his father's ankles securely to a ring in the keel.

"Can we hack through it?" asked his uncle.

"It'd take an hour—maybe more," said Duncan.

Then he had an idea.

"Uncle, cast us off and take me up close to the first soldier, the one spluttering the most."

His uncle asked no questions. He rowed alongside the soldier. Near panic, the soldier clutched at the gunwale of the boat. Duncan drew his claymore.

"Give me the key—or die!" he screamed at the soldier, holding his claymore at the man's throat.

"He's only a kid," called the other soldier. "Don't give it to him."

Duncan brought the blade closer. "The key or yer life!" said Duncan steadily.

The man dug in his coat, keeping one hand on the gunwale.

"T-take it!" he called, extending the key in a shaking hand toward Duncan.

Duncan grabbed the key and threw the man a barrel fishing float. His uncle turned the boat and rowed rapidly back to the yawl. With his father free and now safely on board his uncle's sloop, they trimmed sail and stood out to sea on a southeasterly course.

"Without muskets, they won't give chase," said Duncan. He couldn't stop grinning at his father; there was so much he wanted to say.

"Aye, and the breeze is freshening out of the north east," said Uncle Hamish, eyeing the sails and easing the mainsheet. "Ye're a free man again, brother Sandy, a free man."

"And I'm not unaware, Hamish, that this cost ye a good deal," said Duncan's father.

"Aye, it's like to be my neck," Hamish said with a laugh. "But yer lad, Duncan, he wouldnae let me alone about helping to free ye. And seeing that lot take their morning swim— I wouldnae have missed it for the world!"

HAGGIS

*It is good to hoist up sail and make out
when fair wind and a strong tide calleth.*
Samuel Rutherford

Father and son could do little more than sit grinning at each other. There was so much to say, but for those first few moments no words seemed to come. For a terrifying instant Duncan was afraid he'd been playacting again or that it had all been a dream. He studied his father's emaciated frame. If this was a dream, it was the best dream he'd ever had. His father had never seemed so real. He looked more closely. A month of prison and foul, inhumane treatment had taken its toll. He grabbed his father's hand, his work-hardened, honest hand. No, he wasn't playacting.

"I can't fill my eyes with enough of ye, Duncan," came his father's voice over the hissing of the sea and the thrumming of wind in the sails. "And my mind fairly overflows with gratitude to the heavenly Father who's seen fit to rejoin me with my son. But I'm thinking ye look like ye've had a rough go, lad."

"Nothing to what ye've been through, Father," was all Duncan managed to reply.

"Tell me all, lad," said his father. "Tell me all. Oh, and ye might just throw in the bit about the puppy, here. I'm wanting to ken how ye come by having a wee puppy."

Duncan frowned. Trying to take his mind back over the last month wasn't going to be easy. It had been a very long month.

"Begin after the battle," urged his father. "I ken the battle."

Duncan told all. And when he finished he blurted the one question that had been troubling him more than any other.

"But, Father, if our cause is just . . ." He glanced toward the stern where his Uncle Hamish made out to be preoccupied with steering. "If the cause of the Covenant is just, why, Father, why didn't God hear our prayers and deliver us from our enemies? All our Psalm-singing about triumph over enemies and God's deliverance, it all rings cold and far away. Why? Why did so many good men die? Why did Mr. Crookshanks die and Mr. M'Kail—and my friend Matthew Paton? Why?"

His father listened intently to his question. He looked tenderly into Duncan's tear-stained face, and for several minutes he said nothing.

"Duncan, ye or I donnae ken the ways of the Lord, now do we?" he said at last. "We so want our heaven just now and here on this earth. But God has ordained crosses for our greater sanctification, lad. Worthy Mr. Rutherford put it this way: 'The cross of Christ is the sweetest burden that ever I bear; it is such a burden as wings to a bird or sails to a ship, to carry me forward to my harbor.'" He looked up at the brown sails of the fishing sloop as he quoted.

Duncan didn't quite understand how losing the battle and all those men executed was like sailing away to a safe harbor with his father.

"Remember, lad," his father continued, "'events are God's,' but we're always wanting to grab the helm and steer our own course in this world. Don't chafe against God's wisdom and authority, Duncan. 'Let him sit at his own helm.' Ye see, lad, God's ways are high above our ways, but we like to turn that order around and imagine that seeing only with the eyes of our sight we ken what's best for us. But we don't.

"The servant's not above his Lord, Duncan. And ye ken what they did to yer Lord? Aye, they mocked and beat him and crucified him on a gibbet for all to see and scoff at. And don't ye think Jesus' disciples thought his death a great defeat that day?"

"Aye, sure they did," Duncan said.

"And didn't the enemy of our Lord—didn't the devil himself think it a great triumph for their side?"

"Aye, I suppose he did," said Duncan.

"But was it?"

"No."

"Then, lad, yer task here is to lay what ye cannae see at the feet of God who is so big and who has plans for ye that are so glorious ye cannae be seeing them yerself—and trust him in faith. And, Duncan, ye can rest assured that all God's enemies 'shall lick the very dust.' But God will bring them low in his time. Ye let him do it, lad, without thinking ye could steer the ship better than God."

"Bass Rock off the port bow," called Duncan's uncle from the helm. "Word among seaman is they've plans to use it as a final stop for all traitors—as a prison—" he eyed them both, "—a prison, as ye can see for yerself, from which no one will ever return alive."

The rock islet jutted defiantly out of the frothy green sea like a sentinel. Duncan shuddered as they sailed past the scarred and barren crags. He studied the grim place: no trees, no heather, not even tufts of grass. Sea birds circled and dove near the stained and precipitous sides of the island. He didn't think he'd ever seen a more dismal place.

"We'll do our best to make Holy Island before nightfall," continued his uncle. "We'll tuck away on the inside of Burrow's Hole for the night."

As they sailed farther out into the open North Sea, the waves rose higher and hissed and foamed as the little sloop rose and plunged with each swell. Duncan felt a thrill shudder through his spine as they surfed down the leeward side of the waves. The wind blew favorably, and they were on their way home.

"Oh, I nearly forgot," said Uncle Hamish. "A merry Christmas to ye both!"

Duncan looked at his father. Covenanters didn't celebrate Christmas for fear of making too much of one day above another. But here they were at sea, Duncan's father just freed from the yawing clutches of the Bass Rock, and on their way home. They had much to celebrate.

"God kens I'm most grateful for the birth of the sweet Lord Jesus," said Duncan's father. "And he kens I'm most grateful to ye lot for rescuing me. How then did ye propose, Hamish, to be making merry?"

"With the victuals Duncan's daft friend Lindsay sent along," said Uncle Hamish, pointing at the basket of food.

"She's not daft," retorted Duncan. He colored and wished he hadn't spoken.

"Ye left out part of the story, then," said Duncan's father, his eyebrows raised inquiringly. "Who's Lindsay?"

"A bit lass," said Duncan. "A lass who helped me find ye . . . A lass without whose help I'd never have freed ye . . ."

"Jailer's daughter of all things," said Hamish to his brother.

"Aye?" said Duncan's father.

"Aye," said Duncan.

"Yer mother was 'a bit lass,' once," said his father, a twinkle in his eye as he opened the basket of food. "God be with her and the wee bairns," he added with a stitch in his voice.

Duncan and his father sorted through the feast Lindsay had prepared: cold peat-smoked mutton, bread, pickled onions, boiled turnips, Crowdie cheese—

"And haggis!" said Duncan, hungrily.

"Aye, haggis, indeed," said Duncan's father, gazing longingly at three oblong-shaped sheep stomachs, stretched tight and full with oatmeal, herbs, and finely chopped sheep innards.

"Did I hear ye say, haggis?" asked Uncle Hamish eagerly.

"Aye, ye did," said Duncan's father.

"Well, that lass is not so daft, then," said Hamish.

Duncan snatched up a note that Lindsay packed with the food. He turned aside and opened it. "I'm right about Christmas, too!" it read. Duncan smiled as he refolded the note and tucked it in his sporran. Maybe she is, he thought as he looked back at the feast.

Duncan's father lifted up his hands as he prayed with the most heartfelt gratitude for their meal, and with deep longing, he petitioned the Lord to bring them safe together again with the rest of his family.

And then they ate. It was a meal the likes of which Duncan and his father had not enjoyed for over a month. Paton sat impatiently on the floorboards waiting for scraps.

"Ah, then," said Duncan, "I'd forgotten how good food tasted."

"Aye," said Duncan's father and uncle together.

Duncan looked at the foaming lines of their wake, and his gaze followed the rocky coastline disappearing astern. Suddenly a thought occurred to him. He sat up.

"Uncle Hamish, what happens if they follow us?"

THOUGH HE SLAY ME

Help me, as you have taught,
To love both great and small,
And, by your Spirit's might,
To live at peace with all.

Johann Heermann

O
ch, Duncan," replied Uncle Hamish, looking derisively at his nephew. "I ken this coast better than
most. Smuggling hasn't thrived in these waters for no
reason. We'd have more than a dozen wee inlets and coves to
hide out in if it came to that. Have no fear."

"We're grateful to ye, Hamish," said Duncan's father. "Ye
are God's means of delivering us, and we're most grateful to
ye. But God is our refuge and our strength, aye, Duncan?"

"Aye, Father," said Duncan. He knew what came next.

Accompanied by the music of the waves, and the rhyth-
mic snapping and creaking of sails and rigging, they sang
together:

God is our refuge and our strength,
In straits a present aid;

Therefore, although the earth remove,
We will not be afraid

Unto the ends of all the earth
Wars into peace he turns:
The bow he breaks, the spear he cuts,
In fire the chariot burns.

Be still and know that I am God . . .

As nightfall approached, the ancient monastic home of
Celtic Christian missionaries, Holy Island, came into view.
Lindisfarne Castle stood guard as they sailed into the calm
protected waters of the bay. Duncan caught a glimpse of the
eleventh-century arches of the ruined priory as the sloop
nudged the sand nearby on the mainland.

"Will ye bide for the night, Hamish?" asked Duncan's father.

"No, I have work to do," said Hamish.

"Work?" asked Duncan.

"I return to harbor with no fish in my boat," said his uncle, "and I'll have some fast talking to do. Loaded with fish—
all will seem as normal."

"God be with ye, Hamish," said Duncan's father, gripping
his brother's hand. "I ken ye've done this because I am yer
brother. Oh, how I long for ye to do great deeds such as this
because he is yer King."

"Who is my king?" said Hamish.

"Aye, that's the question, brother," said Duncan's father.
"Who is yer King? May King Jesus be with ye, Hamish."

Duncan and his father gathered their things and made
their way across the sea grass broken only by white humps
where sheep lay bedded down for the night. Paton crouched
low and began a waddling sort of stalking toward the nearest

clump. Suddenly the clump exploded into three or four frightened sheep scurrying in all directions.

"Paton's keen, lad," said Duncan's father. "He'll make a good sheep dog."

"Aye," said Duncan, smiling at the round black-and-white bundle making mad dashes at the fleeing sheep. "Aye, and like me, he's got a wee bit to learn yet."

***

One thing consumed Duncan and his father as they set out for the River Tweed to follow it inland: get home. And they would let nothing get in the way of their return to Glenkens and their family—not hunger, not exhaustion, not a full army of mad dragoons, nothing.

That night, weary though they were, and Duncan's father weakened by his imprisonment, they did not stop until they collapsed under the partial protection of one of the stone arches of the ruined abbey at Kelso. They had marched nearly twenty miles.

Avoiding bigger villages known to have Royalist garrisons, they still did their best to pick up bits and pieces of information as they traveled.

Dalyell had called for a widespread destruction of all Covenanters, including their wives and children, and all who rendered aid of any kind to them. At this news Duncan and his father drove themselves on. Barely sleeping at night, they ate only when they could safely find food from those known for their loyalty to Christ and Covenant. They sang, they prayed, they read the Bible. And they ran.

As they entered the shire of Galloway, signs of pillage and plunder lay on every side: cottages burned, crops destroyed, slaughtered sheep; and Belties, their black-and-white bodies swollen, lay strewn along their way. The English had outdone themselves in their cruelty.

Duncan and his father ran up the hill to their croft. Dread and fear crowded out all hope as they ran. Unspoken, but looming in each of their minds: with all this devastation, how could anyone from their family be alive?

Duncan arrived first. He halted stock still in his tracks. His father joined him an instant later. With a groan, his father fell to his knees, tears streaming down his cheeks. He raised his peace-loving arms in anguished, silent petition. Blackened timbers were all that remained of the roof. Fire had consumed all the heather thatch. Finally all the rats are gone, Duncan thought bitterly. The door hung sideways from one hinge, and splinters from the chairs and table littered the ground near the door.

Though they feared the worst, they took some small comfort in finding no dreaded evidence of the family inside the charred walls.

The same sight met their eyes when they reached Ancient Grier's croft. The fire had burned up onto the hillside, blackening the gorse and heather.

"All is lost," said Duncan, hoarsely.

They stood in silence for several moments.

"What now, Father?" asked Duncan.

"Though he slay me," said Duncan's father, anguish and grief lining his face, "and though he slay all that I love . . . yet will I trust in him."

When they had the strength to investigate further, they found evidence of many horses having trampled the ground around the two crofts. But by the feel of the hoofprints, it had been more than a week since the burning took place.

"We must check one last place, lad," said Duncan's father.

"My passage in the mines," said Duncan, dejectedly. He'd seen the relentless destruction the English left in their wake throughout all Galloway. How could anyone hiding in his silly passage have escaped the determined retaliation of the English? They were like rat terriers when it came to destroying those they hated. Though hope seemed futile, they turned their steps toward the ruins of Dunfarg Castle.

Then, from inside the remains of Grier's croft, Duncan heard a sound. He looked around. Paton had disappeared.

"Where's Paton?" he said.

ANGUS MAKES A DEAL

O what wonder! How amazing!
Jesus, glorious King of kings,
Deigns to call me his beloved,
Lets me rest beneath his wings.
                              Mary D. James

Where's Paton?" Duncan repeated.

"I think I hear him nosing around inside the wreck of Grier's place," said Duncan's father, striding into the croft. Duncan followed.

"Paton! Stop that whining and scratching about," scolded Duncan, catching sight of the young dog in the dim light.

Paton paused, sat on his haunches, and stared at Duncan. Then he gave a yap, stood up, and resumed digging against the back wall of the croft.

"I thought he was keen," said Duncan, grabbing Paton by the scruff of the neck and yanking the dog after him. "But ye're daft—daft clean through. Let's go."

"Hold on, Duncan," said his father sad. "Take a look at this!"

"It looks like a wee door," said Duncan. "I've been inside

262

Grier's croft a hundred times, but I've never seen that door before."

"It's where he stacked his peat," said Duncan's father, nodding. "The pile of peat covered the door. That's why ye never saw it before now."

Suddenly an idea occurred to Duncan. Maybe Ancient Grier *did* know about the passage all the time.

"Do ye think this door might lead," said Duncan, excitement mounting with every word, "right into the mines?"

"It might," said Duncan's father. "It just might."

"It has to!" said Duncan, hardly able to contain his excitement. "That's why Ancient Grier was so all knowing and mysterious about it when Jamie and I first told him."

"If it does," said Duncan's father, hope and longing animating his eyes, "having a way in and another way out would make yer mines an even better place for hiding from the king's merciless dragoons."

"Aye," said Duncan. "And with Jamie and the others," he went on, "they'll have been protected by men with weapons guarding the tunnels."

Hope grew as they pried on the door with Duncan's claymore.

"It sure looks like the end of a tunnel," said Duncan, peering into the darkness when they got the door opened. "Let's go."

Duncan's father hesitated.

"A sentry might hear us coming," his father said slowly, "and think we are the dragoons."

Duncan hadn't thought of that. He knew that if Jamie and his father were inside, they'd put up a sturdy defense against anyone they thought might be an intruder.

"What do we do?" he said.

"We march in singing," said Duncan's father. "Dragoons don't descend on women and bairns while singing the

Psalter." He struck a light and made a hasty torch out of scraps of wood and cloth left after the sacking of Grier's home. Paton scurried ahead into the darkness.

Duncan felt his heart pounding with a mixture of hope and dread. What if the English had found his mother and sisters and little Angus? Take him—take his father—but not his mother and the children.

"It's certainly an old mine," said Duncan's father as they followed the blasted-out stone corridor deeper into the darkness. "And it goes in the direction of yer old castle."

"Looks like someone's recently cleared a path through this rubble," said Duncan, his voice sounding hollow against the jagged walls of the tunnel. Ahead, he heard Paton sniffing and then lapping at what must be a puddle of water. The sound of steady dripping grew gradually more rapid. As they came nearer, it sounded almost like the steady gurgling of a stream.

"They'd have drinking water," mused Duncan's father to himself as they passed the stream. It cascaded down the side of the passage and emptied into a narrow channel running along the left side of the dark corridor.

Paton stepped out of the stream and nearly lost his balance, shaking water from his black-and-white coat. "Hey!" yelled Duncan as cold water sluiced on his legs. Then he added as they continued, "Stay close, Paton."

"I'd say we'd best be singing," said Duncan's father. "We've come far enough that if they're lying in wait for us, we're done for unless we let them know ahead that we're not the English."

No sooner were the words out of his mouth than they heard a "Twang!" and then the clattering of something along the sides of the cave.

"Sing! Duncan, sing!" said his father.

Ye gates, lift up your heads;
Ye doors, doors that do last for aye,
Be lifted up that so the King of glory enter may!
But who is He that is the King?

"Twang!" went another missile ricocheting off the crude walls.
"Hold yer fire!" boomed Duncan's father.
"Twang! Clatter, clatter, clatter."
They both fell facedown on the damp stone floor.
"Sing!" he yelled.

The Lord of hosts, and none but He,
The King of glory is.
The Lord of hosts, and none but He,
The King of glory is.

"Don't ye let fly with that bow again," Duncan and his father heard the scolding voice of a woman distorted by the
twists and turns of the passage. "And whose singing, then?"
"Mary, Mary." Duncan's father sprang to his feet, Duncan
at his heels. "Mary, blessed be God Almighty who's heard my
prayers. He's kept ye safe! He's kept ye safe!"
"It cannae be true!" Duncan heard her say. "Oh, Angus,"
she continued. "Ye've been shooting arrows at yer own father.
Sandy, is that ye—in the flesh?"
"Aye, and Duncan at my side," he called.
Within moments they covered the one hundred yards of
tunnel separating the family, and while everyone talked at
once, tears of joy and thanksgiving flowed unabated down
every cheek. Fiona and Jenny soon joined them, as did Jamie
and his family, Ancient Grier himself and several other fugitive families who had for over a month hidden safely in Duncan's secret passage. With the cacophony of still more excited

265

voices echoing off the damp walls of the passages, the only objective information that could be conveyed was joy—gleeful and giddy, unmitigated joy.

Duncan's mother pressed her tear-stained cheek against his and held him. She called him her baby and generally cooed and coddled. Then she sniffed twice and said, "Duncan, lad, how ye can go getting yerself all over covered so in dirt I'll never ken. Ye're wearing half the brae just on yer neck!" Then she kissed that same neck again and again.

Fiona threw her arms around her brother, and though she said no words, her eyes danced eloquently as she held him at arm's length and then hugged him again. Jenny blubbered and sobbed, and then abruptly stopped and asked him how many English he'd managed to whack with his claymore.

Duncan felt a tugging at his sleeve. He turned and looked down. Little Angus, with lips bulging in concentration, pulled back and held the taut string of his bow and a blunt wooden arrow in his pudgy fist. The toy bow quavered as he strained under the effort, the folds of his right cheek distorted with the pull. One eye squinted tightly shut as he sighted menacingly with the other up the stubby arrow trained on Duncan.

"Whence and whither bound?" he lisped.

***

Around a small peat fire in the gallery that night, stories were pieced together. One week after Duncan and his father had last seen their family, Mrs. Nothing sneaked up the brae under cover of darkness with the news that Archbishop Sharpe, as punishment for the rebellious rising, had ordered the wasting of all Galloway. Commander in Chief Dalyell wanted all Covenanters—men, women and children—exterminated, and where better to begin than in Glenkens. Fiona

267

led the family to Duncan's mines under Dunfarg Castle, and soon other wives and children joined them. Ancient Grier told them of the other entrance from his croft, and with his claymore the old man became the self-appointed protector of them all. Two days after the battle, men trickled back to the moors and hills surrounding Glenkens and the now wasted village of Dalry. Jamie and his father were among them. Around the clock, men stood guard at either end of Duncan's sanctuary mines. When dragoons approached, these men scattered to the rugged moorlands, leading the bloodthirsty soldiers way from the women and children. But the sentries were growing lax: no redcoats had been seen for over a week. Perhaps the English assumed there was nothing left worth plundering in the devastated region.

And after the stories were told—they ate. Bowls of steaming Scotch broth, smoked mutton (they decided to kill some of the sheep before the English got them; smoking the meat preserved it for use through the winter), boiled turnips, pickled onions, and his mother's own oatcakes.

After the meal Duncan's father read from the Bible. "Better a patient man than a warrior . . ." he read. Then in hope they sang:

> God shall arise and by his might
> Put all his enemies to flight . . .

As he sang, Duncan longed for the day when God would deliver them from their enemies—but he also felt stirring in his soul the beginnings of a more patient trust in God's authority, his all-wise and sovereign will concerning when he determined to set about putting all his and their enemies to flight.

When all was quiet in the crowded gallery, Duncan lay back on his fleece with a sigh. Clasping his hands behind his head, he stared into the darkness. He wondered how he could feel so happy. Neilson was dead, Hugh M'Kail was dead, Mathew Paton was dead, and John Ross of Ayrshire was dead, along with so many others. He felt for Ross's Bible at his side by his claymore. It was too dark to read, but what was that text he'd opened to that night on Arthur's Seat? "And they overcame him by the blood of the Lamb, and by the word of their testimony; and they loved not their lives to the death." He sighed again. They died for Christ and Covenant, and now they were at rest and free of all these troubles. But Duncan wondered: this side of heaven, would Scotland ever see the end of all these troubles? He longed for the day.

Duncan sighed. He felt as though he'd lived a very long time—in the last month. And he was tired. A delicious numbness began seeping into his muscles. Then, just on the verge of sleep, like a steel gong, rosy cheeks, dancing eyes, and bouncing red curls suddenly crashed into his consciousness: *Lindsay.* Ah, me. Now he was wide-awake. Sure, she'd helped him free his father. Fact is, he might never have done it without her. But she was a Royalist jailer's daughter—an *Anglican.* Och, then, she'd maybe been right about some things. But it didn't matter. He was sure to never see her again . . . Besides, she was just a lass . . . just a bit lass . . .

Contented little groans rose from where Paton lay curled up on Duncan's chest. The puppy stretched, and yawned, and soon lay still. Its breathing came in deep draws and squeaking sighs.

Then out of the darkness next to him, Duncan heard a faint clinking of metal. He couldn't see anything in the darkness. Again he heard it. His claymore. He reached out and clutched at the basket hilt of the sword. A pudgy fist was clamped tightly around the weapon and was slowly inching it away from Duncan's side.

"Aa-ngus," said Duncan warningly.

"Dunckle?" hissed Angus. "Dunckle?"

"Aye, Angus, I hear ye," he replied, patting the fist still locked around the sword hilt.

Angus snuggled close and hissed in Duncan's ear.

"I'll swap ye for yer claymore," he whispered confidentially.

"Will ye?" answered Duncan with a yawn.

"Aye," said Angus.

Duncan heard him shaking his head up and down vigorously. "But what have ye for trading with?" asked Duncan softly.

"Hold out yer hand," whispered Angus.

Duncan heard eager grinning in his little brother's voice. He opened his hand and extended it warily into the darkness.

"What is it, then?" asked Duncan.

"This," said Angus. "I got lots of 'em."

A cool, slimy object plopped onto Duncan's palm.

"What is it?" hissed Duncan, now fully awake and sitting up.

"Rrribit, rrribit," broke the stillness.

"Puddock!" said Angus.

"A *frog?*" said Duncan in disgust.

"Aye," said Angus defensively. "Now gi'me the sword."

A WORD ABOUT THE CHARACTERS

The defensive rising, the battle, and subsequent executions described in this volume are real events that occurred at real places and involved real people who lived and died because of their loyalty to Christ's Crown and Covenant. Duncan M'Kethe and his family, though fictional, represent the faith and struggles of many during those trying years of persecution in Scotland. Listed below in alphabetical order are the names of historical figures that appear in the story (an * marks the prominent characters).

Arnot, Captain
Blackadder, John
*Crookshanks, John
Dalyell, Lieutenant-General
Deanes, Corporal George
Drummond, assistant to Archbishop Sharpe
Gordon, John
Gordon, Robert
Gray, Captain Andrew
*Grier, Ancient
Guthrie, John
Henry, George

Learmont, Major
*Maclellan, John, of Barscob
M'Cormick, Andrew
M'Culloch, Major
*M'Kail, Hugh
*M'Kail, Matthew
*Neilson, John, of Corsock
Paton, Captain John
*Paton, Matthew
*Peden, Alexander
Robertson, Alexander
Ross, John
Semple, Gabriel
Sharpe, Archbishop
Short, John
Sorwich, John
Thomson, Alexander
*Turner, Sir James
*Wallace, James
Welsh, John

GLOSSARY OF SCOTTISH TERMS

Aye: yes
Bairn: child
Bannock: flat oatmeal cake baked on a griddle
Bonnie: pretty
Brae: hillside
Burn: stream
Claymore: heavy Scottish sword of choice with basket hilt
Croft: small, low farmhouse
Daft limmer: crazy woman
Didnae: did not
Ding me daft: drive me silly
Dirk: a short straight dagger
Doesnae: does not
Donnae: do not
Dry stane dykes: stone walls, laid without mortar and used for
    fences
Glen: valley
Hae: have
Haggis: ground sheep organs and oatmeal boiled in sheep stomach
Hasnae: has not
Ken: know

Lad: boy
Lass: girl
Loch: lake
Lug: ear
Muckle: much
Non-compearance: failure to conform to Anglican worship
Och: expression of dismay, woe or dismissal
Pate: head
Plaid: long, cross-patterned, wool cloth worn over the shoulder
Quarter: mercy granted in battle
Redress: compensation for a loss or wrong a person has experienced
Sporran: leather pouch worn at the front of a kilt
Wee: little

TIMELINE OF SCOTTISH COVENANTING HISTORY

1610   James the VI of Scotland becomes James I King of England

1611   Bishops appointed to rule in Presbyterian Scotland

1618   Five Articles of Perth: James I further imposes Anglican worship in Scotland

1625   Death of James I; Charles I crowned

1637   Rejection of Laud's Liturgy (Jenny Geddes heaves her stool in St. Giles)

1638   Signing the National Covenant at Greyfriars Abbey

1639   Bishops' Wars begin

1642   Civil War begins

1643   Westminster Assembly; Samuel Rutherford and Scottish commissioners to London

1643   Solemn League and Covenant signed (English Puritans and Scottish Presbyterians pledge their nations to Presbyterian uniformity in religion)

1649   Charles I executed

1651   Covenanters crown Charles Stuart; Oliver Cromwell defeats Scottish army

1660   Restoration of monarchy; King Charles II betrays the Covenant

1661	Anglican worship re-imposed
1662	Faithful ministers ejected from their pulpits; Field preaching begins
1663	Persecution and plunder by James Turner begins with a vengeance
1666	Pentland Rising; Battle of Rullion Green

ACKNOWLEDGMENTS

I am indebted to my proofreaders, Laurel McCoy, Mike Pfefferle, Lorna Arnold, and Mary Jane Bond, as well to Douglas Lamb and Robert Rayburn for their expertise on Scotland and the Covenanters, and their generous supply of books and sources. Heartfelt thanks also to Eric and Irene MacCallum and Angus and Mae Steel for their Scottish hospitality while I retraced the route of the rising and stomped with the sheep around the battlefield featured in this story.

Douglas Bond, a high school history and English teacher, has done extensive research on Scottish history, and has traveled many times to Scotland. He is the author of the Mr. *Pipes* series of children's books. Bond has earned an M.I.T. in Education from St. Martin's College. He lives with his wife and four children in Washington state.

CROWN & COVENANT SERIES

Duncan's War (Book 1)
King's Arrow (Book 2)
Rebel's Keep (Book 3)

How to order:
P&R Publishing:
(800) 631–0094
www.prpbooks.com

Learn more about the author,
Doug Bond, and his
Scottish Adventures!
www.bondbooks.net